DEEPEN MY DESIRES
SEBASTIAN & LOLA PART III

STEELE INTERNATIONAL, INC. A BILLIONAIRES ROMANCE SERIES BOOK 6

CHARMAINE LOUISE SHELTON

CONTENTS

FREE BOOK!

PREQUEL
NEVER
RELEASED!

EXCLUSIVE FOR SUBSCRIBERS!

A Trilogy of Desires Roger & Leonie Parts I-III

A Trilogy of Desires Malcolm & Starr Parts I-III

Series Extras

Series Playlist

STEELE INTERNATIONAL, INC. - JACKSON
CORPORATION

A BILLIONAIRES ROMANCE SERIES CROSSOVER

Tempt My Desires Lachlan & Haley Part I

Tease My Desires Lachlan & Haley Part II

Grant My Desires Lachlan & Haley Part III

Intrigue My Desires Harris & Kat Part I

Decode My Desires Harris & Kat Part II

Honor My Desires Harris & Kat Patt III

A Trilogy of Desires Lachlan & Haley Parts I-III

A Trilogy of Desires Harris & Kat Parts I-III

Series Extras

Series Playlist

ABOUT STEELE INTERNATIONAL, INC. A BILLIONAIRES ROMANCE SERIES

Welcome to the titillating world of the multibillion-dollar global company and the love affairs of the family that controls it.

STEELE International, Inc. is a series of interconnecting Billionaire romance. Follow the Steele family as they fly around the world chasing the women they love and their happily ever afters. Get ready for glitz, glamour, and steamy romance books. What's better than that? The Jet-set Lifestyle has never been hotter...

The Desires Series is not for the tea set; it's for the top-shelf vodka straight up in a pretty crystal glass coterie!

Don't miss any of the sizzling romance books in the STEELE International, Inc. A Billionaires Romance Series:

Discover My Desires Sebastian & Lola Prequel
(Available Exclusively to Subscribers)

Fulfill My Desires Sebastian & Lola Part I

Heighten My Desires Sebastian & Lola Part II

Ignite My Desires Roger & Leonie Part I

Stoke My Desires Roger & Leonie Part II

Justify My Desires Roger & Leonie Part III

Deepen My Desires Sebastian & Lola Part III

Capture My Desires Malcolm & Starr Part I

Embrace My Desires Malcolm & Starr Part II

Cherish My Desires Malcolm & Starr Part III

A Trilogy of Desires Sebastian & Lola Parts I-III

A Trilogy of Desires Roger & Leonie Parts I-III

A Trilogy of Desires Malcolm & Starr Parts I-III

Series Extras

Series Playlist

ABOUT DEEPEN MY DESIRES
SEBASTIAN & LOLA PART III

The white-hot love affair of Sebastian and Lola—who can't get enough of his controlling ways—concludes with a final fight for their happily ever after in their soul mates romance story.

The sparks fly once again when a lover from Lola's past threatens to upend her lovefest with her new hubby when Simon demands more than her luxury lingerie company's partnership… He wants Lola.

What's a girl to do when her hormones rage and the man she loves questions her loyalty?

Join their Sexy Fantasy as Sebastian and Lola face their biggest hurdle as this love triangle takes them around the globe!

Sebastian and Lola's love story is a standalone trilogy in the series. Get a glimpse of their dynamism in other books.

Anthem: "Deeper and Deeper" Madonna
https://www.youtube.com/watch?v=sJV29ZQIUhs

Playlist:
https://www.youtube.com/playlist?list=
PLXwYvn0e218Chf-HjF7o7_s0BxYm-WNL9

Visit CharmaineLouiseBooks.com

LOLA

"*I* want to have a baby with you, Lola."

Sebastian Steele—the former multibillion-aire playboy now my husband of eighteen months—murmurs to me as he traces shapes with his fingertips on my bare, flat belly.

Shocked to hear his words, I stiffen. An ice bucket of water douses the fiery heat swirling around our post-climax bodies.

We just made passionate love, and my core still buzzes from Baz's skillful touch—mouth, lips, tongue, fingers, ten-inches…

I roll over to face him in bed at my best friend turned sister-in-law Leonie Steele, formerly Beaulieu, and Baz's second younger brother Roger's new, multimillion-dollar chalet in Verbier, Switzerland. I need to know how serious Baz is about a baby.

As I stare into his dove gray eyes that shine in the

moonlight from the wall of windows in our suite, I search his handsome face for any sign of a joke. No guile, only earnestness, and dare I think hopefulness show.

Damn.

Why now?

I thought we addressed this issue months ago.

First Baz only hinted at a baby all nonchalant like. A reference to the need for the next head of STEELE International, Inc., his family's multigenerational, multibillionaire dollar luxury real estate development and management corporation based in New York City.

Baz, previously president of the Retail Properties Division, earned the CEO role when his father Morgan announced his retirement and named Baz his successor at our wedding, as Morgan's father named him. Each of his siblings works at STEELE: Malcolm, second oldest, president of the Entertainment Properties Division; Roger, president of the Residential Properties Division; Harris and Haley, youngest and fraternal twins, co-founders of the subsidiary STEELE Technology and Cyber Security.

Who needs "the next head of STEELE" only eighteen months after being appointed and Baz is only thirty-seven years old now, nowhere near retirement age? Really? Cue the biggest eye roll of the millennia…

I didn't open my mouth.

Then a couple of months passed, and he mentioned having a baby outright.

I told him we should spend our first few years as a couple, no need to rush into a family. We'd rushed enough

—meeting one week; living tougher the next week; a couple for four months before our disastrous breakup…

Plus, we have our career goals that dominate our focus. The growth of Lola's Coterie my luxury lingerie and now evening wear collection boutiques and Baz as CEO and Chairman of the Board. We're both driven and acknowledge the importance of our businesses. Particularly since my growth ties in with STEELE as their retail spaces serve as my boutique locations around the globe.

Baz agreed. That is, until he brought it up again just now…

I blame Leonie and Roger for running around proud parents of identical twin boys, Rodolphe Beaulieu Steele and Gaspard Beaulieu Steele. They just turned three-months old and nothing is more adorable than The Twins. To see my bestie so ecstatic with her husband of four days, Roger, and her *beaux fils*—beautiful sons as the Parisian and Tunisian beauty in her own right calls them—makes my heart swell with love.

Since Leonie and Roger prove a young couple can successfully balance a family while they excel in their careers—Leonie as a megamodel turned interior designer with her newly created division at STEELE—influenced Sebastian clearly. Not to mention how they cannot keep their hands off each other. Who said babies end a steamy sex life?

Can I see Baz and me like Leonie and Roger living their best lives? Hell yes! But…

I can't get over the loss of my parents in a tragic car

accident when I was seventeen years old and left all alone in the world.

The thought of having children only to leave them makes me violently ill. Sweat breaks out on my skin and dry heaves rack my body, dizziness overtakes me. Realistically I know there's no way to see the future, and no one has kids expecting their own deaths, but it's hard for me, even fifteen years later.

The upside came from my friendships with Luc Montaigne and Leonie, who he introduced to me eight years ago. Luc became my mentor, Vice Chair of Lola's Coterie, and a father figure. That is after I literally bumped into him one evening in Paris where I was an apprentice at a lace atelier after graduating from the Fashion Institute of Technology in my native New York City.

Le Renard Argenté, fifty-two and the multibillionaire CEO and Chairman of the Board of his family's multigenerational banking empire Banque Montaigne headquartered in Paris with branches worldwide, took me under his wing. The Silver Fox lives up to his name as a sexy and fit older man who is the last *duc* of his family's noble line.

When he introduced me to Leonie, she agreed to become the spokesmodel for Lola's Coterie. It was one move that skyrocketed my company to the stratosphere. To have *The Lion*—the world renown face of fashion houses and cosmetics companies—represent my lingerie brand made Lola's Coterie a household name.

Luc and Leonie became my surrogate family along with Leonie's parents, *Papa* Guy and *Maman* Joséphine. Sadly,

Luc lost his wife and son in childbirth one year before he met me. We helped each other to survive our shared grief of losing loved ones unexpectedly.

So while I'm super happy for Leonie and Roger, I'm still hesitant to move forward with a child. I've put off thinking about it. But they influenced me, too. Especially since we arrived in Verbier yesterday to celebrate not only their marriage, but Christmas and New Year's. Spending time at the Christmas market and at dinner makes me want what they have for Baz and me.

"Babe, don't look so stricken. Just think more about it. For me, for us. Okay?"

Baz's softly spoken request pulls me from my musings. His eyes now fill with concern and a touch of sadness.

My throat clogs, and my chest constricts. I can only nod in response.

"Words, Little Pet. I will have your words," Baz corrects me in his commanding Alpha Dom voice.

I shiver and bite my lower lip as a thrill rushes through me.

To think just over three years ago I was first introduced to a D/s relationship by my onetime lover Simon Blanchett. The hot AF Alpha Dom spanked me before giving me the most intense orgasms and sense of release I'd ever experienced. He awakened the need in me.

Until Baz… The only man I submit to now after my Independent Woman realizes I can still roar in the board-room, but purr in the bedroom. I give Sebastian control with our fucking willingly, but with enough sass I'll forever need a spanking. Indeed, a total win-win situation. Give it to me, baby!

"Yes, Sir," I answer firmly.

"Good. Now go to sleep, you earned your rest, Little Pet," Baz says with a smirk.

He kisses my lips, but ends with a nip for a touch of pain with the pleasure before he rolls me back over to spoon again.

I lie wrapped in his warm, loving embrace as my mind continues to work over the issue.

Once his breathing evens out, and his hold lessens, I slip from our bed.

I pad to the bathroom to clean up, then put on one of Lola's Coterie cashmere lounge suits and matching slippers. A quick peek at Sebastian assures me he's still fast asleep. For a moment, I stare at his gorgeous face, so peaceful. I love this man with all of my heart and soul and want both of us happy.

With a sad smile, I turn for the suite's main door.

The massive chalet sits quietly. How's the Christmas tale go? Not even a mouse stirs. Dim lighting from wall sconces and ceiling pots make my way visible. It's a comfy and chic custom-built chalet with all the top amenities and accoutrements expected by a posh family.

Roger gifted it to his new bride as one of his wedding presents. Leonie whose favorite holiday is Christmas named it *Chalet de le Joie* since it's the time of year most filled with joy.

Verbs, as the in-the-know jet-set call Verbier, is a town

in the Swiss Alps. A part of the Valais canton in the south-west of Switzerland, France borders Verbier to the west with Italy to the south. It's the most exclusive ski destination in the world.

It's the winter version of Monaco, with the difference being people who go to Monaco want to watch or be watched. Whereas Verbier has an understated style where wealth is glamorous, stylish and tasteful. People are here for the reasons one goes to a ski resort—the superb skiing. Not to mention the phenomenal bars and restaurants; the après-ski is perfect for party lovers. Verbier is a glamorous winter playground.

Leonie and Roger's luxury chalet occupies the area south of the Médran lift. They're slightly away from town along Rue de Médran, where the extra space means they are rarely overlooked and have a private, exclusive vibe. The residential compound is opposite to the STEELE Verbier Hotel & Resort that's closer to the heart of the village square. The concept is for the STEELE Verbier Chalets to access the resort for its five-star amenities. The most important include the luxury thermal bath spa and the three Jackson Corporation restaurants headed by the Steele siblings' cousin Lucien the *Sexy Chef* as he's known by his millions of followers.

The STEELE Verbier had its grand opening during last year's ski season. They planned the Residential Properties Division's completion of the by-application-only compound of ten state-of-the-art chalets and private clubhouse to take occupancy for this year's season. As always, both top-notch properties deserve the STEELE stamp.

I make my way down the back set of stairs that open out on a windowed walkway. It connects the huge chef's kitchen and butler's pantry with a cluster of rooms.

Not that Leonie cooks! Over the years, *Maman* Josy taught their Tunisian family's traditional recipes to me since cooking is one of my favorite pastimes.

A giggle bubbles up as I think about the time Leonie burned water… Yeah, she boiled it right out of the pot and burnt the whole kit and caboodle! *Maman* Josy banned her from *Le Beaulieu Manoir's* kitchen for a week. It's surprising Leonie didn't burn down her family's ancestral mansion on the westernmost part of the outskirts of Paris in Neuilly-Auteuil-Passy. The majestic property features manicured park-like grounds, stables, tennis court, swimming pool and cabana, and a palatial French Rococo mansion. A part of the 16th arrondissement, it's in the wealthiest neighborhood.

They built the hamlet between the thirteenth and seventeenth centuries. Later, during the reign of Louis XV, it became a fashionable country retreat for French elites. The Beaulieu's twenty acres of land border Bois de Boulogne with parts of the acreage awarded to their ancestors by the monarch.

So growing up überwealthy, Leonie really does not need to cook at *Le Manoir* or here. Not that I did either with a mother who was a high-powered medical attorney and my father was one of the world's top cardiologists.

They were multimillionaires. I just love to cook and enjoy the fruits of my labor, and Baz loves my curves.

The fully stocked pantry offers tons of options for a warm cuppa; I opt for chamomile tea. Once it's ready, I return to the walkway and curl up on a settee. Then bundle an oversized cashmere throw around me; it engulfs my petite body.

Listlessly, I gaze out the windows as the early morning light sparks beyond the Swiss Alps. So lost in thought, I don't hear anyone approach.

"Hey. What are you doing up so early?"

I glance over my shoulder to find Leonie.

The sad expression on my face makes her pause.

"What's wrong?!" She asks urgently as she sits beside me hurriedly. "Why are you out here and not upstairs with Sebastian? Did something happen?"

Her feline amber eyes narrow as she searches my face for the cause of my distress. We've become one another's defenders over the years. To take on boyfriends and touchy-feely fans in a heartbeat.

I sigh and wipe a hand over my heart-shaped face. With a smile, I shake my head. The glossy raven tresses sway with the movement. "Sebastian and I—"

"I'll kick his ass! I don't care if he's Roger's brother! What did he do to you?!" Leonie demands, her French accent thickening with her emotions as her eyes glow fiercely.

Another giggle surfaces through the pain, and I hold up my hands to stop her.

"No. It's not what you guess," I say. "He wants to have a baby for a while now. At first he only hinted at it, later he mentioned it outright. Now, being around The Twins and seeing how happy you and Roger are and how you're making the family thing work, Baz brought it up again earlier this morning. I couldn't fall sleep. I stayed up thinking long after he fell asleep. So I came down here for some chamomile tea."

I twirl a strand of hair around my fingers. My gaze goes back out the floor-to-ceiling windows and to the beauty of the snow-covered Swiss Alps beyond. Puffs of snow fall from a leaden sky.

It's Christmas morning and a picturesque wintry day. My best friend knows I should enjoy a cuddle with my hubby instead of sitting down here all alone. She waits for me to continue.

Moments later, I shift on the settee to face Leonie.

"I do want children, and I know we can make it work, too," I start. Again, I look away. "But I'm scared about them losing one of us like I lost my parents at seventeen. It's really so hard..."

My voice cracks and tears fill my hazel eyes as my lower lip trembles.

Leonie scoots closer and pulls me into an embrace. Her maternal instincts make her rock me and hum softly as she rubs my back soothingly.

I'm sure she's thinking about how I felt that night when the police came to my family's apartment on Manhattan's Upper East Side. Only a few hours before, I'd wished my parents a good time at dinner with their out-of-town friends.

I give Leonie a squeeze before I sit up, drying my eyes with the backs of my hands. I take a deep cleansing breath like Starr Knight—our close friend and yogi, who helped me get through the rough patch after I left Baz early on—taught us. On the exhale, I nod, the decision made.

Again, Leonie waits for me to speak, knowing her BFF so well and how I like to think things through uninterrupted.

"I can't not live because of a what may happen. I want what you and Roger have just as much as Sebastian. Hell, probably even more"—I chuckle and clasp her hands in mine—"What do you think? Am I being silly?"

Leonie squeezes my hands and shakes her head. Her long mahogany waves settle around her like a lion's mane.

"Absolutely not! You had a traumatic experience that's not so easily overcome. Luc and I helped you and being around my parents did, too. But it still had to be hard"—she squeezes my hands again and continues—"But now, you have a man who loves you madly and an even bigger family with the entire Steele clan. You have the support of many loved ones. 'Live. Live. Live' as Auntie Mame says!"

I giggle again at her reference to one of her favorite movies about the eccentric, carefree socialite who let nothing or anyone make her change course—much like Leonie.

"There you are!"

"We've been looking all over for the two of you!"

Sebastian and Roger stride down the hallway, their long legs make quick work of the distance between us. Baz cocks his head to the side and narrows his eyes when he notices my tear-stained face.

"What's wrong, baby? What happened? Are you sick?" He asks rapidly as he rushes to kneel before me.

Leonie pats his shoulder and squeezes it. He glances at her, puzzled.

"Take her upstairs. Despite how nice it is for us to have some BFF alone time, I'm positive Lola would rather be with you than in this walkway with me," she says grinning.

Baz nods and scoops me in a bride-like hold. I wrap my arms around his neck as I nuzzle against him, breathing in his sexy cologne that's imprinted on my brain as love and safety. Creed Aventus. The iconic name derived from ventus—the wind—illustrating the Aventus man as destined to live a driven life, ever galloping with the wind at his back toward success. How apropos.

Roger claps him on the back as we pass.

Sebastian acknowledges him barely as he murmurs soothing words in my ear.

In what seems like no time, we're back in our suite. Baz stands me by the bed and strips the lounge suit from my body, then tucks me under the covers. He takes off his long-sleeved t-shirt and sweatpants.

My body instantly responds to his muscular six-foot-four-inch frame and massive cock, even flaccid it's major.

He catches sight of my hungry gaze—knowing how my other favorite pastime is to suck him off—and smirks.

"First, tell me why you left our bed and ended up in the walkway in tears, babe," Baz says as he scoots under the bedding beside me.

We promised one another honesty above all, a lesson we learned after our breakup.

"I'm scared to have children only for them to lose me or you like I lost my parents," the words tumble from my mouth in a rush.

Baz nods and cups my face to pin me with his intense gaze.

"My love, I cannot imagine your pain. I can only try to ease it with my love for you"— he says then kisses me deeply—"But we have to live our lives and not let the past, no matter how tragic, stop us. Yes?"

I take another cleansing breath as I say a silent prayer to my parents for their strength.

"Yes, Baz. Let's have a baby, my love."

The most beatific smile crosses Sebastian's face, lighting his gray eyes to the color of molten platinum.

"Second, let's get started right. Now."

LOLA

"Hey! Starting without me, I see!"

The tinkling laughter of my buddy Starr makes me laugh in my crystal tumbler filled with a Manhattan cocktail over ice.

I flew out to the West Coast for business at my Lola's Coterie Beverly Hills and Las Vegas boutiques. My marketing team and I plan to review campaign locations for my new collections along with vendor meetings I'll handle in person.

My personal assistants Blair Thomas and Billie Chandler accompany me. Blair came from New York City with me on Baz's Gulfstream 650, and Billie joined us from Las Vegas. It's funny how all these years later, after denying to Luc I needed an assistant and insisting I could take care of all aspects of my company, I have two.

It's been five years since Luc made the referral for Blair.

As the daughter of an English manufacturing magnate, she comes from a wealthy family and really doesn't have to work. But she set her heart on being in the fashion industry. So Luc did his friend a favor and introduced his daughter to me.

At first I was hesitant until Blair flashed a determined expression with her cerulean blue eyes. Her gusto and attention to detail won me over quickly.

Like Blair, Billie chose not to follow in her family's footsteps to pursue her love of fashion. Her family comprises affluent Southern politicians. Billie—who reminds everyone of a petite Tyra Banks with her wavy, medium-blonde balayage hair, pecan-colored skin, and green eyes—was tired of being arm candy for her ex-boyfriend. She moved to Vegas. Shortly after I began construction on my boutique at STEELE Las Vegas, Malcolm introduced me to her. Here we are three years later.

Although I wonder how much longer either will remain as my PA since they paired off with Luc and Patrick Rockett, respectively. When Billie started dating Patrick, Sebastian nearly had a coronary as Rockett Construction is STEELE's top competitor, not to mention how Pat was interested in being my Dom initially... Fortunately, the brawny multibillionaire Scotsman became enthralled by Billie's siren song.

Along with Leonie and Haley, Blair, Billie, and Starr have become my girls over the years. We can't wait to get tougher for a Girls' Night Out or a Girls' Getaway—especially if it's one of Starr's international luxury fitness retreats. Tonight is no different, minus Leonie, since the Hot Mama is still on her honeymoon.

"Hey yourself! You're late and the party starts once I arrive!" Billie jokes as she stands to hug Starr.

Blair rises, too, and quips, "Yeah, and you know I cannot resist my Whiskey Sour for too long! My Scottish blood from my mother's side demands it as soon as I enter a bar!"

I wave my hand and add, "*Voilà!* Your drink mademoiselle, nice and fresh just how you prefer it!"

The server appears to place Starr's favorite mojito cocktail in front of her. She grins and raises it for a toast.

"Here's to good friends and excellent drinks. May they forever be as one!" She winks, then adds, "And here's to our girl Leonie who's definitely having a hotter time than us right now!!"

We burst out into giggles while the other patrons at the restaurant in STEELE Rodeo Drive glance our way. The vibe is elegant, but relaxed, so they smile at our joviality. The restaurant run by Lucien through Jackson's partnership with STEELE is a popular Michelin-starred eatery like his other establishments.

When Sebastian and I travel, we stay at a STEELE property—being they own so many worldwide, we never run out of options. Hence, with my frequent trips to the West Coast, the Penthouse Suite here has become my home away from home.

While in town, my peace of mind and workouts happen at my yogi buddy's Starr Light Fitness & Wellness Beverly Hills. For my thirtieth birthday twenty months ago, I attended her first international retreat at the private Laucala Island in Fiji. I was like Humpty Dumpty since Starr had to put me back together again after my breakup with Sebastian.

"Okay, ladies, time to dish about your fabulous holidays in chichi Verbs!" Billie says as she claps her hands once the server completes our order. "Then Blair, you must admit to some details about your time with *Duc* Luc, give us some tiny morsel for a change. After I'll tell you all about my Highland adventures!"

Starr and I share some highlights from our fabulous Winter Wonderland Christmas and New Year's.

Happily, I note how her sorrel brown eyes sparkle whenever she mentions Malcolm. As Baz's doppelgänger—same six feet, four inches in height; gray eyes; black hair; clean shaven or 5 o'clock shadow covers a firm jaw—I can understand her pleasure. Only two years apart, some confuse the brothers for twins.

I smile to myself and wonder when the next of the STEELE Quaternity will be off the market. The media dubbed Baz, Malcolm, Roger, and Harris as the STEELE Quaternity—the most sought-after of the world's eligible billionaires. Since my marriage and now Leonie's, the number has diminished by half. I expect Malcolm in a matter of time…

"Er, Lola? Who's—"

Blair's words get cut off by a sexy French accent in a baritone that once made my pussy juices flow. Shocked, I turn and look up six feet, three inches of a well-formed male into the ice-blue eyes of drop-dead gorgeous Simon Blanchett. They bore into my hazel orbs. I'm spellbound.

"Lola?"

Caught gaping at him, I flush from my hairline to my chest. Damn! Even after all these years, Simon's dominant masculine presence still takes my breath away. What the hell is wrong with me??

"I thought that was you, *belle*," he continues in French with a smirk.

My attraction obvious as he bends over to double kiss my cheeks. He's like a great white shark in open water that scents one drop of blood.

Baz is the only man for me. My body just had a visceral reaction to my original one-night Dom who helped me to discover my desires for BDSM. I shake my head to dispel the fog. *Get it together, Mrs. Steele!* I chide myself.

"Simon… Bonsoir," I respond as my fluency in French takes over. "How nice to see you. Allow me to introduce my friends."

I use the introductions to get my head together and regain control of the situation.

We chat for a moment and learn we're in town on business for the next week. His eyes light up.

"How fortuitous! I have a business proposition to discuss with you. Rather than interrupt your evening, have dinner with me tomorrow night. We can meet in the lobby if you prefer, then go to Spago. I remember how you enjoy large cuts of meat," Simon says.

Damn.

He has a way of making innuendos so effortlessly.

But I am intrigued since I've been considering ramping up Lola's Coterie online presence. Who better to partner with than Blanchett Retail Enterprises, SAS, the largest online luxury retailer in the world?

I first met the commanding self-made multibillionaire at a retailers' event in London three and a half ago. He was persistent then, just as he issued his directive to me now.

With that mastery and confidence, it's no wonder Simon could build his online shopping platform with a few thousand dollars and no formal college education. Three years before we met, he was already generating millions of dollars in revenue. Soon, his company will surpass Amazon —a feat.

I like to tell myself his brilliant business acumen drew me to him—I thought I could learn a lot from his success and apply it to Lola's Coterie. But I fooled myself. I desired his controlling ways.

Even though that's in the past, if he has an idea for me, I won't pass it up. Of course I'll tell Baz. After I find out the details…

"Sounds intriguing, Simon. Seven works for me. I'll meet you by the concierge desk. Good night," I respond confidently as my Independent Woman charges to the forefront.

"*Bien, jusque-là, belle,*" he responds. His glacial eyes pin me to my seat. Then he turns and bids the girls a good evening.

I watch—like other women in the room—as he strides to a table with well-dressed men in bespoke business suits. My designer's eye can pick up on the high-quality tailoring and fabrics. When my gaze returns to our table, the girls stare at me with wide eyes. It's pretty comical.

"Oookay, then..." Starr says, fluttering her eyelashes dramatically.

Blair and Billie mimic her movements, and they laugh.

I wave my friends off and assure them nothing is amiss. I don't mention my brief relationship with Simon. Although I know Malcolm and Patrick are Alpha Doms, and I'm positive Starr and Billie partake in their sexual pursuits, we've never spoken about it.

Dinner continues with delicious dishes, fine wine, and pleasant conversation.

But Simon has my mind on overdrive, more than likely on purpose. I push the distracting thoughts aside and refocus on my friends. Tomorrow will take care of itself. *Be present*, a Starrism I've adopted.

"YOU LOOK WONDERFUL, Lola. The photos do not come close to your radiance. Married life has given you a special glow."

Interesting. Simon must follow me in the media. Why else would he mention photos?

Not that I was by any means attempting to impress him, but I put a bit more razzle-dazzle into my outfit.

A white wool-crepe midi dress with an off-the-shoulder neckline artfully folded to frame my collarbones. The nipped-in waist and darts at my hips highlight my curvy figure. Plus the color stresses my sun-kissed skin from the week Baz and I spent aboard *Serendipity*, his parents' megayacht cruising the Mediterranean Sea after we left Verbier.

I kept my hair and makeup simple with an upswept style and a natural palette, matte red lipstick for the zinger. To add height to my petite frame sky-high, glittery Swarovski crystal strappy sandals adorn my feet.

Most importantly, I wore my elaborate diamond hand harness attached to my eternity band and my Ice Rink engagement ring. My Captain Caveman wanted to ensure no one would mistake me for a single lady. And I want to drive that point home to Simon tonight.

I am here for business only.

"Yes," I respond, then lean forward to pin him with my hazel stare. "Tell me about your business proposition."

A smile plays at the corners of Simon's full mouth as he runs his fingers through his wavy flaxen hair. A lock falls over his eye and it reminds me of how I slipped it behind his ear that night in his Parisian penthouse.

I glance away.

"Of course," Simon replies. His eyes scan my face before he continues, "Lola's Coterie could benefit from being a part of the new luxury e-commerce portal my company plans to launch in the next six months. The brands represent the absolute best in their categories and offer exclusive and unique items sought after by the highest echelons of the überwealthy. We handpick the brands and the clients must apply to the portal, then pay a significant annual access fee."

Simon pauses to gauge my reaction. Then adds, "Ordinarily you would sign an ironclad or rather a steel-clad nondisclosure agreement being your husband's company includes a retail division."

He stops again and pins me with his mind-blanking stare, the blue of his eyes turns dark sapphire at the edges.

"But you and I have a history built on trust. I can still trust you, *non, belle?*" Simon asks.

I swear my body temperature rises instantly and my underarms prickle. The heat on my face lets me know my cheeks flushed from his reference to that night.

Damn! Simon took control again.

I lift my glass of Marcassin Estate Chardonnay to my lips. The movement catches his eye. Good. Before the rim touches my alluring, red-stained mouth, I stare directly into his hooded eyes, then respond.

"Yes, Simon."

This time I speak those words, I know the sub always has the true power in the D/s relationship. I set the limits and can choose to stop at any time. I'm in control.

The smile stretches from one corner of Simon's lips to the other and his eyes sparkle in delight. With a nod, he lifts his wineglass in salute. Touché.

We spend the rest of dinner discussing the venture's details. He answers the questions I think off the cuff knowledgeably. This dinner was no ruse to get in my panties again.

It appears a sound opportunity that would increase Lola's Coterie's exposure on the Internet and add another stream of revenue—the potential remarkable. I let him know the need to speak with my team and Sebastian about it.

Simon agrees. Then tells me he'll be in New York City next month so we can schedule a meeting at his US offices. At that point, we'll sign NDAs prior to the presentation. Our assistants will organize the best date for all parties.

When we return to STEELE Rodeo Drive, Simon walks with me to the elevator bank for the VIP suites. As it so happens, he's in the other Penthouse Suite that's accessed by the rear door of the elevator I use to access my suite.

"I won't ask you to tell me your reason for ignoring my calls, text messages, and visits to your flagship offices after our magnificent night together. I respect you, Lola, and your decision not to be my sub. No matter how much I wanted to continue our relationship," he says as we part through the separate elevator doors on the top floor. "But I will tell you Steele is a very lucky man who better treat you right."

I stare at the man who had I met later when I was in a different mindset could have been the one. With a nod, I hold out my hand.

"*Bonne nuit*, Simon."

"*Bonne nuit fais de beaux rêves*," he replies as he clasps my hand between his much larger ones.

I can only hope Baz's dreams are sweet after I call him to say I had dinner with Simon, albeit it for business.

Fuck. Me.

Simon Blanchett is the man who introduced my wife to spanking. The man who owns the largest fashion e-commerce platform in the world on which many of STEELE's brick-and-mortar clients host their online presence.

Not a direct competitor to our Retail Properties Division per se, but on a personal degree, he's my archrival…

Almost three years ago the woman who fell into my arms at LEVELS New York—the flagship location for the global, luxury, members-only BDSM/dance clubs created by Malcolm and Lucien—took my breath away. My body jolted from her touch and my cock sprang to life from her sinful little body—my Petite Seductress.

Before our scene Lola told me her last lover was a Dom who spanked her for the first time and she enjoyed it. A feral growl ripped from between my clenched teeth. I wanted to rip his fucking head off. Mine!

Now I'm going to rip the head on his shoulders and the one in his pants off.

To have the absolute audacity to approach my wife—business opportunity or not—goes beyond the code. No Dom addresses another's sub without explicit permission. As an experienced Dom, without a doubt he's aware of that respectful conduct.

It took every ounce of my control not to call my second flight crew to file a plan for an immediate trip out to LAX. But for the fact Lola asked me to trust her—the basis of our relationship, marriage and D/s—I would have been at Blanchett's suite door in a matter of hours. He's lucky I didn't have his ass kicked out of my hotel.

Instead, I called my personal trainer and former MMA champion Borya *The War Defender* Alexeyev to our session an hour early. The big Russian grumbled to meet at 4:15 in the morning, but complied since I pay him a sizable salary to be on call.

Our sparring gave me a chance to release the tension—and need for reckoning—before my workday began.

That was a month ago.

Lola, Luc, Blair, and I sit across from Blanchett, our respective teams beside us. Not in his offices as he planned originally. Rather in the conference room of STEELE's twenty-ninth floor executive floor where Lola has her suite of offices down the corridor from mine. This meeting occurs on my territory, no power exchange with Blanchett ever.

My forebears chose this Billionaires' Row location at the corner of Fifty-Seventh Street and Fifth Avenue to build the modern, gray-tinted glass fifty-seven story mixed-use skyscraper. It's function to impress clients and to intimidate competitors.

Through its floor-to-ceiling windows, the city stretches out with unobstructed views. Central Park to the north, the Hudson River to the west, the East River opposite, and the rest of Manhattan to the south from Midtown to Battery Park. On a sunny, cloudless day like this morning, the panoramas are riveting.

The decor—as sleek as the exterior—features platinum silk wall treatments, ebony wood floors, dove gray and white leather furniture, crystal light fixtures, Lucite tables, steel accents, and original artwork. The reception area has a spacious desk. Three attractive receptionists with head-sets in their ears and custom-tailored light gray dress suits and skin-tone heels that serve as uniforms sit behind it.

The majesty of our power awes all who enter SI's head-quarters.

It's the exact chord I want to strike with Blanchett. Despite his nonchalance, I sense his vulnerability at being in my presence.

When Lola told me who he was to her, I had my guy do an extensive background check on Blanchett. Nothing unseemly stuck out: thirty-nine; street smart; tech savvy;

philanthropic; respected by his employees and peers; in between subs he usually keeps for a few months.

But his Achille's heel lies in his feeling less than since his formal education ended at eighteen. Whenever he's interviewed, Blanchett scoffs at those with higher levels of education and throws shade on them. He prides himself on being self-made through his grit and "not a fancy degree that hangs on a wall collecting dust and not money."

A dominant man such as myself who comes from a wealthy family and attended Harvard University, both undergrad and Business School—as my family's legacy—irks Blanchett. Not to mention Lola denying him as her Dom, yet she's with me.

My guy also found Blanchett holds a Global All Access membership to the LEVELS clubs—New York, Paris, London. Lola told me he wanted to take her to the Paris location, but she freaked out after their encounter and never returned his calls. Good!

Blanchett's behavior during this meeting will be the deciding factor in his interest of Lola's company or of the woman herself.

Game fucking on.

"Mr. Steele, the nondisclosure agreement is acceptable."

STEELE's General Counsel for New York brings me back to the conference room.

I thank her, and her administrative assistant passes a copy to each of us. Once they're signed, my gaze goes to Blanchett.

"You may proceed," I tell him.

Only a slight change around his eyes hints at his irritation with my undisguised command. His expression shutters as he recovers quickly. Blanchett signals to his team lead, and their presentation begins.

During the course of the ninety minutes, I observe Blanchett. He keeps to a professional demeanor and addresses Lola appropriately. It appears his interests lie in the new portal and a partnership with Lola's Coterie.

Luc and I ask questions along with members of Lola's team and STEELE's marketing team. Blanchett allows his people to answer, but adds to their responses as necessary. His display of leadership and grace combined with the solid opportunity prove a partnership with his company has the potential to be worthwhile.

The CEO of STEELE International, Inc. in me sets personal issues aside. I acknowledge the deal could benefit Lola's Coterie significantly. The potential for other STEELE retailers not already associated with Blanchett Retail Enterprises could increase their revenue, too.

As it always concerns me: does the deal have a high profit margin and will it add to STEELE International's bottom line? Yes, well, it's a go. No, then no go.

Lola expresses her likelihood of participating and tells Blanchett we will discuss it amongst ourselves, then get back to him next week.

After we married, Lola was appointed to STEELE's board of directors as I was to Lola's Coterie. I've taken on an advisory role to her similar in capacity to Luc. Final decisions lie with her ultimately.

Blanchett nods his acceptance, and the meeting ends.

"Luc, do you plan to attend the Hearts of Love Foundation Gala?" Blanchett asks in French as he strides around the table to where we stand. "I sit on the board and see Banque Montaigne listed as a sponsor this year."

Luc pauses in his conversation with Lola to face Blanchett. Then assesses him coolly as only aristocrats can without coming across as rude.

I have to laugh to myself when I realize two men from Lola's past stand before me.

Luc, who I swore wanted to fuck her despite being her "mentor." Fortunately, I've let go of my jealousy of her relationship with Luc. For one since she wears my rings and two since he and Blair appear to be an item.

Blanchett, well…

"Yes. Where I invest my money, I invest my time," Luc responds.

Being fluent in French—Italian and Russian—I understand what's spoken and Blanchett's subtle attempt to isolate me from the conversation, not realizing my language abilities.

Rule Number One: never underestimate an opponent.

Rule Number Two: know your opponent's allies.

Luc responds in French, but shifts his stance to encompass Lola, Blair, and me. He knows my fluency and undoubtedly what Blanchett sought to accomplish.

I reconsider my thought of this being strictly business. It's obvious Blanchett still has some degree of interest in Lola, or he's just pissed I got what he wanted.

As a dominant Alpha male, I don't blame him. But oh the fuck well. Lola is mine.

However, I would never hamper my wife's business goals. So I won't speak on Blanchett's behavior with her further. Rather, I smile and join in on the conversation; Blanchett attempts to hide his surprise.

Rule Number Three: keep them on edge.

Rule Number Four: remain vigilant at all times.

One wrong move and both heads will roll.

THE SENSUOUS PULSATING rhythm of the music combined with the moans of those being pleasured or punished strum through my body. Lola and I enter the BDSM dungeon known as the Cellar at LEVELS New York for a night of hedonistic passion.

The flagship is situated inside a multilevel brick warehouse in the historic Manhattan neighborhood of the Meatpacking District as a play on the area's name. Put a club where men pack their meat into willing women, and willing men allow women to pack them with their toys.

The historic reference continues with the decor. The lobby is minimal and industrial. The fixtures and furniture that appear well worn are high-end, modern replicas used to add authenticity without the grime of old pieces. The two sides have coordinating greeter stations that allow access to the separate Dine & Dance levels and the BDSM levels.

All Access members can choose from any of the seven

levels. While the Dine/Dance members only have access to the party levels—Sky Lounge, Dance Club, and Level 4 Restaurant. For consistency and members' comfort, locations share the same layout with varying views:

Seven levels: 7th Sky Lounge that offers for the Meatpacking location a stunning, 360-degree view of Manhattan and across the Hudson River to New Jersey's shoreline, a bar, restaurant by day dance club by night, a coverable pool that's open during the warmer months, and a glass-retractable roof; 6th and 5th multilevel dance club with two bars and a lounge for food and drinks; 4th Level 4 Restaurant and bar open for breakfast, lunch, and dinner; 3rd has twelve private suites for members to continue their pleasure apart from the BDSM levels; 2nd Peepshow for BDSM with seating alcoves, primary stage, mini-stages, performance rooms, and a bar that serves non-alcoholic mocktails; below ground the Cellar a BDSM dungeon with mocktails bar.

Since the club caters to the crème de la crème of society, male and female. Members include the likes of US Attorney Generals, international politicians, royalty, and high-powered industry titans. Entry is rigorous and participation consensual. The most wealthy and influential prefer their sexual proclivities remain private.

LEVELS offers a judgment-free safe haven with the relative protection one can expect from the signed ironclad nondisclosure agreement required from every member and their guests. Patrons relax and indulge their every whim or socialize at the dance clubs or restaurants.

Tonight Lola and I plan to indulge.

Recently I've loosened up and agreed to join the public spaces sans masks. Lola complained I was being overly Captain Caveman since we only ventured out during Masquerade Night.

True, after we married, I didn't want another man seeing what is mine. But she pointed out the fact we didn't wear masks before and she was mine. Thus our faces remain uncovered and it's a regular night.

Even though her tantalizing curvy body is on full blast in her Lola's Coterie playsuit. If you can call a black satin belt with continuous holes that winds around her body from her neck to the outsides of her lush tits, doubled below them to wrap around her slim waist and ample hips then to cup her crotch for a naughty bondage look a suit of any kind. Her nipples and areoles covered by diamond pasties and her bare pussy by a sheer flesh-tone crotchless thong. Her shapely legs lengthened by matching fuck-me mules.

She wore her raven hair out in lustrous waves that skim her ass as her hips sway. Her mouth a pouty red I can't wait to see stain my cock.

Above the belt, my diamond collar adorns her neck. The pavéd center loop connects to a thin platinum chain I hold in my hand as we walk. The Cellar's lighting makes my collar sparkle, leaving no doubt Lola is my sub.

When we come out to play, she wears a platinum band

that matches mine instead of her wedding jewelry to avoid any damage to the pieces.

As Lola removed her wool cape at the Cellar's double doors, my lower jaw hit the floor and my dick hardened down my leather covered thigh. I had to adjust its length in my pants because of the uncomfortable confines. I understood then why she wouldn't let me see her before we left our duplex penthouse.

Naughty Pet.

My cock twitches at the thought of spanking that luscious ass and watching the flesh jiggle as it blooms from blush pink to crimson red. Oh, she'll wear my marks tonight.

I also know Lola did it on purpose to incite a punishment. My woman loves the release I help her reach.

Naughty, Naughty Pet.

My smirk falls off my face when I spot Blanchett in the center of the dungeon. He's standing on a demonstration stage with a vamp red leather spanking bench and a petite raven-haired woman who stares up at him adoringly. From this distance I can't discern his words to the members gathered, but the hairs on the back of my neck rise all the same.

This motherfucker.

He has a sub who bears an extremely close resemblance to my wife!

What. The. Fuck?!

"Sir, what's wrong?"

Lola's pillowy tits press into my back, the heat of her

body seeps through the thin cotton of my lace-up, long-sleeved shirt. She rises on her toes to whisper in my ear since I halted abruptly, and she bumped into my back.

I narrow my eyes at Blanchett while I reach a hand behind me to hold Lola in place. Damned if I'll let him see her half-assed naked! He may have had sex with her years ago, but this is now. And I'm not having it.

Mine!

Lola being busy as usual slips around my other side. She peers up at my face, then her gaze follows mine. When she sees Blanchett strapping the sub to the bench, Lola's eyes widen in shock.

Quickly, she glances at me to gauge my reaction. Her mouth set in a perfect O, and the wrong cheeks redden as she flushes with embarrassment. Lola also picked up on the startling resemblance between her and Blanchett's sub.

Since Blanchett's background check noted he's in between partners, he must have requested of the LEVELS concierge an introduction to a woman fitting Lola's description, or he happened upon this one. Either way, this clears shit up for real.

He's not over Lola at all.

SEBASTIAN

"*Joyeux Anniversaire!*"

"Happy Birthday!"

My parents, the Beaulieus, and Luc celebrate The Twins' six-month birthday the day after Roger and Leonie return from their two-month-long honeymoon in Verbier.

Lola and I flew into Paris last night for the party, to update Roger on another bullshit legal claim, and for a meeting with Blanchett to complete the deal with Lola's Coterie.

Yeah, like I said, I don't let personal impede a sound business deal. So, Lola's moved forward with the partnership.

However, I made it clear to her should Blanchett so much as smile at her in a way I find inappropriate, I will finish him. Then I'll buy his fucking company and enfold it within STEELE International.

Fuck with a Steele and see what happens.

However, I refuse to let my mind dwell on any negativity right now. I'm here to celebrate my adorable nephews.

We're in Roger and Leonie's triplex penthouse in The STEELE Tower Paris gathered around the dining room table with Rodolphe and Gaspard sitting in their high chairs. They're bedazzled by the flickering candles on the identical cakes before them.

As everyone sings, The Twins bounce and wave their arms in amusement. Each has one little tooth that gleams in the light. All the drooling and tears led to their first tooth. Each time I see them, they surprise me with their growth.

I still can't believe it's been half a year already and three months since Lola promised we'd start a family of our own.

As Roger and Leonie bend over to blow out the candles, a pang hits my chest when they lean in to kiss The Twins' chubby cheeks and Gaspard says, "Dada, dada!"

Roger looks stunned.

"Dada, dada."

Everyone looks over to Rodolphe, and he waves his arms, repeating the words.

Roger has tears in his eyes as he lifts first Gaspard, then Rodolphe into his arms. He kisses their cheeks and holds them close.

Leonie wraps her arms around the three of them. Roger buries his face in her hair. It's an unexpected, momentous occasion that overwhelms the first-time parents.

The room is silent save The Twins and their baby sounds.

"Well, Dada, don't get all sappy on us!"

We glance at Harris, who laughs.

"I'm ready for some cake, bro!"

Everyone laughs at the jokester.

While Roger continues to hold The Twins and turns to me, Lola helps Leonie cut the cakes made by the Twins' *grand-mère* Josy.

"How's married life treating you, bro?" I ask as I reach for Rodolphe, then nuzzle his cheek, inhaling his baby scent.

"Incredible, man! Now I know why you went all loopy after you married Lola!" Roger chuckles and his eyes dance. Then turns serious. "I never would have thought I could be so happy. Having my wife and my sons makes me complete. I won't allow anyone to harm them or to come between us, ever. They're mine, all mine."

Then he glances towards our wives and back at me.

"So, how's progress on fatherhood for you?" He asks, his famous intense stare locking on me. "You guys seemed pretty eager before you left Verbier."

I take a moment to consider our progress. Lola had just taken her three-month birth control injection before we left for Roger and Leonie's wedding. Since we agreed to have a baby, Lola told me the other day she didn't renew it this month when I asked her about it.

So I'd say we're making excellent progress. I can't wait to have a sweet-smelling bundle of my own.

As if agreeing with me, Rodolphe raises the same gray eyes as mine to gaze at me so like his father. Then the mini Steele laughs, drool slipping down his chin.

I laugh and wipe his mouth as I tell Roger he won't be the only dada for long!

We spend the next half an hour opening presents. With The Twins' development in mind, the gifts include stacking toys with different-sized rings and multi-colored cubes; cars, trains, and balls that roll, light up, and make music to encourage crawling; roly-poly toys; sturdy toys that encourage pulling up to standing; to keep them entertained, colorful board books.

The Dynamic Duo give them some gadgets claiming one is never too young for technology.

Luc bought them their first stock portfolios. The men were more impressed and had a lengthy discussion about the growth potential.

Afterwards, we go to the cinema room with aperitifs.

Haley surprises Roger and Leonie with a compilation movie of our first family Christmas and New Year's. No one even realized she was taking footage while we were together. Some scenes from us skiing, the angle straight on as though we were still on the piste; making s'mores at the outside firepit; The Twins first snowfall; the New Year's Eve fireworks in the village.

She has it set to some of Leonie's favorite Christmas

songs, including "Christmas Canon" and Andrea Bocelli and Céline Dion's "The Prayer."

She gives Haley an enormous hug as tears well in her amber eyes.

Haley impresses everyone, and we request copies. Always prepared, she hands out artfully packaged copies to each of us.

Then everyone departs since we have a busy workday tomorrow.

My parents and Lola and I take the family's private elevator to our respective penthouses on the two floors below Roger and Leonie. Our residences occupy the top floors, twenty-eight through thirty-two.

The Tower is in the Front de Seine district of Beaugrenelle in the *quinzième*. Like its New York City counterpart, it's mixed-use with commercial and residential space plus the largest mall in Paris. The views of the Seine and of the Eiffel Tower are incredible, especially at night when the spectacular light display flits across the monumental iron structure.

Malcolm, Harris, and Haley return to their suites at the STEELE Place Vendôme. Guy and Josy leave for their family's ancestral home, *Le Beaulieu Manoir*. Their driver will take Luc to his mansion first as both live in the posh *seizième* arrondissement.

"Good night, sweethearts. I can't wait for our next grandchild!" My mother Shelley exclaims as she hugs Lola and me before we step off the elevator.

"Now, do not pressure them, Shelley," my father

admonishes.

She lowers her eyes, but winks at us.

I'll never get over how my father and mother share a D/s relationship, too. In the bedroom, since my mother is as independent as Lola. I guess our kids will wonder the same about us I chuckle to myself.

I give my mother a squeeze and whisper in her ear, "Me, too."

Lola's smiles, but remains silent.

I clasp her hand and lead her off the elevator. Once inside, we go to our bedroom.

"I can't believe how much Rodolphe and Gaspard grew since we saw them. What do you think Roger and Leonie feed them?" I stop when I realize breast milk. No need for the visual of my brother's wife.

Lola makes a noncommittal sound as she walks into the bathroom. She tosses her dress onto a chair. Her round ass beckons to me as I watch the thong disappear between her ample cheeks.

The water turns on from the shower.

I follow her, my cock hardening at the thought of her luscious body slick with water and soapsuds, steam playing peekaboo with her curves. As I stroke my bulge through my boxer briefs, I slip behind Lola where she stands at the sink wiping her makeup off.

"How about we make a baby and give The Twins a cousin, hell, maybe two?" I murmur against Lola's neck as my lips trail open-mouthed kisses to her bare shoulder.

My hands cup her natural D-cup tits. They're more

than a handful, even for my sizable hands. I heft their weight and tweak the plump nipples that sit high on the pillowy mounds until they harden to points, pulling on them persistently.

"Mmmmmm… Baz," Lola mewls, grinding her hips against my tented boxer briefs. "Please fuck me, Sir."

With a low growl, I nip the sensitive skin where her neck meets her shoulder. Lola cries out, and I smile satisfied against her skin before I lap at it to soothe the bite of pain.

"So tender, so sweet, Little Pet," I croon seductively.

Lola squirms, and I spank her ass in quick succession, one cheek after the other. She rises on her toes and braces herself against the vanity top. Her hips roll with each slap.

"Aaaahhh… Yeeesss, Sir," she moans.

My hand snakes around her hip to cup her mons through the silk thong, stroking my thick, long middle finger along the damp crotch. The tip of my nail scrapes her swollen clit beneath its hood.

Lola yelps as her body jerks in response.

I continue to play with her nipples as I grind against her, driving Lola's hips into the edge of the counter. My body folds over hers as I force her to bend at the waist, her torso parallel to the vanity top and her lower half pinned by my muscular legs.

A swift kick to widen her stance allows me to move between her legs, humping my groin against her ass.

Fuck, she feels so good. I growl in her ear to let her

know just how pleased I am with her delectable body. It's my playground.

When I sense Lola's on the cusp of an orgasm, I stand abruptly and rip her thong off, then toss her over my shoulder. A smack to her ass settles her in place as I stride to the steamy glass-enclosed shower.

Once inside, I place Lola on her feet and angle the showerheads to rain water on her. Then lather the lusciousness of Lola in the enticing bodywash she uses. Its sultry bergamot, lemon, ylang-ylang, peach, and green notes drive me wild.

My fingers slip over her slick skin as she writhes with pleasure, eyes closed and head tilted back. Her soft sighs make my cock throb. But her pleasure first, as always.

I dip my fingers between her folds, now even more wet from the shower. Lola mewls and tightens her grip on my shoulders as she rises to her toes to wrap one leg around my hips.

A swat to her ass stills her pussy undulating against my palm as she attempts to ride my fingers.

"I will give you your pleasure, Naughty Pet."

The rumble sends a shudder through Lola. She presses her torso against mine as she wraps her arms around my neck. Anchored to me, her needy whimpers thrum in my ears.

My gentle thrusts in her pussy increase in pace and pressure. When a third finger joins the other two, Lola's inner walls tighten and flutter with her impending orgasm.

I coat the thumb from my left hand with some of her

pussy juices, then press the tip against her bottom hole. The tight ring of muscles gives way to my invasion of her most private hole as I alternate thrusts to her pussy with those to her ass. The erotic, tight fit proves too much for Lola.

"Cum for me hard all over my fingers, Little Pet," I command. "Cum. Right. Now!"

I punctuate each word with deep thrusts.

Lola throws her head back and keens as wave after wave of her climax racks her body. She quakes in my arms. Her greedy pussy and ass muscles clench on my fingers over and over.

All the while, I continue to move within her holes rhythmically and murmur provocative words to inflame her passion.

"Splendid girl, Little Pet," I praise Lola.

"Thank you, Sir," she whispers as her heated forehead rests on my chest.

I kiss the top of her silky head and steady her as I rinse the suds off. A slap of my palm against the panel turns the water off, and I help her from the shower. Wrapped in a warm bath sheet, I dry Lola off and sit her on the oversized terrycloth ottoman. Then I strip out of my boxer briefs and towel off.

Lola's lust-filled hooded stare watches my every move. She never fails to tell me how much my sculpted frame turns her on just as much as my ten inches.

I stroke my length and smirk when the gold in her hazel eyes spark with renewed carnal interest.

"Oh, my Little Pet, you will have my cock deep inside of you. It's time my seed fills your womb and takes root," I say advancing on Lola.

For a brief moment, the spark dims in her eyes. I dismiss it in my heightened state and pick her up to carry her from the bathroom. Lola tenses when I place her on our bed, but relaxes when I kiss her silly.

Lola falls back against the pillows when I crawl up her lush body, trailing kisses in my wake. Her knees fall apart as the head of my cock nudges her swollen seam.

We groan in unison when I breech her tight pussy with my wide girth. I set a pace of long and even strokes, sure to touch every surface of Lola's warm, wet sheath. The sensation sends ripples of ecstasy along my spine.

Lola cries out as her pussy spasms with another orgasm. It squeezes my dick like a vice.

I want to make it last, so I dip my head to pull her turgid nipple into my mouth. As I suckle deeply, just the way Lola likes it, she bows her back and digs her nails into my scalp to lock me to her breast.

"Ooohhh... Baaazzz. So good, baby, so good," Lola moans as she meets each of my thrusts with one of her own.

I reach beneath her and cup her round ass in my hands to keep her in place. Unable to hold back any longer, I drill her into the mattress repeatedly. The frisson of my climax starts at my toes and works its way up the backs of my legs. It increases the force of my pistoning strokes into Lola's sopping wet pussy.

Her pussy grips my cock and hungrily draws me further inside until I hit her cervix.

It's the trigger to my release.

My speed increases as I growl through each spurt of my release, "Take it. Take every last drop of it, and give me a son, Lola!"

The copious amounts of my seed shoot deep in her womb, bathing it thoroughly. The caveman in me throws his head back and roars.

"Mine, Lola! You are mine and only mine!"

Images of Blanchett with Lola run through my head. Followed by thoughts of him fucking a sub who resembles my woman drive me over the brink.

Yeah, I want a baby with Lola. But I also want to make her belly swell with my seed as a sign she is mine completely.

Like Roger said, *"Having my wife and my sons makes me complete. I won't allow anyone to harm them or come between us, ever. They're mine, all mine."*

That just about sums it up.

LOLA

"*L*ola!!! What. The Fuck?! Are you serious with me right now?!"

I jump ten feet when Sebastian's angry bellow startles me. I damn near stab myself in the eye as I apply mascara at my vanity in my dressing room of our New York City duplex penthouse in The STEELE Tower.

Simon and I signed the contracts last month during our meeting in Paris. Today, we have our first gathering with our combined marketing and sales teams.

Obviously I need both eyes…

Sebastian storms in. Through the reflection I notice his face is an angry shade of red and his dove gray eyes flash daggers in my direction.

Oh fuck…

"What—"

"NO! Just stop! You fucking lied to me for weeks now! All the millions of times we were 'making a baby,' you laid beneath me and lied!! How could you, Lola?! Do you think this is some sort of a game? All you had to say was *I need more time*!! We've been married for damn near two years. What would another six months matter?! We promised we would always tell each other the truth. And. You. Fucking. Lied. To. Me. Lola!!!"

I can only sit in astonishment. Never has Sebastian spoken to me in this manner or been this furious. My mind runs through reasons and comes up blank. What the hell did I lie... Oh no. There's no way he could know...

"Yeah you know, don't you?! I can see it in your face, Lola!"

He folds his arms across his massive heaving chest and stands with his feet planted wide, staring down at me. The look of pure disgust on his handsome face makes me flinch.

We stare at each other, knowing who speaks first loses leverage. Our relationship started with a deal, and we always fall back on the rules of engagement.

But I'm at fault, so I give in. I won't lie further and can only pray he'll forgive me.

"Baz, I just need more time, especially with the new e-commerce portal partnership. To get pregnant now wouldn't let me get the work done. I—"

"Are you serious with me right now?! You lied to me about stopping your birth control injection so you can WORK?! No fucking way, Lola! That's a poor-ass excuse!!!" Sebastian shouts as he throws his hands in the air.

The veins in his neck bulge and the corners of his lips

turn into a sneer. He looks me up and down, shakes his head, and strides from the room.

"Baz!! Wait!!!" I scream as I leap from the tufted stool. It crashes backwards to the hardwood floor. "Sebastian, I'm SORRY!!!"

His long legs carry him from our bedroom to the outer sitting room swiftly. I rush to reach him. He slams the door shut behind him, and the wooden frame shakes with the force. It stops me in my tracks.

Damn!

I take but a moment to fling the door open and race out the door. I glance towards the stairs as I hasten in that direction, only to hear the ding of our private elevator down the hall.

He's leaving our home!

With a burst of speed, I run to catch Sebastian. Our eyes meet through the two inches before the doors close as I skid to a halt in front of them. When I see tears in his eyes, I cry out in agony and slap my palms against the wood.

Oh, no… What the fuck have I done???

A sob tears from between my lips as I crumble to the floor. Pain like I've never known pierces my heart. It's as though a piece of my soul ripped from the deepest part of my body, leaving me with an irreparable void.

I have no idea how long I sit there with tears streaming down my cheeks. Minutes? Hours?

When the house phone rings, I drag myself to my feet and go into the closest room to answer. It's Blair. She had the concierge call since I didn't answer my mobile. I left it in my dressing room.

The meeting starts in fifteen minutes.

Damn.

I reason with myself Sebastian won't speak to me at this moment, so I ask Blair to buy me time. Twenty minutes, and I'll be ready. Back at my vanity after washing my face, I check my mobile and only see missed calls and text messages from Blair—nothing from Sebastian.

Again, I tell myself it's best to let him calm down before I contact him. In reality, I don't want to miss my meeting. Besides, Sebastian of all people understands the importance of being professional and accomplishing one's business goals.

Hell, I should be upset he's upset. I wouldn't stop him or expect him to get pregnant with an important deal to finish.

The idea of Baz pregnant makes me giggle.

We'll be all right.

"WHY DON'T we continue these discussions over dinner? We can order some food in and knock this out."

Blair's suggestion would make sense if Sebastian and I hadn't argued this morning.

I pause to consider my options. I haven't heard from him all day. When I dropped by his office, Melody Lawson —one of his two personal assistants—told me he was out at appointments for the rest of the day followed by a business dinner.

Either I could go home and wait for him or get this done and get home around the same time as him. We can talk then.

I ignore the niggle in my chest and shoot Sebastian a text message to let him know I'm working through dinner and will see him after his business engagement.

"Excellent recommendation, Blair! Lola, you agree, *non?*" Simon says. His ice-blue eyes regard me intently.

I shrug off any hesitation and smile brightly, "Of course! Let's get this done!"

Simon beams, and Blair pulls up the menu for our favorite Thai restaurant.

The time flies as we work and eat and work some more. Before I realize it, four hours pass. Shocked, I check my mobile for any communication from Sebastian. Seeing none, I turn my attention back to the others and finish the last bit on the plan.

Thirty minutes later, Simon and I stand at the private elevator that connects the STEELE offices to the family's residences. I smile up at him.

"That was incredibly productive!" I say.

"*Oui*, we accomplished much," Simon begins, staring at me. "But you seemed distracted at times. Are you all right? Nothing wrong at home I hope."

Surprised he caught my lack of focus and would ask about my personal life, I glance away and shake my head.

"I have quite a few projects going on. But all run

smoothly. I appreciate your concern," I tell him, purposefully ignoring the "at home" comment. Like I need another reason for the Wrath of Captain Caveman…

"Simon, I'll walk you to the main elevators."

Blair's voice interrupts Simon's next words.

He closes his mouth and nods. Then he bows to me before he strides in the direction Blair indicates. With his back to her, Blair raises an elegant eyebrow at me in question.

I ignore her, too, and place my palm on the elevator call panel as I bid them good night.

When I step off on the fifty-fifth floor for the second level of our duplex, a sense of sadness overtakes me. I haven't heard from Sebastian. He didn't respond to my text message. I murmur a prayer he'll forgive me as I walk through our darkened sitting room. Just as I reach the bedroom door, a lamp flicks on.

"Where have you been, Lola?"

Once again, Sebastian startles me. I glance over my shoulder to find him dressed as earlier, seated on a chair by the fireplace. He has a crystal snifter of amber liquid in his hand—undoubtedly his favorite Jackson Special Blend Scotch.

I swallow as I take in the closed expression on his face and the aloof body language. He's not letting me in. My mouth sours as a wave of nausea hits me.

"In my offices. We worked through dinner. I sent a text message to you. Melody said you were out at appointments, then had a business dinner. So I figured we would catch up later." The words tumble from my lips in a rush.

Sebastian lifts the glass to his mouth and sips as he peers at me over the rim. His unchanged gaze locks on me.

"With Blanchett?" He asks, watching me closely.

"Yes," I reply. But when a flash gleams in his eyes, I add, "Of course, with both of our teams present the entire time!"

Sebastian merely stares at me; no response or reaction to my statement.

I swallow and press on.

"How—" I have to clear my suddenly dry throat. "How do you feel now?"

He continues to gaze at me as he swirls the liquid, then puts the snifter on the knee of his leg crossed over the other. Pointedly, he pushes the sleeve of his suit jacket back to glance at his Audemars Piguet watch. The birthday gift I gave to him and said, *"You are priceless to me, Sebastian. Nothing in this world or beyond compares to you. Think of my love whenever you glance at the time."* Moments after, he proposed to me in front of our family and friends in Positano.

Fuck…

"Well, considering it is after ten at night and my wife just returns home after we had our first major argument this morning because she lied to me, I could be better," he replies in a bland tone.

I cross the room in a hurry and drop to my knees in

front of him. I clasp his free hand between mine and stare up at him beseechingly.

"Baz, my love, please forgive me. I did not intend to hurt you… hurt us. I was selfish and should have been honest with you. Will you please forgive me?" I plead.

Sebastian stares back at me, then takes a sip of his Scotch before he places it on the side table.

"I forgive you, Lola. I know how important your company is to you," he stands and looks down at me as I continue to kneel before him. He scans my face, then he continues.

"You let me know when you are ready to have a baby, Lola. You already know I am. I will not ask again," Baz says.

I watch as he walks to our bedroom without a backwards glance. Then cover my face with my hands and cry, knowing the irreparable void just widened.

I cannot believe how easily Lola lied to me. Looked me dead in my face every single fucking day for weeks and lied with no remorse whatsoever. Not a tell to observe. Her nonchalance shocks me.

Had the receptionist at her gynecologist's office not called the duplex's landline and I answered, I never would have known. Ever.

Fortunately for me, my sneaky wife left her umbrella at their office yesterday. Bad luck for her.

All I could see was red. A swirling cyclone of anger centered on the vortex of how Lola would lie to me after all we've been through. So. Fucked. Up.

But the reality hit me, and it hurt so badly I had to get away before the pain of anguish took over from the blinding fury.

We've known each other for nearly three years and married for twenty-two months. I told Lola from the start a D/s relationship requires trust and open, honest communication. If having a baby now is a hard limit, then I would respect her wishes.

Those same principles apply to our marriage. Without them, it dooms the situation for failure and pain of another sort. Heartrending doubt in us.

I'm no wuss and can't remember the last time I cried. But the idea Lola cares so little for us and what we're trying to achieve as a couple cut me to the quick.

Prior to Lola, I never had a relationship beyond satisfying my Dom needs and physical release with a woman one night, maybe two. Lola changed my playboy ways, and I don't regret it. Her love gave me reason to settle down.

But her actions make me wonder if I should have kept to the course I set for myself: remain business focused. I adjusted my ways for her—for us—and she could care the fuck less. Her work is still more important to her than our marriage.

And that's what's so messed up. I give in to change so our relationship can work, and she stays the same for selfish reasons.

Obviously we're in this marriage for better or for worse. But I needed time this morning, and I need it now. The scheduled ten days of business travel couldn't have come at a more opportune time.

So I stalk into my dressing room and continue to pack my luggage as I started an hour ago.

"Wh... What are you doing? Where are you going, Sebastian??"

Caught up in my thoughts, I didn't hear Lola enter the room. I turn to find her clutching her hand to her chest and her eyes wide, glistening with tears. Her gaze bounces between my open garment bag and wheelie.

I don't answer right away. Let her wonder, get a sense of my pain.

Again, she's so self-absorbed she forgot I leave for visits to several STEELE properties in South American cities tomorrow morning. She begged off accompanying me because of the meetings with Blanchett—how fucking convenient.

A vicious growl rumbles from my mouth at the thought.

Lola gasps, assuming I directed the feral sound at her.

I have to stop myself from rolling my eyes in annoyance. Instead, I respond snarkily, "South America for business. Remember? Oh no, that's right, you're too focused on your more important work with Blanchett. Nothing compares, right, babe?"

A subtle jab at her claiming nothing in this world or beyond compares to me

As I stride into my bathroom for my toiletries kit, I throw a scowl at her over my shoulder. At this point, I don't give a damn how immature I behave.

"Baz," Lola cries as she hurries behind me. "That's not fair! You're more important to me and nothing compares to you!"

When she reaches for me, I jerk away and snatch my kit off the shelf.

"Lola, listen, I get it. Don't worry yourself. Why don't you go get ready for bed?" I face her and add, "The jet departs early, so I'm sleeping in one of the guest suites. Wouldn't want to disturb your rest for another long work-day. Good night, sweetheart."

* * *

THE SORROW in Lola's eyes as she stood at our elevator watching me leave for Teterboro at 4 a.m. still stings twelve days later. Some issues arose that kept me longer than expected. With the time changes and how Melody packed my schedule to avoid a lengthy time away, Lola and I communicated little.

On the flight back, I vowed to settle this and to move forward. I let emotion cloud my judgement and didn't give her a chance to explain fully. Not that I won't be pissed, but we can talk it out like adults.

I last told her I'd arrive tomorrow morning. But the meeting moved up, allowing me to arrive earlier than expected. I picked up some dinner from Mr. Chow's Lola's favorite high Chinese cuisine restaurant before my driver Edgar Gonzalez took me home. The delicious food has my mouth watering, along with the thought of Lola doing her happy dance, shimmying her grip-worthy hips.

Now, my driver pulls up to the residence side of The STEELE Tower. As we near the curb, I notice a tall, blond man in conversation with a petite raven-haired woman.

Something he says makes her throw her head back and laugh; his eyes fill with mirth.

I blink to make sure I'm not hallucinating since I didn't even know he was still in New York City. No. Fuck me if it's not Blanchett and Lola standing in front of the entrance to our home.

A string of expletives falls from my mouth. I can't catch a break with bullshit, can I?

Rather than asking Edgar to continue on past the building, I have him pull right up next to the gleeful couple. As my mother says, never air your dirty laundry in public. I'll put on an Oscar-caliber performance: husband returns home from a business trip and sweeps wife off her feet in front of her former lover, leaving him with his dick in his hand.

I don't wait for Edgar to get the door; he can give my luggage to the bellman who will leave it at the penthouse's service entrance. Jumping out, I grab the bag of food and saunter over to Lola and Blanchett a broad grin on my face.

"Lola, sweetheart!" I call as I near them.

Her head swivels in my direction. Wide eyes full of surprise blink at me—she must not believe her eyes either —and her mouth forms a perfect O.

I don't allow my gaze to shift to Blanchett until I wrap my arm around Lola, place my hand on her ass, and kiss her possessively. With my lips still on hers, I glance over at him. Then I stand to my full height, an inch taller than him.

"Blanchett, how good of you to walk my wife home

from the office. The progress of the portal pleases me. What are the latest updates?" I ask.

Rule Number Three: keep them on edge.

They stare at me, unsure how to respond.

Blanchett recovers first. His eyes slide to Lola and back to me before he answers.

"Steele, what a surprise. Lola did not mention your return," he says.

I grin wider and ask, "You don't believe Lola tells you details of our private lives, now do you?"

"Of course I don't!" Lola exclaims as she peeks up at me, eyes searching mine for a clue to my true mood.

To dispel her anxiety, I chuckle and bend down to kiss the top of her head. I eye Blanchett. "Well then, we'll bid you a good night!"

I nod at him, and without awaiting his response, I hustle Lola along with me as I stride past the doorman into the building.

She keeps up on her sky-high stilettos and doesn't utter a word until we're on our elevator.

"Sebastian! You're home early! Why didn't you tell me? I would have fixed dinner for you," Lola says hurriedly, staring up at me, then tilts her head down. "Oh, is that Mr. Chow?"

She squeezes my side where her hand rests to get my attention.

I glance down at her and search her face.

And the winner for best performance in a love triangle drama goes to Sebastian Steele…

Lola fell for my act.

"The better question, how much time has Blanchett spent at our home while I was away on an extended business trip?" I ask her.

She stumbles backwards as though the words knocked the breath from her lungs. Her mouth opens on a gasp and closes as her eyes scan my face.

Lola sputters, "Wh... What do you mean? How can you think I'd allow any man to spend time at our home, Sebastian?"

I cock an eyebrow.

"Sebastian," she says, exasperated. "We need to talk."

The elevator doors open to the first level of our duplex, and I gesture for her to go ahead of me.

"That was my plan and why I picked up food from one of your favorite restaurants. How the hell would I know you and Blanchett had other plans?" I say as I follow her to the entry double doors.

Lola spins and glares at me. The gold flecks in her hazel eyes blaze.

"We didn't have 'plans,' Sebastian! Simon just walked me around the corner from my boutique! How the hell can you call that 'plans'?" She demands, glaring at me, face flushed scarlet with anger.

Oh, so she's upset? How rich!

I ignore her and slap my palm on the entry pad to unlock the double doors. Then without looking at Lola, gesture for her to go ahead of me into our duplex. As she passes, I swear I hear her growl. To keep from chuckling, I bite the inside of my cheek and shake my head.

She drops her handbag on the side table and drapes her coat on the chair beside it before she bends over to remove her over-the-knee boots. The roundness of her ass and the curve of her hips in the black leather pencil skirt call me to push her against the wall and fuck her raw.

It's been too long since we last had sex, and my cock weeps in dismay. But I'll be damned if I give in to the temptation of Lola's lush little body. I'm still pissed with her, and we need to resolve this situation before we can move forward.

So I drag my hungry gaze away. Once again I shake my head, then discreetly adjust my throbbing length.

"Listen, Lola. I'm calling it as I saw it," I respond as I stride past her to the kitchen. "Let's eat before we get into it."

"Fine," she huffs as she follows me in her stockinged feet.

We wash our hands and fix our plates in silence. Not the comfortable silence of a happily married couple, rather the tense silence of an ill-at-ease pair.

Lola heads to the kitchen banquette with our plates.

My eyes rove over her voluptuous figure as her hips sway. My dick tents the front of my tracksuit pants.

Down, boy! Not now.

"White or red?" I ask as I clear my throat.

She glances over her shoulder and bites her plump lower lip in consideration of her wine choice.

I can think of another pair of lips I'd like to bite. And suck. And lave... My facial expression must give away my carnal thoughts based on the sudden heat in Lola's hazel orbs.

Her scorching gaze takes me in from top to toe, hesitating on my enormous bulge. She licks her lips and flares her nostrils. More than likely her thoughts run to her love of sucking me off.

My dick twitches, and she smirks.

"Red, please," Lola murmurs seductively.

Ah, the color of passion. How apropos.

I take another moment to watch her sashay to sit down, then turn to the Sub-Zero wine storage. Along with the bottle, I grab two glasses and pocket the opener. When I place the bottle and glasses on the table, Lola inclines her head towards me with another smirk.

"Happy to see me?" She asks. "Or is that a corkscrew in your pocket?"

I cock my head and grace her with my smirk as I quip, "Wouldn't you love to know?"

Quick as a flash, Lola snakes her hands inside my pants and grips my junk. Her small, soft hand glides along my hard length and squeezes my ample girth. When she rubs her finger across my weeping tip, I grunt and my hips jerk of their own accord.

Lola shifts on the bench and uses her free hand to tug my pants and boxer briefs to drop at my feet. On a satisfied sigh, she leans forward and engulfs my cock with her warm, wet mouth as her hand grips my thick base. Her tongue swirls around the shaft, lowering until my bulbous tip hits the back of her throat. Her gag reflex kicks in, but she doesn't stop.

Instead, Lola lifts her hooded gaze to mine and hums.

The vibrations rock me to my core. My hands dive into her hair to hold her head in place as my hips piston forward. In fast, out slow, in fast, out slow. Long and even strokes. I maintain the controlled pace, barely giving Lola time to catch her breath.

Her splutters and strips of saliva clinging from her lips to my cock fuel my drive. As the first tingles of my orgasm begin at the base of my spine, I increase my pace and rise onto the balls of my feet.

Lola's hands wrap around the backs of my thighs, pressing into the taut muscles. Her whimpers around my dick zing along my nerve endings. Her blown pupils stare up at me.

Fuck!

My hips buck and I plunder her mouth, losing all control. My only thought centered on the orgasm charging through my body, from down my spine and up from my toes to join at the base of my hard-as-steel cock and heavy balls.

"Take it… Take every inch of me… Fuuuckkk!" I bellow as I throw my head back and roar my release, my body shuddering from the force.

My vision blackens and my hearing dulls as I collapse forward, slapping my palms on the wooden table and on the suede bench back.

Slowly, I return to myself to feel Lola licking my spent dick and massaging my empty balls leisurely.

"Mmmmmm… Better than Mr. Chow's any day, Sir," she moans in a low and throaty voice, well-fed by me filling her belly with my seed.

I can only grunt in response as I pull away with a pop.

Her hazel eyes dance in delight as she wipes the corners of her mouth with her pinky finger.

For the third time, I shake my head. Damn, what this woman does to me. As I've always told Lola, she has the power in our relationship. She just took control and brought me to my knees.

"Yes, well, eat up. We still need to talk," I say as I tuck my now happy cock back in my pants.

Out of my periphery, I notice Lola's shoulders sag before she rearranges herself on the bench. Ordinarily, I would never leave her unfulfilled. But where we are is not normal. We need to clear things up so we can get back to that happy couple. Pronto.

I take my seat opposite her and pour the wine in our glasses. My heart tugs when I see Lola glance at me wistfully.

"Sebas—"

"Lola—"

We speak at the same time.

I tilt my head towards her and sit back.

Lola clears her throat and starts again, "I am so very, very sorry, Sebastian. Never should I have lied to you. Ever. Nor do I blame you for being angry with me."

She takes a sip of wine for fortification and continues, "I do want to have a baby, babies, with you. With no doubt."

Lola pauses to lean forward and reaches for my left hand. As she stares at it, she rubs her thumb over my platinum wedding band. Then her tear-filled eyes lift to me.

"I love you, Baz. Only you, forever you. Not Simon or anyone else can ever compare to you or what we share," Lola whispers, her voice warbles with emotion.

She entwines our fingers and brings our joined hands to her lips to kiss them. With an imploring look, Lola stares into my eyes.

"Please, Baz, I want to finish this project first. It launches in five months. Can we please wait until then?" She asks as she squeezes my hand.

I contemplate her request and her actions that led us to where we are now. It is not my wish to interfere with her business, and I understand her commitment. The kicker is, I'm more committed to us than Lola. However, I won't belabor the issue. But I will get my point across.

"One would think after all this time, their loved one would be honest," I respond. "All I ask of you is your honesty, Lola. Had you discussed your decision with me, we would have avoided the argument."

The tears spill from her eyes and my heart clenches. I wipe her face with my other hand and nod.

"As I said before I left, we can wait until you're ready. However, going forward, let's decide together, Lola, as a couple, not as individuals. Do you agree?" I finish as I cup her cheek in my hand.

She turns her face to kiss my palm, then nuzzles against it with her eyes closed on a sigh. Lola rises from her seat to embrace me.

I stand and pull her into my arms. With our bodies fully pressed together, Lola wraps her arms around my neck and nods with her forehead against my chest. Her tears wet my long-sleeved t-shirt.

Petting her back, I say, "Words, Lola. I will have your words."

She pulls back and rises onto her toes to look me square in the eye.

"Yes, Sebastian, my love. Absolutely, yes."

SEBASTIAN

"Sebastian, we've known each other for a very long time. There is absolutely no way you can hide your feelings from me. So don't even try it. Spill it, buddy."

I'm at Quality Meats for lunch with Lydie Jackson—the eldest of the Jackson siblings and my childhood friend for whom I've become a confidante since we're in the same position. She's working to take over the helm at Jackson Corporation from her father, just as I did with STEELE from mine. Both of us consider ourselves the leaders of our siblings and responsible for their wellbeing.

Over the years, she's turned to me for advice, especially since she craves approval from her father, Connor. Lydie will do anything to prove she's as good as a son to lead. The son in question is Lachlan, my best friend and the second oldest of the Jackson clan. He's one year younger than Lydie and their father's preferred heir. But Lachlan is a reluctant heir apparent because he loves his older sister more than he wants to please Uncle Connor. He refuses to hurt her, knowing how much she wants to run their company.

For now, Uncle Connor is holding out on making his final decision since he's not retiring for a few months—it's been up in the air the last couple of years. He continues to hope Lydie will marry and turn to her family life and Lachlan can step up to CEO.

Despite being a stunningly gorgeous woman—only six inches shorter than me in high heels, waist-length dark brown hair, and intelligent green eyes known as the signature Jackson family trait—I've never felt a sexual attraction to Lydie.

Lola however thought differently and broke up with me because she mistook my conversation with Lydie as an affair—albeit from Lola's perspective, the visual was rather damning. From the moment they met, Lola perceived Lydie wanted more and only held back because I hadn't made a move and was a serial playboy who fucked different women without commitments.

Little did I know Lola was correct, and Lydie confessed. She thought I solved her problem since her father would accept me as her behind-the-scenes co-head of Jackson Corporation—the perfect merger of STEELE and Jackson.

Uh, not.

I told her under no circumstances we would ever be more than friends, and Lola was the only woman for me. In the end, Lydie realized her errors and apologized to Lola and me. After which, Lola and I renewed our relationship and married months later.

Understandably I'm more than hesitant to disclose the baby drama Lola and I are dealing with to Lydie. Not to mention the fact Lola would have my balls and thus would end any chance of me carrying on the Steele line. So instead I feign work-related stress.

"You're right. I have a new deal in the works that's proving to be more of a headache than I expected. We have delayed the conclusion for the foreseeable future because of outside forces. So don't mind me," I respond, partially true since the new deal is having a baby obstructed by Blanchett.

Lydie arches her elegant eyebrow and narrows her emerald eyes as she scans my face for any fakery. A full minute later, she nods and lifts her glass of 2007 Sassicaia to her full, ruby lips.

"Okay, let's go with that then," she says with a wry smile. "So tell me, what else is going on with you?"

We fall back into an easy conversation no different from the ones we used to have prior to Lola and I dating. Every month Lydie and I would meet for lunch or dinner and talk on the phone between face time. With Lydie spending more time on the West Coast and focused on her new boyfriend plus me with Lola, our schedules don't allow our get-togethers.

The conversation goes from catching up on our lives since we last saw each other at Roger and Leonie's wedding seven months ago to a business proposal for another STEELE-Jackson partnership. It's light and enjoyable.

Time passes quickly as we chat and eat. I walk Lydie to her car where her driver holds the door open. She turns to me before she gets in.

"It was so good to see you, Sebastian. Perhaps the next time Chase is in town, the four of us can go to dinner," Lydie says with a bright smile.

"That would be nice. And I can give him The Talk, even though I'm sure Lachlan did it already," I smirk.

Her laughter floats around us as I kiss her cheek. "You know he did! Even Laurent had his say in the matter. It's a wonder Chase didn't run away!" Lydie shakes her head as her lustrous hair sways with the movement.

"Excellent," I chuckle. "I'll let Lola know about dinner."

I step back and watch Lydie's Duo-tone cognac and black Bentley Mulsanne glide into traffic. Then stride down Sixth Avenue to head back to my office.

Yeah, it was good to see Lydie. And even better to see her happily involved with another man.

"So, how was your lunch with Lydie?"

I glance at Lola, fork midway to my mouth, as we sit on the terrace off the living room eating the dinner she made and set up like a picnic.

Over the past month she's been extra attentive: sending text messages to me during the day to check in; coming home by six each evening; cooking dinner a few times a week; vamping up her Petite Seductress. I in turn have moved forward and not mentioned a baby or my concerns about Blanchett. So it's been nice and we're back on track.

"It was good. She asked about you and suggested we have dinner with her and her new boyfriend Chase the next time he's in town," I respond, then hold back my chuckle when Lola's eyes widen, and she sputters her wine.

"Yup, Lydie has a new beau who appears serious. Serious enough, her brothers gave him The Talk, and I told her I would, too," I add.

Lola's head bobs, and she claps her hands in glee.

"That's the best news ever! Now she won't have time to moon over you… Sebbie," Lola gibes in reference to Lydie's childhood nickname for me that Lola despises.

I shake my head as I roll my eyes. Women.

"Tell me about your day. How's the progress on the portal?" I say, changing the subject deftly.

Lola smirks in acknowledgment of my tactic, but goes on to answer in lengthy detail. Then mentions a business trip to Paris for meetings with Blanchett's operations and tech teams next month.

"I want you to come with me. Tina checked your calendar and said your schedule could permit the trip," Lola finishes expectantly having spoken with my second personal assistant.

My teeth grind at the thought of her going to Paris to be with Blanchett. Paris, where they fucked. You can bet your ass I'll be there.

Besides, it's our two-year anniversary. I wonder if Lola even remembers since she didn't mention it…

"Of course, babe, I'll confirm with Tina in the morning and ask her to arrange the G650," I answer in an even tone.

"Thanks, baby, you're so good to me!" Lola squeals and climbs onto my lap. "Now it's time for dessert… Sir."

Her seductive purr coupled with her round ass grinding on my groin makes my cock spring to life. From alfresco dining to alfresco fucking. Our penthouse duplex on the fifty-fourth floor with no other buildings around has its perks.

I stand and carry Lola to one of the double-size chaise lounges to spread my tempting treat before me.

I set Lola on her feet. My hands glide along her flanks, hips, and legs to pull the hem of her silk maxi dress up and off. One tug and the tiny scrap of pink lace covering her pussy falls to the floor. Lola in all her luscious naked beauty takes my breath away.

I bow my head to her full D-cup tits to draw a plump nipple into my mouth, puckering in the cool night air. A few lusty sucks followed by sharp nibbles of first one then the other tasty morsel have Lola shifting from one foot to the other as she gasps. I growl and stretch her out on the chaise lounge.

Time to partake.

Her raven hair fans out to frame her gorgeous face flush rosy from her arousal. She bows her back on a throaty moan as she looks down her body at me on my knees between her legs, open wide in full invitation.

"Look at my pretty, little, pink pussy glistening so wet for me, Pet"—I lean forward and brush my nose along her slippery seam and inhale deeply—"Mmmmmm. And it smells delectable. Let us see just how delicious it is, Pet."

Lola writhes and mewls as I lave from her puckered hole along her slit to her clit in one long swipe of my flattened tongue. The tip teases her bundle of nerves until it's engorged, and her thighs clamp around my ears to lock me against her honeypot.

With a wicked chuckle, I nip her inner thighs, place my palms on them, and brush my fingertips against her puffy pussy lips as I press her legs apart again. I watch as her pussy quivers.

"Ooohhh… Sir… Please…" Lola moans, her hips lifting from the chaise lounge to seek my mouth.

"Ah, ah, ah, Naughty Pet," I chastise, then smack her throbbing pussy three times in quick succession.

The squelching and her breathless cries make my cock ache.

But her needs come first—literally. I lift her legs to rest the backs of her thighs on my shoulders as I reposition myself to continue my ministrations with gusto. My determination to bring Lola to orgasm three more times becomes my sole purpose. Groans fall from my mouth in pleasure as her musky and sweet taste cross my palate.

"Ohhhh my Go—"

Her strangled cries cut off as her body shudders from the strength of her climax. Heels knock against the back of my neck as she bucks against my mouth.

I don't let up.

"Aaaahhh… Sssirrr… No more, please!" Lola wails after one orgasm follows another.

She tosses her head from side to side and digs her nails into the cushion. Her inner thigh muscles strain to clench around my head.

Instead, I hold her legs apart while I lap up her juices as she rides out the waves of her climaxes.

"So sweet, just like fresh honey. Tell me your pussy is my personal honeypot, Pet," I growl, my eyes traveling up her body to her reddened, dewy face. "Open your eyes and tell me. All mine!"

Lola's eyes flutter open. Her unfocused expression lets me know she's past a coherent state. But she attempts to follow my command.

"Yes, Sir," she whimpers. "All yours, Sir."

With a satisfied nod, I rise to my feet above her, sprawled out on the chaise to strip out of my clothes. I make quick work of the linen sweater and trousers as I kick off the slides. My clothes land on top of Lola's dress as I discard them without a care.

Single focus: bury my turgid length balls deep in Lola's sopping wet pussy.

I take a moment to stroke my cock. The bulbous tip a vivid red and dripping pre-cum. As my gaze travels over Lola's lush body, so ready for penetration, my dick swells and hardens further.

She must sense my need and lifts her arms in welcome.

On a primal growl, I pounce. Lola squeals.

One hand fists my thick base while the other grips her hip in preparation. I glance at her face and pause. Lola's nod unleashes my pent-up passion.

"Hands above your head, Pet, against the back of the chaise. Do not move them, no matter what happens," I command in my stern Alpha Dom voice.

"Yes, Sir," Lola pants, fully aroused and ready for more.

One brutal thrust, and I make my mark—tip against her cervix and balls slap against her ass.

"Fuuuckkk... Feel so good," I bark, buried deep within Lola's tight core.

"Fuck, yesss!" She screams once I bottom out. "Oohhhhhh..."

My hips take on a mind of their own as they pull back, then slam forward over and over again. I plunder Lola's pussy as she braces herself against the chaise lounge. The grip on her hip increases painfully, sure to leave a bruise.

My other hand lowers to above her shoulder to prevent Lola from sliding back and forth as I piston inside her throbbing pussy.

Looking down at her, I snarl, "You are mine, Lola. You know that, do you not?"

So caught up in our carnal pleasure, she's unable to respond verbally. Her head bobs as her mouth hangs slack, issuing soft mewls and moans.

Enthralled by her big tits bouncing with each thrust, I lower my head to latch onto one pebbled nipple. My tongue flicks, then wraps around the pert tip to suck hard.

The action triggers Lola to buck her hips as her pussy

walls flutter then clamp down on my cock. She orgasms again with a carnal scream.

My dick swells unbelievably in response.

Her nipple drops from my mouth with a pop as I throw my head back and let off a feral roar. No longer even strokes, my movements become unhinged with the need to reach my release. Caveman grunts and growls fill the air around us as my peak draws near.

"Cum for me, Pet. Cum with me now!" I snarl ferociously.

Lola keens and stiffens as her entire body jolts with one last orgasm.

"Good, girl," I praise her as I bury my face in her sweaty neck, overtaken by my toe-curling climax.

She shudders beneath me.

Fuck Blanchett. Lola is mine, all MINE!

SEBASTIAN

"The inventory systems for the portal will connect seamlessly with your Paris, London, New York, Las Vegas, and Beverly Hills warehouses' tracking systems to ensure delivery of packages to clients within the specified distances. The New York and Paris warehouses will coordinate the shipping for international deliveries. This program proves most effective and efficient for other partners with similar locations to yours. Just as important, we put extensive cyber security measures in place to prevent information breaches. Any questions?"

Harris and Haley flew over to Paris with us to take part in the technology portion of Blanchett's meetings. As the Dynamic Duo—tech and hacker wizzes, respectively—the twins were best suited to handle this presentation.

They question Blanchett's team while Lola, Luc, Blair, and I listen on.

As it turns out, the timing for this trip coincided perfectly with a legal update for Roger and STEELE Paris. Yesterday morning, we met with Blanchett. Later that afternoon, our father, Malcolm, our Paris and New York legal teams, and Leonie gathered in Roger's offices. Afterwards we had dinner with our mother, Lola, Guy, and Josy joining the rest of us.

Blanchett Day Two ends with this meeting.

Fortunately, he's been professional and allowed his teams to run the meetings. Occasionally he's glanced in Lola's direction for longer than necessary. But averted his eyes when I glared at him across the conference room table.

Fucker.

I'm keeping it civil for business sake.

Lola appears oblivious. Her attention focused on the presentations and discussions. Her rapt concentration and well-thought comments and suggestions prove her business acumen.

Luc and I exchange looks of pride.

"If this satisfies Haley and Harris, then I give my approval to move forward. However, I require coordination with STEELE Technology and Cyber Security on all matters. Their team will keep me abreast."

Lola's command of the conference room would make anyone doubt she's a sub in the bedroom, I chuckle to myself. Her Independent Woman is at the forefront to handle her business.

The contradiction makes my cock pulse.

"Although my team comprises the best in the field, I will agree to your request," Simon responds.

I note he said request as opposed to Lola's requirement. A glance at her proves she didn't miss his word choice either.

"While I am sure your team is excellent, my business reputation is of the utmost importance. I trust Haley and Harris to handle my technology affairs implicitly," Lola states with her hazel eyes locked on Blanchett unwaveringly.

He has the grace to nod and break the standoff.

Blanchett better had or I would have stepped in. Or Luc from the way he leaned forward zoning in on Blanchett.

"Of course. Whatever Lola wants," Blanchett quips with a wide smile.

I have to contain my need to punch him in the mouth for using my phrase for my wife. Instead, I turn to Lola.

"Are you satisfied with the progression or do you have any other concerns before the meeting ends?" I ask, wanting to get the fuck out of here before I lose my hold on civility.

Lola glances at me and smiles.

"Yes, you and Luc?" She asks.

Out of my periphery, I catch a glimpse of Blanchett tightening his jaw in a struggle to hold back a comment. I play it up to spite him.

"I agree with you regarding the tech responsibilities and find the launch well in hand. Luc?" I respond.

Luc shares his feedback and adds some suggestions that

everyone agrees would benefit the portal overall. Blair adds some thoughtful insights, and her marketing acumen shines through. Luc smiles at her in adoration.

I grin to myself knowing that look firsthand and cast one at Lola who smiles back.

Then she turns to Blanchett.

"This has been a productive two days, Simon. We appreciate your teams' efforts and their work towards a successful launch," Lola starts as she glances around the room at each face. "Unless you have additional information, we can adjourn our meeting."

Blanchett shutters his emotions when he senses my assessment of him, then smiles brightly.

"Lola, as always you hold the power, and we are at you will—"

"What exactly do you mean, Blanchett?" I demand as I rise from my seat and lean towards him with my palms on the table. I'm poised to leap across and knock the shit out of him.

This motherfucker has just shredded the last thread on my civility.

Our eyes lock. A momentary flare of anger sparks his icy eyes before he holds his hands up in capitulation.

"I mean no disrespect, Monsieur Steele. I merely mean our partner's wishes take priority," he says. Then adds, "Nothing more, I assure you."

A small hand on my arm and a discrete cough from Harris ease me down several notches. But not completely.

"Be sure to respect my wife, Blanchett. I give zero fucks

whether you respect me," I respond as I stand and take Lola's hand.

I turn to his team and add, "Thank you for your time and work."

Lola, Luc, Blair, Harris, and Haley rise and gather their things. They thank Blanchett's teams before he and his managers walk us to the elevator.

"We'll provide the weekly updates as scheduled. Safe travels home," Blanchett says as he shakes our hands.

I give him an extra-firm squeeze as a reminder. Then usher Lola through the elevator doors.

"Well, that was entertaining," Harris quips when the elevator descends.

Lola snorts, and everyone laughs heartily.

* * *

So Lola didn't forget our second wedding anniversary after all I smile to myself as I stretch out on the oversized beach towel after thanking her sufficiently.

I glance over at my wife, still buzzing from making love under the warm sun of the Maldives as the Indian Ocean waves caress our toes.

Lola surprised me with a trip to a private island for the next ten days.

"I want us to leave everything and everyone behind as we celebrate our anniversary, my love."

My eyes close as I revel in the aftereffects of our love-making. Nothing beats Lola on my lap, wrapped in my arms, held with her back to my chest while our bodies connected, taking in the incredible sight of the expansive turquoise, aquamarine water. Not a soul for miles as we rocked in rhythm with the water lapping around us.

The ultimate in peace and tranquility.

"Mmmmmmm, Baz… Can we stay forever?"

I chuckle as I roll over and plank above Lola. Her hooded hazel eyes meet mine, darkened yet again with erotic lust.

She slips her arms around my neck and pulls herself up to slant her mouth over my lips. Our tongues tangle as we explore one another. The taste of the tropical fruit juice still lingers. I lap at it with a hum.

"Mmmmm… Yes, babe. Forever and ever," I respond, desperate to show Lola just how happy she makes me.

I lose myself in her body once again. Slowly I sink my cock within her core, still soaked from our combined essence. Her greedy pussy grips me as I slide deep.

Both of us groan when I bottom out.

Intent on making it last, I hold still to allow us to feel our intimate connection. Right now, it's not about fucking until we're breathless and spent. We need to reaffirm our vows. Take time to just let go and feel.

I told Lola that from the moment she asked me to teach her the ways of a D/s relationship. In almost three years we've been to together, I remind her regularly. Today makes it extra special since we became husband and wife two years ago. Bound forever as one.

Soft sobs bring me back from my musings.

I lift my head from Lola's neck to find tears falling from the corners of her eyes down the sides of her face. My heart constricts.

"What's wrong, baby?" I ask, concerned by her abrupt change in mood.

Lola shakes her head. But I urge her to speak with murmurs of love and reassurance. She raises her gaze to me.

"I love you so much, Sebastian. I hate we argued. I never want us to part at odds again"—she takes a deep breath and continues—"Promise me, please."

An overwhelming desire to engulf Lola with my ever-lasting love overtakes me. I groan and start to move within her, hoping my actions speak better than any words I can offer, as choked up as I am by raw emotion.

With my face buried in her neck, I slip my arms under her shoulders to cradle the back of her head. Steady strokes of my cock as I pull out to the tip, then slide back in at a slow pace cause Lola to bow her back. Her contented sighs replace the soft sobs.

I shift the angle of my penetration to nudge her most sensitive spot with each inward stroke. Lola feels so fucking good I can't help the nonsensical words and sounds emanating from my mouth. She's right there with me as she coos against my damp hair.

We reach our climax as one on strangled cries of ecstasy. My cock jerks and shoots my seed deep within her womb as Lola's pussy flutters along my length, milking every drop.

On a groan, I collapse on top of her, my breath blowing her hair from her cheek. My lips find the delicate area where her neck and shoulder meet. I trail open-mouthed kisses up her throat, tasting the salty flavor of her sweat-covered skin, until I reach the shell of her ear.

"I love you so much, too, Lola. I promise to never part from you at odds ever again," I thrum against her lobe in a voice deepened by desire.

Lola

The sound of Baz's laughter as he cracks up at my corny joke makes my heart swell with love. His gray eyes shine brighter than the sun as it sparkles on the infinite expanse of azure blue waters in front of us.

We have one more day in Paradise, and truly I never want it to end. I wasn't joking when I asked him if we could stay forever. I mean it even more now than I did that first day.

It's been a peaceful time for us to reconnect and to lose ourselves in each other. No distractions and no interference, just like our honeymoon two years ago. Beyond perfect.

I know Simon still bothers Baz, and he's making every effort to not let his Captain Caveman loose. When Simon referenced "Whatever Lola Wants" followed up with his "power" comment, I could feel the heat radiate off of Baz. The temperature in the room increased tenfold in seconds, then plummeted when Baz stood to face off with Simon.

Without a doubt, Baz would have throttled him right then and there had I not placed my hand on Baz's arm to pull him back from the battle. He was ready to strike. With his MMA training and his possessiveness of me, Baz would have decimated Simon. Then again, Simon is a worthy opponent with his knowledge of Krav Maga. Alpha males…

Thankfully, nothing worse happened.

I meant it when I said I love Baz so much. It's so true, and it's made me feel horrible about the baby situation. Once Lola's Coterie completes the portal, things will be better. Baz and I will be better, that I vow.

"Babe, you're too much!"

Sebastian's words draw me from my musings, as do his continued chuckles.

"Come on, Ms. Jokes. Let's go for a swim," he says, standing to his feet and pulling me up to mine. "I want to check out the reef one more time."

He hands my snorkel tube and mask to me. Then he places his set on his face and carries our fins to the water's edge. We make quick work of donning our gear, before we dive into the crystal-clear, warm water of the Indian Ocean.

Baz's playful mood extends to its depths. He makes faces around his snorkel while his gray eyes dance behind the mask. As we near the reef, he swims after the colorful fish as they scatter from our intrusion of their watery home.

I can't help but to join in his friskiness. The sunlight filters to the bottom, and we swim around in the brilliant rays. I flip my legs as I channel my inner Ariel mermaid to race past Baz to the coral reef ahead of us.

After we investigate the nooks and length of the reef, we resurface to float on our backs lazily. The tranquility of the water lapping around our buoyant bodies lulls us in the heat of the sun.

Suddenly, the water erupts with loud splashes and whistles. Startled, Baz grabs me and pulls me to his chest as he treads water. I screech and cling to him with my face buried in his neck.

My God, what the hell is—

Baz's laughter cuts my thoughts off. He loosens his grip and turns me around.

"Spinner dolphins! It's a pod of dolphins! Damn… I didn't know what the fuck was happening!" He exclaims pointing at the offensive creatures excitedly.

I let go of the breath I was holding and throw my head back, laughing. All I could think of was Jaws and how no one would ever find us.

"Holy crap! I almost keeled over from fright!" I yell. "Damn if they didn't sneak up on us!"

The dolphins swim and leap in the surrounding air, but are careful not to do any harm. The majestic mammals take my breath away. I've never been this close to them before.

Baz reaches over and skims his hand along the back of

one as it passes by. I mimic his movement and touch the slick side of one near me. Their whistles and clicks increase as they continue to romp around. Then, as unexpectedly as they appeared, the pod dives below the surface.

We put our masks back on and watch as the dolphins swim away. Once they're out of sight, we resurface, and Baz kisses me silly.

"I love you, Mrs. Steele," he murmurs against my swollen lips.

"I love you more, Mr. Steele," I whisper as I stare into his hooded gray eyes.

It's a magical end to our enchanted anniversary getaway.

LOLA

"*Chérie!* It's so good to see you!"

I glance over from the white board covered in ideas for the latest pre- and postnatal collections to see Leonie padding towards me. We're in the conference area of my atelier above Lola's Coterie New York, and Leonie just arrived for the first of several meetings planned while she and Roger are here. Next month the entire Steele clan, Josy, Guy, Luc, Blair, Billie, and Patrick will go to Steele Southampton Village for their annual Labor Day fundraiser.

Even though it's only been a month since we last saw each other, it feels like forever. Since I moved to New York, then married Baz, Leonie and I have gone from practically spending every day together in Paris to a few days a month or so. Now she's married to Roger and has The Twins leaving even less time.

I miss her and jump up to pull her into a tight hug.

89

"Hey! You're early! When did you get in?" I ask.

Leonie tosses her mahogany mane of waves over her shoulder and smiles brightly. Her amber eyes glow with mischief as she rubs her hands together.

"I told Roger not to tell Sebastian so I could surprise you! We arrived last night and made sure the coast was clear before we entered the family's private elevator," she exclaims gleefully. "Surprise!"

We laugh and hug again.

"Well, well, well… The gang's almost all here! Only Haley is missing."

Leonie and I part to find Billie and Blair heading towards us, beaming.

"You weren't due in until later this afternoon!"

They embrace and catch up a bit before we settle at the table with my design team. We proceed with the meeting for the new pieces, including the ones Leonie sketched. After we separate the yeas from the nays, we impress everyone with the final selection.

"I love the new collections, *Chérie*. Well done!" Leonie says as she does our happy shimmy dance. "When will you have the samples ready? I can't wait to see the outcome."

I nod in agreement. The collections are fantastic and go along with the concept of sexy mamas with a need for functional lingerie before and after childbirth.

"Yes, this turned out well! We should have the samples to the—"

"Pardon me, Lola. I didn't realize you'd be in a meeting."

I shift in my seat. Another surprise—it's Simon. I rack

my brain for a memory of an appointment scheduled with him and come up empty. I turn to Blair and Billie, but they shake their heads and stare at me in wide-eyed shock.

Quickly, I recover and stand to greet him.

Simon pulls me in close and kisses my cheeks, close to the corners of my mouth. When he steps back slightly, I notice Leonie's raised eyebrow and questioning look. I blink and return my gaze to Simon.

"Hi, how are you? Did we have a meeting scheduled? I don't recall one in my calendar," I stammer.

Simon smiles and his ice-blue eyes glitter.

"*Non, belle.* I have business in New York and thought I'd stop by to see you. Ask you to lunch so I can update you on the portal," he says with his hands still holding my arms. "But if you are busy, let's have dinner, *non?*"

I blink again, unable to formulate a sentence.

"*Excusez moi, monsieur.* I'm Leonie Steele, Lola's sister-in-law. We are in the middle of a meeting now and we have plans with our husbands later. Too bad you came all of this way for nothing, *non?*" Leonie smoothly intercedes as we often do for one another when faced with unwanted attention.

I smile at her and nod. She gave me time to get my word together.

"Yes, Leonie is correct, Simon. Now is not a good time, and I jam-packed my schedule. If the update is urgent, Blair may be available to discuss it with you as she handles the portal," I respond.

Silently Simon stares into my eyes, piercing my soul

with his now arctic blues. Then he inclines his head and releases my arms before he steps back further.

"I see," he starts. "I apologize for my intrusion. I will have my assistant touch base with yours regarding the update. Next time, I will make certain to get on your calendar, Lola. I'd hate to disturb your work or family plans."

He turns to nod at Leonie, who stands beside me, after to Blair.

"I bid you all adieu," Simon says before he pivots and strides to the elevator.

Once the doors close behind him, I stalk to my office with Leonie on my heels. I close the door behind us and sag onto the sofa, throwing my head back and screaming silently.

Damn, that man gets to me every single time!

When I raise my head, Leonie sits across from me on a chair, assessing me with feline eyes. She cocks her head to the side.

"Spill it, *Chérie*," she demands.

I tell her how things are going with Baz, me, the baby, and Simon in a non-stop stream of confessions. It's been forever since we last spoke about our lives and I need to off load in the worse way.

Thankfully, Leonie lives up to her BFF status and sits in silence nonjudgmental while I let it all out. Once I'm done, she takes a moment to absorb it all before she speaks.

"I understand, *Chérie*. But I must agree with Sebastian. Simon wants you back and being an Alpha male, he won't let up. Be firm with him and make it very clear you are no longer interested in him beyond your professional partner-ship," Leonie says.

She arches her elegant brow when I don't respond right away.

"Yes, yes, of course! Baz is the only man for me, Leonie," I say as I rise to my feet to pace the floor. "I just don't want to mess up this deal. It's important and I want nothing to go wrong. I'll speak with Simon."

I stop to face Leonie, and she eyes me for a moment again. Then she nods and rises, too.

"*Bien!* Now, let's review the photo shoot details. I miss being in front of the camera, you know!" She says with a wink as she sashays out of my office.

Visions of Sebastian's head exploding if he saw Simon holding me flit across my sight. I shake my head to rid it of the terrible thoughts before I follow Leonie through the door.

God forbid…

* * *

"Lola!!! What the fuck?!"

"What are you yelling about?! I'm the one who should be pissed since you had me fucking followed, Sebastian Steele!!"

Sebastian and I snarl at one another as he throws photo after photo after photo of Simon and me: Simon touching my lower back; me laughing at whatever the fuck he said;

Simon staring at me with my back turned; me leaning over his shoulder at something he's holding.

Un-fucking-believable!

My husband had me tailed by his guy for weeks. Weeks!! Capturing damning photos of Simon and me in scenarios that were innocent!

"How could you, Sebastian?!" I shout as I pick up a photo and rip it to shreds angrily shaking my head. "This proves nothing! Do you hear me, N-O-T-H-I-N-G!!"

"Yeah?! Then you explain to me why the fuck Blanchett has his hands all over you? Huh? Why, Lola?!" Sebastian shouts back, waving one of the four-color pieces of "evidence."

I glare at him as my nostrils flare.

"Yeah. Thought so. No answer," Sebastian says as he throws the photo on the table between us.

I watch it flutter to land on top of the others. My eyes fill with tears, but I'm determined not to let them fall like the photo.

A deep inhale and exhale does little to calm me down. I turn my back to Sebastian and swipe at my eyes.

"You said you were meeting him for work, for business, for the fucking portal. I trusted you to tell me the truth, Lola," Sebastian ends his tirade in a lower tone of voice.

I spin around to face him, angered once again. Damn my tears!

"That is the truth, Sebastian! I never lied to you. It was for work," I say. Then add, "No different from you and Lydie."

Sebastian's face turns the brightest shade of crimson imaginable. Smoke tendrils seep from his ears. For a second I fear he'll combust.

"Are you seriously comparing my longtime family and business relationships with Lydie to you and Blanchett?!?!" Sebastian shouts.

When I nod, his eyes widen, then narrow to slits. His lip curls into a feral snarl.

Uh oh. I brace myself. But nothing could prepare me for the words that drip from his mouth scathingly.

"I… Never… Fucked… Lydie."

My knees buckle, and I have to grab ahold of the table's edge to prevent myself from collapsing to the floor in a broken heap.

"But you fucked Simon. Did you not, Lola?" Sebastian pauses to look me up and down. "So no. You cannot compare my situation with Lydie to yours with Blanchett."

The tears that threatened to spill now fall unceasing from my eyes. I drop my chin to my chest and sob.

I cannot believe this has gone so far. How could I have known Sebastian would react in this manner. He won't listen to anything I say. It's beyond the simple point of "let's move on."

His anguish is deep-seated. His assigning someone to follow me shows how far Sebastian's trust of me has fallen. Then to throw my one night with Simon in my face. Too low of a blow.

I can sense Sebastian watching me, waiting for a

response, any answer. But I can't give it to him right now. I need some space.

Without a glance in his direction, I straighten my spine and stride from the room. When I reach the entry foyer to our duplex, I grab my handbag from the console. My hand stops inches from the front door's knob.

"So, that's it? You're going to leave as usual. Not even stick around to clear this shit up?" Sebastian asks from behind me.

When I don't answer, he sighs and continues.

"Well then go, Lola. If Blanchett is in town, go cry on his shoulder. No doubt he will welcome you with open arms," Sebastian says, then walks away.

My heart clenches. But I leave despite the pain in my chest that chokes words from my mouth that could end the pain for both of us.

Time. I just need some more time.

Weeks later, I sit at a conference room table in Paris. I have the final run-through of the e-commerce portal. Luc and Blair sit with me at Blanchett Enterprises, SAS, while Haley and Harris join via video conference. Sebastian has business engagements he couldn't break.

After I left our duplex, I checked in at the St. Regis Hotel New York for a few days. I needed the time to get my head together and for Sebastian to calm down. So I sent a text message to him to let him know I was in the Presidential Suite. Prior to my deal with STEELE, the suite served as my home in New York whenever I came in for business.

Sebastian acknowledged my text with a brusque, *fine*.

Over the weeks, I went to work and threw myself into the photo shoots, collections finalizations, and the contentious portal. I just wanted it done already. I kept the end goal in mind each night I laid my exhausted head on the pillow when I came home late from the office.

Often Sebastian was already in bed or soon returned home from his late hours at STEELE. He never mentioned that night to me or asked about my work activities. It wasn't as though Sebastian was rude, he just refrained from speaking too in-depth about anything. He stuck to the basics. And we made love rarely.

Occasionally, I would catch Baz staring at me with a raw expression of hurt. But he would turn away or leave the room before I could address it.

A mirthless snicker escapes my lips as I recall the somber times we've had recently.

The incessant drone of voices around me stops. The sudden silence pulls me from my thoughts, and I glance around the room at the concerned faces staring at me.

Damn.

"Lola, are you all right?" Simon asks from across the table. "Does the presentation displease you?"

I straighten in my leather chair, then clear my throat as I touch my fingertips to it.

"Ah, yes. I mean no. I'm fine and so is the presentation. I had a tickle in my throat. Excuse me," I respond with a slight cough.

I can sense Luc and Blair eyeing me, but I don't turn to them.

"Kindly continue, thank you," I add, then smile.

Simon stares at me for a second longer than necessary. His ice-blue eyes scan my face before he inclines his head and motions for the marketing vice president to continue her slideshow.

Periodically, he glances in my direction. But I avoid his questioning gaze.

When the veep finishes, Blair asks questions regarding the promotional campaigns. An in-depth discussion ensues. The suggestions she makes are on point. As always, Blair impresses me with her acumen.

The financial presentation occurs next. Numbers are my kryptonite, so I leave them to Luc to handle. He points out improvements, and the team makes the adjustments. When he's satisfied, Luc turns to me, and I agree. He proclaims the structure sound, and Simon concurs.

Haley and Harris make last-minute tweaks to the tech aspects that Simon's team missed. He teases how he must become a client of the Dynamic Duo's subsidiary. Everyone laughs, and once again Simon's eyes land on me.

I avert my gaze and squirm under his intense stare.

Luckily, the last presentation begins, and I focus on the operations team. Billie takes over for Lola's Coterie since that area falls in her wheelhouse. She too makes amendments to the Blanchett team's process. Billie's knowledge proves as impressive as Blair's.

After hours of review, the meeting ends. Haley and Harris sign off from New York. The rest of us stand and stretch from sitting for so long. Luc, Blair, and Billie chat about their evening plans. Luc and Blair intend to hang out at Luc's mansion while Billie goes to dinner with Patrick, who flew in with her from Las Vegas.

"What are your plans, Lola? Do you want to join us?" Billie asks.

"Actually, I reserved a table at Arpège for dinner to celebrate the portal's completion," Simon interjects. "I know it's your favorite restaurant, Lola."

Luc makes his patronizing Gallic "*Bof*!" He narrows his eyes at Simon and opens his mouth.

I cut him off, "Sounds good. What time shall we meet?"

Simon smiles broadly and tells me he'll pick me up from The STEELE Tower Paris at eight o'clock. Then we part.

I ignore the looks from Luc, Blair, and Billie. I know what I'm doing.

"You look lovely, *belle*."

I glance down at the black figure-hugging crepe dress that's ruched to highlight my waist before it falls to an asymmetric split hem. I paired it with black stretch satin above the knee stiletto boots. I left my hair to cascade down my back in waves and my face with natural hues of makeup.

"Thank you, Simon," I respond as I fall in step beside him. I choose to ignore his proffered arm.

We leave the lobby of The Tower residence and slip into his chauffeur-driven Rolls-Royce Phantom. We keep the conversation easygoing as we make our way through the Parisian streets. The traffic is light, so we arrive at the restaurant in no time.

Once seated, we order, and I select one of my favorite dishes, Coquilles Saint-Jacques à la Bretonne. Simon opts for the grilled abalone with garlic buckwheat. The sommelier returns and pours the wine.

As I sip my Chardonnay, I observe Simon over the rim. He chats amicably with the sommelier while they discuss the merits of the wine selection. Simon's hearty laugh fills the surrounding air.

Women flick their gazes in his direction like moths to a flame. Some even eye me as competition.

Simon will never lack a woman's attention.

I smile against the rim and take another sip.

The sommelier leaves, and Simon turns his attention to me.

"Tell me, *belle*. Are you happy?" He asks softly, his eyes boring into mine.

I cock my head to the side and stare back at him. I hazard a guess he's not asking about the portal, but I feign ignorance.

"Simon, the portal is brilliant. It further proves how astute you are as an entrepreneur. Thank you for thinking about Lola's Coterie. It's the perfect opportunity for a conducive partnership," I respond and lift my wineglass in salute.

He raises his and smiles. Then shakes his head after he takes a sip.

"*Belle*, I am happy the outcome pleases you. You are never far from my mind. However, my reference was not to the business, rather to you and your personal life"—he takes a sip of his wine before he continues—"Are you happy in your marriage, *belle*?"

The sip of wine sputters as I gasp at his inappropriate question. I never thought Simon would come right out and ask such a thing. But then, he is a dominant and never hesitates to go after what he wants. Apparently, he still wants me as Sebastian guessed.

Damn.

I dab my lips with the linen napkin, then meet his heated gaze.

"Simon, that is not an appropriate question for you to ask—"

"You did not answer my question, *belle*. Are you happy in your marriage?" He queries again. "If not, leave Steele. I will take care of you like the treasure you are to me."

I push back from the table and rise.

Simon hastens to stand and catches my wrist as I turn to walk away.

"Lola, wait. I do not mean to upset you. Please sit down," he beseeches me. "You appeared sad at the meeting, and I know the only thing to hurt you and cause you to disregard your business is your husband."

I glance at Simon over my shoulder and lock blazing hazel eyes with him.

"I am extremely happy in my marriage, Simon. I am not at all happy you would ask such a personal question of me," I state emphatically.

He has the decency to lower his gaze, then he glances back up at me.

"I apologize, *bell*—"

"Also, do not call me *'belle'* anymore, Simon," I correct him sharply.

He nods, then says, "Come. Finish dinner, and I will keep my comments to myself. We have much to celebrate. *D'accord?*"

I appraise him for a moment, then nod when I note sincerity in the depths of his blue eyes.

"*D'accord*, Simon."

He helps me back into my chair and sits across from me. Simon continues as the perfect gentleman for the rest of dinner. The conversation is stilted at first. But after more wine, we relax into a friendly banter. We finish with delicious millefeuille croustillant and soufflé au citron Meyer desserts.

Once we stop in front of The Tower residence, Simon shifts in his seat to face me. His eyes shine in the dim interior lighting.

"Lola, it pains me I missed my opportunity to be with you"—he holds up his hand to stop me from interrupting him—"I will forever wonder what our lives would have been like had we been in a relationship. I respect you and will not make another advance towards you. But do know, I stand by my words. Should Steele muck things up, I will always be there for you, Lola."

Simon smiles sadly and steps from the car. He helps me out and walks me through the lobby to the private elevator.

I turn to him and smile softly.

"Thank you, Simon. Know that had you and I met later

than we did, things may have been different. I love Sebastian, and he is my heart, my soul mate. You will find a woman who has that same love for you. *Bonne nuit*," I respond.

Simon bows, and I step into the elevator.

The doors closing signal the end of that chapter in my life. It's time to get home to my love.

"Aaah... Lola... Babe..."

I slide my tongue along the slit of Baz's cock, swirling and tasting him as he lies in our bed asleep. The weight of his dick growing as it goes from flaccid to hard in my mouth.

After I returned to our Paris penthouse, I called for the jet. One minute I was in Paris, the next I was racing through the door of our New York bedroom. Relief flooded through me when I saw Baz asleep in bed, in all his naked glory on his back with one arm thrown over his face, the other resting on my pillow. Gorgeous.

A smile lifts the corners of my lips when my name falls from his mouth. Even in sleep, he wants me only. My husband. My lover. My Dom.

I purr around his thick girth, and he pumps his hips as his fingers clasp the back of my head. I relax my jaw muscles and allow him to use me for his pleasure.

Still asleep partially, Baz groans and guides my movements to match his pace.

His taste of musk and of his bodywash makes my

mouth water. I slip a finger in and out of my slippery wet folds in time with his thrusts. Our moans and groans ring out in the room.

"Fuuuck, babe! You feel so fucking good... Mmmm-mm," Baz grunts as he begins to piston and hit the back of my throat.

Offering no resistance, his shaft slides down my throat on each reentry. The sounds of his pleasure bring me to climax. My shuddering body triggers his release with the thickening of his massive dick in my mouth.

"Yeeessss... Aaaahhhh!!!" Baz roars as he holds my head still and his seed shoots down to my belly.

When his grip lessens, he pulls me on top of his heaving chest. Our bodies line up, and he nuzzles my neck.

"I missed you, Lola," he murmurs in a voice rough from sleep and his cries of passion.

"I missed you, too, Baz," I respond, content to be in his arms again.

Then I straddle him and lean over to place my hands on either side of his head. I brush my nose against his and grind my pussy against his still hard cock.

"Next time, I want your big dick inside of my greedy pussy so your seed can fill my womb. I want my belly full of your baby, not just your cum, Mr. Steele" I whisper.

Baz stiffens beneath me, then bolts upright, wrapping his arms around my waist. He leans back to stare into my eyes.

I smile at the shock in his gray depths, and I nod.

"Yes, Mr. Steele. Give me your baby, your heir."

On a whoop, Baz flips us over and aligns his pelvis with mine. Notched together, he slams into me on a guttural, feral growl.

My Captain Caveman makes good on my request and fills me with an abundance of his seed all night into the early morning.

When my body can take no more, Baz rolls to his back and tucks me into his side. As we drift off, I tell him I won't get my birth control injection next month.

It's time we make our family and deepen our love at last.

LOLA

"I love the different shades of ocean blues around the Hamptons. Mixed with the warm tones of caramel and orange and a base of eggshell white, it's the perfect palette for a beachfront home."

Roger smirks, "Really? Well, you told me you're not interested in redecorating our home at the compound. So, what's with 'the perfect palette'?"

Leonie nudges his side with her elbow and rolls her eyes.

"Just a comment, smarty pants," Leonie responds. "Is that all right with you?"

"*Just* saying…" He quips. "You declined the opportunity, babe."

Baz and I along with Blair, The Twins, Nanny Grace, Roger, and Leonie are on board the STEELE Sikorsky helicopter heading to the Southampton Village Heliport. Billie will fly in with Patrick on his helicopter later this afternoon and stay at his beachfront property.

Already at the beachfront compound are Morgan, Shelley, Malcolm, Starr, and Harris. Haley and her "we're just friends" Callum also left early. They're prepping for tonight's sunset dinner on the beach—a traditional New England Clambake. And I cannot wait, yum!

Leonie's parents and Luc should have landed by now at the private airport for the Hamptons. They flew in on Luc's new Gulfstream G700. He heard how much we enjoyed our flights for Verbier in the STEELE jet, so he ordered one even though he has a plush G650. This trip his excuse to try his new toy. Leonie and I teased he's a spoiled *duc*!

"Bro, it's been eight months. You haven't learned, yet?" Baz chuckles. "Sometimes you have to not say a word!"

"Yeah. Happy wife, happy life and all that," I say, glancing up from her laptop.

Then I turn to The Twins in their car seats and add, "Learn that lesson now, Little Pumpkins, and you'll be all right."

Rodolphe waves his car in the air while Gaspard claps and says, "Dada, Dada!"

"Yeah, Dada," Leonie laughs and points to Roger as she claps.

Everyone joins in, and The Twins' laughter is the sweetest of all.

Malcolm, Harris, and Haley meet us at the heliport with two Black Badge Rolls-Royce Cullinans and a Suburban.

The guys load up the Suburban with our luggage while Blair and I hop into the back of Malcolm's SUV.

Nanny Grace and Leonie secure The Twins in the middle row of the SUV Haley drove. Then Nanny Grace slips onto the third row, and Leonie sits between The Twins.

When Roger opens the driver's door, Haley crosses her arms over her chest and cocks her head to the side, peering up at him.

"Oh, so you think you're just going to bogart my ride, Big Brother?" She asks.

Roger pinches her cheeks and grins.

"You're so cute when you're annoyed, Baby Sister," he says wiggling her face. "I love you with all my heart. But I will drive any vehicle with my wife and sons in it."

Reluctantly, Haley relinquishing the SUV to her brother. But not without giving him the stink eye as she walks around to climb into the passenger seat.

"Don't feel bad, *Chérie*," Leonie tells her. "Roger does the same thing to me. He refuses to let me drive The Twins anywhere. Either he drives or Eric. *C'est la vie.*"

Haley nods, then says, "Only because of my nephews did I give in to you, Roger…"

He winks at her and starts the engine.

We pull up to the compound's private road. A security guard in a gatehouse triggers the oversized wooden gates set between stone pillars with wrought iron lanterns to swing open. A long driveway of pressed oil and natural stone rolls out before us like the yellow brick road.

We're not in Kansas! This is Southampton luxury living at its finest.

Once past the impressive gates, it's another world. The property rests on ten acres all beachfront. Its incredible surroundings include native trees, grassy areas, and closer to the ocean sandy dunes. The briny scent of the ocean through the open windows fills my lungs. The calls of seagulls ring out.

On either side of the primary driveway, secondary ones appear as we drive along. Malcolm pulls off to one on the right. Roger turns onto one of them to our left and Harris follows.

A shorter driveway ends in a circle before a classic Hamptons-style three-story mansion. Sea green shutters lean against gray weathered shingles. Beneath the windowsills flower boxes filled with yellow and red blossoms add to the beauty of the home.

"Here we are," Baz says as Malcolm pulls to a stop at the front door.

We hop out, and I wrap my arm around Sebastian's waist as I gaze at the house. Atop the widow's walk, an antique weathervane idly switches direction with the breeze. The top half of the dark green Dutch door stands open. It's absolutely picturesque.

I glance up at Baz to find him staring at me with a soft smile. His aviator sunglasses reflect mine. He drops his head to kiss me sweetly.

"All right, see you guys at the main house," Malcolm

says before he continues along the circular driveway with Blair.

"See you later!" She exclaims as she waves.

We stride through the front door where the interior doesn't disappoint. It's a center hall with a double staircase rising along the walls. The cream, pale green, and dusty yellow hues complement the stone floors. Canvas covered furniture with the accent colors fill the great room. It's comfy and elegant.

But as always, the view of the ocean out of the wall of windows takes my breath away.

Drawn to the endless expanse of the Atlantic Ocean, I walk over to step onto the deck. Out on the private beach, caterers prepare for the clambake. They dug the pit and lined it with large stones and wood. The fragrant scent fills the air. I love being in Southampton Village!

"Come, let's get settled, then meet up with everyone at the main house," Baz says.

I nod and follow him back inside.

We spend the next hour getting situated. I ordered some new bikinis with matching pareos and workout clothing. The staff put everything away before we arrived.

The day turns into evening, and we go to the beach for a seafood feast with the backdrop of a spectacular sunset. The perfectly steamed clams, lobsters, potatoes, and corn on the cob topped with melted butter and paired with local beer and white wine make for a scrumptious meal. Dessert options include warm blueberry and apple pies with vanilla ice cream. Afterwards, we sit around the bonfire chatting.

I smile over at Rodolphe and Gaspard asleep in their mesh beach cots, Blair found online. They enjoyed their first taste of seafood. The greedy little monsters wanted more! So with full bellies, they doze during the rest of our beach time.

"Time to make our baby, Mrs. Steele," Baz murmurs against my windblown hair as I sit between his legs and lean my back against his broad chest.

Wrapped in the warm cocoon of Baz and an oversized blanket, I don't want to move. But nod, and we gather our things and bid everyone a goodnight.

"Don't forget beach yoga at seven tomorrow morning!" Starr calls out to me, as she sits huddled up with Malcolm.

I give her the thumbs up and loop my arm through Baz's as he we walk along the sandy path to our golf cart. I lean my head against his shoulder as we take the short ride.

When we get home, we take a steamy shower to rid our bodies of the sand before we climb into our bed. We make love with the full moon's light bathing us in its glow. Then we collapse with Baz's body spooning mine.

We whisper I love you and fall into a restful slumber.

* * *

"WHAT A GORGEOUS START to the day! I'm so glad the summer weather continued into September."

"It could stay summer year-round as far as I'm concerned."

The girls and I spread our yoga mats out on the sand at the beach in front of the Shelley and Morgan's house. Originally, Starr wanted us to gather for a sunrise meditation at six-thirty, but after the long night we convinced her to start later—if only by half an hour.

I fold into Child's Pose to release tension and to prepare my mind and body for our session.

After the mediation, Starr undoubtedly has a vigorous flow planned with a dharma talk during Savasana. My consistent Skype sessions with Starr over the last two years increased my endurance and ability to handle more advanced asanas. I look forward to today's practice.

"Let us begin. Come to a comfortable sitting position with your palms face up on your knees, fingers in Gyan Mudra. Center your mind…"

Starr takes us from a reflective guided meditation through a sequence of asanas that build up to the challenging peak pose of Scorpion Handstand.

In practicing asanas, the point isn't to twist oneself into a pretzel and the more you can bend, the better. Rather, the focus on the breath and releasing the mind to move the body.

Starr loves to push our ability to focus, and Scorpion Handstand requires lots of it.

I'm beyond grateful for Savasana as we settle onto our backs. With our eyes closed and our minds open, Starr speaks to us about surrender. Despite the purpose of her dharma talk, I can't help but wonder if she surrenders to Malcolm's Alpha Dom as his sub!

Just as we stand to take a dip in the ocean, here they come…

"Rats, did we miss the yoga?" Patrick jokes in his Scottish accent.

It turns out he and Callum know each other, and it surprised them to find the other with us.

Last night at the clambake, Billie teased how she and Haley are into bangers and mash. The visual of the double entendre made her blush and Callum sputter his ale.

"Of course it's over since I left you snoring almost two hours ago!" Billie replies, her Granny Smith apple green eyes sparkling in the bright sunlight.

With her wavy, medium-blonde balayage hair and pecan-colored skin, everyone says she's Tyra's doppelgänger. Billie is curvy like the megamodel, but a petite version at five feet, four inches. Patrick towers over her by eleven inches.

He scoops Billie into his arms and carries her off to the water as she giggles.

"I saw you with your pussy in the air holding the position for me to come over, grab your thighs, and fuck you until you saw stars in the daytime."

A gasp slips past my lips as my pussy clenches and my nipples pebble beneath my white bandeau bikini. I sway in Baz's sudden embrace as he presses his front into my back with his hands on my lower belly.

He makes his arousal known with his lengthening dick sandwiched between us.

"Can you back up your claim, Monsieur Steele?" I purr.

Baz chuckles, his warm breath tickles my neck. "Absolutely, Naughty Pet. Come back to our house, and I will show you."

"Bye, guys! See you later!" I tell the others.

THE NEXT FEW days are so relaxing. We do more yoga, lounge around the pool, swim in the ocean, or hang out on the entertainment level of the primary house to bowl, play in the arcade, or watch movies.

It's good to unwind with everyone since it's the first time we've all been together in a few weeks.

Baz's laughter comes easily, and he jokes with his siblings. They along with Patrick and Callum played a rowdy game of touch football on the beach.

Between drooling over the gleaming muscles, the girls and I cheered them on. My parents-in-law, Leonie's parents, Luc, and The Twins watched from the sidelines.

Patrick and Callum told them American football sucks and isn't even football since the ball stays in the players' hands more often than not. They insisted on a round of rugby—"the real man's sport."

We couldn't care less as long as the guys remained sweaty.

I giggle about it as I slip into my side-cut-out my white

silk maxi dress. The soft caress of the material swirls around my body as it falls to the tips of my crystal-embell-ished ankle strap sandals.

"You look stunning, Mrs. Steele."

A glance over my shoulder reveals Baz in the doorway of my dressing room.

He's delectable in an untucked white linen button-down shirt with the sleeves rolled midway up his muscular forearms and white linen pants with a pair of white leather slides. The Audemars Piguet watch I gave to him for his birthday on his wrist and his wedding band puts a smile on my face.

His sun-kissed skin makes his gray eyes even more translucent. Two-day stubble covers his cheeks and chin. With his hair combed back, his bone structure stands out. Baz is a sight to behold.

And all mine!

The corners of my mouth lift in a grin, and I twirl for him. As I stop, my hair swings over my shoulder to cascade past my hip in glossy waves. My eyes shine with love for my man.

"I love you," Baz says. "But you're missing something."

He holds up his hand and the light catches the diamonds glittering in his palm.

My diamond and platinum choker—at least that's what those unfamiliar with BDSM would think. Tonight Baz wants me to wear one of the collars he gave to me as his sub.

Okay… So he needs to prove I'm his, huh?

I blush under the intensity of his stare and bow my head. He makes my heart race uncontrollably.

"Come. Put this on and let's get to the party," Baz continues. "Later we'll make our own fireworks."

Now, my pussy throbs. We have hours before the party ends.

Damn.

Baz smirks at me knowingly and puts my collar around my neck before he takes my hand to lead me to the golf cart out front.

A quick ride along a path separate from the driveway—that's lined with cars waiting to reach the party's valets—and we arrive at Morgan and Shelley's house.

The giant side lawn, aglow by thousands of fairy lights and lanterns, has two sumptuous pavilions, one for dinner and the other for dessert and dancing. Beyond it, on the beach, several bonfires burn. Waitstaff mill about with trays of champagne and wines or hors d'oeuvres. To one side a band plays lively music piped through speakers, also out on the sand.

Guests mingle, sipping drinks in the different areas, all dressed in the theme of the annual STEELE White Party.

It's already bustling since it's the party of the season and everyone wants a ticket for a chance to see and be seen amongst the world's elite. Not to mention raising funds for STEELE Foundation.

As soon as we're spotted, people approach to get a word with Baz or to take a photo of us for the society pages.

Automatically, I smile for the cameras and snicker inside. Oh boy…

Baz slips his arm around my side right below my braless boob so his fingers brush underneath it and hugs me close. Did anyone say, "Captain Caveman?"

Finally, we spot people we know and make our way to Billie and Patrick.

"Hey! I love your dress!" I gush to her.

She has on a strapless white-on-white dress that falls to the floor. Her apple green eyes stand out against her tanned skin and twinkle when she smiles.

"Thanks, you look fantastic, too!" Billie responds.

Patrick smiles at her. His hand on the back of her neck slides down as he strokes her possessively.

"Hi! You're finally here!"

I turn to see Leonie and Roger striding over. A giggle escapes when Leonie when she notices my collar. I smirk, and she winks.

We chat for a few minutes, then return to mingle before the waitstaff serves dinner.

I catch sight of Haley and Lachlan talking off to the side. It appears serious, so I don't interrupt them with a greeting.

The Jacksons, who also have a compound nearby, came over for the party. Laurent, the playboy, flirts shamelessly with three female guests. Lydie who seems to be with her new boyfriend Baz mentioned laughs with some industry titans—she's a killer in the boardroom. Lucien, whose Southampton restaurant caters the event, holds court in the dining pavilion for last-minute preparations.

A quick scan of the crowd reveals Leonie's parents in conversation with Connor and Lucie while Morgan and Shelley stand next to them chatting with other guests. The couples make a powerful trio and became fast friends over the past two years.

Baz and I visit a third tent for the silent auction.

Luc offered two weeks at his family's ancestral seat. In his case, it's a magnificent chateau on one hundred acres of park-like grounds and forests once used as royal hunting grounds. Excursions for cooking and wine lessons and tours of the countryside round out the visit.

STEELE went further with a six-week-long trip around the South Pacific. Two-week stays at three five-star hotels and resorts in Fiji, Tahiti, and Hawaii make for a memorable holiday. Plus, use of a STEELE private jet and helicopter to transport the lucky couple. The imagery for the display is so vibrant and romantic, I want to put a bid on it!

The gong rings to announce dinner.

We follow the guests to the dining pavilion and take our seats. The Steele clan disperses across the room, sitting at tables with guests to make everyone feel welcome and included.

Shelley makes her speech, and the emcee keeps the party going through dinner and on to the dessert and dancing. A DJ famous for his skills on the turntables spins popular music that gets the guests on their feet.

The fireworks display from a barge offshore lights up

the inky night sky with vivid sparklers, crowns, glitter, and crosettes. We cheer with each round, delighted by the glitziness.

"I have an explosive pistil with your name on it, Little Pet. Shall we?"

For the rest of the night and well into the early morning, Baz makes me oh and ah in erotic, toe-curling delight. At the rate we're going, I'll be pregnant soon!

* * *

"I can't believe *Mr. Responsible* let you take The Twins and drive into the village without him."

Leonie bites her lip and raises her eyebrows at my comment.

We're heading back to our Cullinan after a couple of hours shopping on Main Street. Baz and the guys went to play golf.

When Leonie hesitates in her answer, I turn to face her.

"Wait a minute. Do you mean to tell me you did not let Roger know?" I ask incredulously, stopping in the middle of the sidewalk.

She shrugs and presses the key fob to unlock the doors.

"Leonie! He's going to be so pissed off with you!" I say as I buckle Rodolphe in his car seat. "And do not give me that *Bof* shrug!"

Leonie laughs and responds, "Don't worry! We'll return before them. So stop yammering and get in the car already.

I took advantage of his absence to prove I can handle driving us around—alone."

I shake my head and step up to the passenger seat.

Along the way, we chat about our final dinner tonight before we leave in the morning. We spent an extra week after Labor Day because it was just so nice to hang out.

"It's amazing how time flies! I cannot believe The Twins will be one year old in a couple of weeks—"

WHAM!

The SUV veers off the road and crashes head-on into a tree. Leonie and I jerk forward as the front end smashes, then bounce back when the airbags deploy. The Twins' cries fill the car along with my pained moans.

My ears ring as my head pounds from my forehead being slammed by the airbag. I try to turn to see Leonie, but can't see, blinded partially by the airbag dust and blood dripping in my eyes.

Relief sweeps through me when the back doors open. Thank God, someone helps us.

"Is everyone okay?" I ask. Still unable to move with my legs trapped by the front of the SUV, I shift my gaze sideways.

The chilling tendrils of horror close in when two masked faces stare at me and without a sound take Rodolphe and Gaspard from their car seats.

"*Nooooooon,*" Leonie yells, now frantic and forcing her body to move. "*Ne prends pas mes bébés!!!*"

Unable to think in English, she screams at them to not take her babies.

I hear a cry and scuffling.

In her haste and limited eyesight, Leonie misgauges the height and falls out of the SUV. I hear her leap to her feet to run after the kidnappers. Screaming, she pounds after them, fueled by the cries of The Twins.

As if in a dream, the kidnappers peel away. Their tires kick up gravel from the side of the road.

I hear Leonie screaming in sheer heart-wrenching agony. Tears stream down my cheeks and my screams join hers.

"What the fuck's going on?"

I demand down the mobile line when I see Roger drop his club and race after Harris. He's already running to their golf cart. Luc and Callum close in on them, the sound going in and out as I run, too.

Behind me, Malcolm and Patrick shout questions.

"Harris! What the fuck is going on?!" Roger yells as he jumps into their cart.

Without taking his eyes from the path, he shakes his head and says, "Your Cullinan crashed."

The world tilts.

Lola!

Frantically, Roger ends my call, and I dial her mobile. No answer. I dial my father.

"Where are Lola, Leonie, and The Twins?" I yell.

He sucks in a shocked breath, then responds, "Dammit! They went into the village. What's happened?"

I fill him in, then my other line rings. It's Luc.

I start yelling over the line, demanding to know where the app places them.

"Where?" I hear Roger ask Harris.

He tells him it's the road from Main Street toward our compound. His app alerted him to the crash along with the STEELE Cyber Security emergency team. First responders are en route to the scene.

"The scene." My nightmare. Bile rises in my throat as my stomach clenches. I pray they're not injured. Especially since Lola's parents died in a car accident. I nearly puke on the spot. I have to pull on my control to keep ahold of my emotions to allow my brain to function like a leader.

When we get to the country club's parking lot, we abandon the cart and race to the Suburban just as Roger, Luc, and Callum jump from their cart. All of them are on their mobiles.

I go for the driver's door, but Malcolm stops me.

"You're too keyed up, bro," he starts, then continues when I interrupt. "I got this, get in."

By the time we get to the car crash, the police cordoned off the area. Fire engines and ambulances line the road. Cars backed up prevent us from getting any closer.

We leave the SUV and rush to the yellow caution tape.

An officer stops us, but Roger and I yell it involves our wives and Roger's sons. When he reaches for his radio and doesn't lift the tape to give us access, I duck under and run to the first ambulance.

My stomach clenches again when I catch sight of the

Cullinan's crushed hood. The force of the impact decimated it.

FUCK!

We step up on the back of the ambulance and see Lola on a stretcher.

Her eyes widen when she sees me. Mine widen when I see the bloody gash on her forehead.

"Leonie? The Twins?" Roger asks.

Lola bursts into tears, and Roger's knees buckle.

I pull him out of the way and climb on board. I don't have time to help him. I have to see to my wife first.

"Lola, baby, what happened?" I ask urgently as I kneel beside her.

"Sir, please give me room. I have to attend to her wound now," a paramedic says as he nudges me.

I swivel my head and give him a death stare.

He doesn't back down and points to Lola's head.

"She can have a concussion, spinal injury, and we don't need the wound to get infected. Kindly step aside," he states.

Lola touches my arm, and I glance back at her. She shakes her head, then winces. The collar around her neck, unlike mine, is there to limit damage to her spine.

I move to allow the paramedic to work.

"The Twins... they kidnapped them!" Lola wails as fresh tears fall from her red eyes.

My heart stops.

The world falls off its axis.

Adrenaline pumps through me, and I race out of the

ambulance, screaming Harris' name. He has the app on his phone and can tell us where The Twins are right now.

"Where are they?" I ask when he runs towards me.

He shows me, then we race to Roger where an officer has him on the side of the ambulance.

"We know where they are!!" Harris and I yell simultaneously.

Officers come running, and Harris shows them another of his apps.

Two dots blink green on a map with heat signatures of four other individuals in various locations. The coordinates place The Twins near to where we stand. The street view shows a secluded house on a private lane.

Just then Roger's mobile rings with a call from our father.

"A person contacted me with a ransom demand of $10 million," he says without preamble. "Each."

"We've got The Twins via their trackers, and—"

"*Quelle? Veux-tu dire??*"

Leonie stands behind the officers with Lola. They clutch each other. At that moment, I notice the bruising on Leonie's face, too.

Roger strides over to her and pulls her into my arms as I embrace Lola.

Leonie peers up at him and asks again, what does he mean.

Tightly holding her, he explains, so only we can hear that every member of our family has a tracker in case we get lost or kidnapped. She questions why he didn't tell her about The Twins having them, and he tells her it slipped my mind.

Then Leonie and Lola frown and ask if they have one, too. We nod and tell them we'll explain after we get them home. Leonie whispers it's all her fault.

Roger tells her not to think such nonsense. Then kisses her head and nods to the paramedic to take her back inside the ambulance.

I kiss Lola and tell her to stay with Leonie and the officers. She clings to me, and I hug her once more before I move to my brothers.

Meanwhile, the officers plan an extraction and send a unit to the compound to monitor the communications from the kidnappers.

Roger, Harris, and I insist upon accompanying the extraction team.

The officers see we won't let them deny us, so they give in on the condition we remain in the patrol car. No one knows whether the kidnappers have weapons.

We agree.

Luc promises to take care of Leonie and Lola. Since he's known them longer than Roger and I combined, we trust he won't allow any harm to come to them.

Malcolm drives them and Callum back to the compound.

"More people arrived at the house!" Harris exclaims as he monitors his app's feed. "What the fuck?! Haley is there now!!"

Roger and I swing our gazes to the front seat where Harris sits beside the sheriff.

"Whaaat?!?!" We yell at the same time.

Then we tell the sheriff to drive faster.

Shortly thereafter, we arrive at the house. According to the app, The Twins still blink green in the same room with a heat signature next to them. However, ten heat signatures surround three others in another room while four appear in a third one beside The Twins.

The STEELE's security team lead for our compound flags us down.

"Mr. Steele," he says to Roger. "We have the situation under control. Ms. Steele alerted us to the kidnapping, and we used the tracking app to locate your sons. They're with the team medic. The kidnappers are being held by other members of the team. Come with me, sirs."

Just as he said, we see our team with three men who sit handcuffed in the middle of the floor. One is jabbering on about not being a part of the kidnapping. His voice gives me pause. It's Antonio Velasquez, the guy from Leonie's school.

What. The. Fuck!

If Delia Shaw, the woman who fucked with Roger is behind this, I'm going to finish the psycho bitch once and for all!

Raised voices draw my attention from the asshole Antonio.

Roger, our security lead, and I rush into the next room. Two of our team members stand aside, but at the ready.

Delia runs screaming like a banshee with her arms outstretched and long nails ready to claw at Haley.

Surprisingly, Haley stands her ground in a defensive posture. No one is prepared for what happens next.

"You BITCH!"

WHAM!

"You fucked with my brother."

WHAM! WHAM!

"You tried to steal my nephews!"

WHAM! WHAM! WHAM!

"Stay. The. Fuck. Away. From. My. FAMILY!!!"

Haley whales on Delia.

"I've got your number, bitch, and it's all legit. You're going away for the rest of your miserable fucking life," Haley ends in a deadly tone made more terrifying after her shouts and thrashing.

Delia—whose face already shows signs of swelling—stares with one open eye up at Haley. Delia's busted lip trembles as she mumbles how sorry she is for all she's done.

Haley refuses to give in and tells her it's too fucking late.

The officers rush in, and we explain what happened. They proceed to arrest Delia, who starts crying assault. When they ignore her and read the Miranda warning, she doesn't have the sense to shut the fuck up.

Instead, she slings more baseless claims against me and curses while they take her away.

Bye, bitch!

"Mr. Steele, your sons are safe and sound."

Roger turns to face the door and sees the security medic as noted by the word on the front of his uniform's bullet-proof vest. He and another team member hold Rodolphe and Gaspard, who wear black adult-size t-shirts.

When they see him, they call out Dada and reach their arms out.

Tears fill my eyes, and my breath escapes me at the sight of their reddened faces puffy from crying. Two strides and they're in his arms. He squeezes them so tightly to his chest they squirm and cry some more.

Never in my life have I been so terrified. All sorts of crazy thoughts ran through my head. Nightmarish and ghastly things are done to children, and I would end anyone who would harm what's mine.

I know for a fact I would be beside myself if something happened to a child of mine.

Harris, Haley, and I enfold our arms around Roger and hug The Twins and him. We're a tight-knit clan, and I feel the love flowing from us to them. Even The Twins calm, hiccups replace their sorrowful sobs.

We take a moment to absorb the intensity of the situation.

Then I squeeze them and look at each of their faces. Mine, like theirs, streaked with tears. But the steely glint in my eyes shows I'm back to business. As the eldest sibling, I always take on the responsibility of my brothers and sister —no matter their ages.

"Let us go. Haley, call Leonie. Harris, you get Dad on

the line. He needs to prep for our arrival"—I turn to the security lead—"I want a full briefing with the team, the police, and the FBI. We will meet in my father's office in an hour."

Big brother, CEO, Alpha Dom, all in one take charge.

When we reach the compound's perimeter fence, armed security members stand spaced in intervals along its full length. At the front gates, two of their armored Suburbans block the entry and dozens more armed members stand around them. We are on full lockdown.

"ROGEEERRR!!!"

Leonie roars as she runs out of the house.

She throws her arms wide, pulling The Twins and him into her embrace. She trembles as sobs rack her body. He murmurs words of love and lets her know they're fine to soothe her anguish.

Josy and Guy join them, and they hug in a unit as he did with his siblings. The pile on continues when they make room for our mother and father.

He notices the others hovering, not wanting to interrupt. So he gives them a nod and suggests we move inside.

We settle in the living room where Leonie and Roger hold The Twins on our laps. She checks them over one at a time, rubbing her hands over their bodies and holding their faces to look into their eyes. He tells her they're fine since the medic did an examination, and he assessed them on the ride over.

But *Maman Lionne* ignores him.

The silence broken by Malcolm.

"That bitch is going to pay," *The Enforcer* declares. "No way will she get away with this shit. I want answers now!"

Everyone shares his sentiment, and we decide to have the briefing here instead of in the office for more space.

Before they arrive, Leonie and Roger take The Twins upstairs to bathe and redress them. The forensics team took their clothes for evidence, thus the t-shirts.

Lola's who's been sitting on my lap quietly turns to me and whispers, "I can't believe this happened. I was so scared, Baz... What would happen if we had a baby and I... I..."

Her words cut off on a choked sob. Lola buries her face in my neck as her body trembles with emotion.

I can only imagine her fright. Instantly I remember her concerns about having a baby and one of us dying to leave the child alone, as happened with her and her parents. My heart breaks.

"Lola... Babe, look at me," I say when her sobs worsen. "Oh baby, listen to me. It's all right now. The Twins, Leonie, you are all safe and sound. Come, let's go home."

I stand with Lola wrapped around me like a monkey clinging to a tree. As I rub her back, I glance at my father and he nods, understanding without uttering a word. My mother also nods and smiles encouragingly.

"We'll let you know if something comes up, son. Go take care of your wife. You've been through a hell of a time," Morgan says gruffly, the Alpha Dom Steele Patriarch as always.

Lola whimpers, and I squeeze her in my comforting

embrace. I have more than enough strength for both of us. I vow to watch over her and our children with my life.

"Baz, I need you… Please."

I wake up two days later to Lola stroking my cock, and her desire whispered in my ear.

Her full D-cup tits press against my back, the points of her peaked nipples jutting into me. Sleep falls away, followed by memories that come back in a flash.

Lola's soft cries as she relived the nightmare of the crash coupled with the pain from the loss of her parents filled the last two nights. During the day, she stayed huddled under a throw sitting on the deck staring out into the distance of the Atlantic Ocean, lost in thought.

Starr came by each morning to do breathwork and meditation with Lola. It helped her to clear her mind, but she remained quiet. Starr assured me Lola just needed some time and not to worry.

I smiled, thinking how lucky Malcolm is to have a woman like Starr in his life. It's time he settled down, too. I chuckled as Starr left the house with Malcolm, and he helped her into the golf cart before they returned to his house.

And she was right, judging by Lola's persistent caresses of my now fully engorged cock.

"Baz, wake up," Lola says louder as my cock jerks in her hand.

On a groan, I roll and plank over her body as I stare into her hooded hazel eyes. They widen with urgency when I hesitate.

Lola reaches up and slips her hands into my hair to tug me down on top of her. She widens her thighs to give me more space to settle against her mound. Lifting her hips, she slides her wet pussy lips along the length of my dick and moans.

"Now… Baz…" she demands.

"Little Pet, who is in control?" I growl in her ear as I lift away from her pussy. "You or me?"

Lola moans incoherently and bows her back.

"Words, Little Pet. I will have your words," I growl, staring down at her.

She licks her lips then pulls a corner into her mouth with her teeth before she nods, "You, Sir. Only you, Sir."

I reward her with a brutal thrust as I lift her thigh onto my forearm and grip the base of my cock. The angle and depth make Lola throw her head back and keen. Her nails dig into shoulders as she clings to me.

Lola needs it rough to take away the pain, just as spankings relieve the tension in her body.

Without hesitation, I give my baby exactly what she needs and more. My hips snap forward and backward as I drive deep within her tight core, not easing up on the demanding rhythm. I rock in and out of her body, entranced by her gasps and the squelching of her abundant juices.

Her pussy muscles clamp on my cock, and it twitches

inside of her core. She can feel every ridge, every vein, and every one of my ten inches as I drill her into the mattress repeatedly.

Lola cries out from her climax, but urges me on by throwing her other leg over my shoulder and tilting her pelvis up to meet each of my pistoning strokes.

"More, Sir, please!" She begs through clenched teeth.

I ramp up my pace and latch onto her pebbled nipple with my teeth, then suckle strongly.

Lola squeals and thrashes beneath me. Her eyes roll to the back of her head and close in pleasure.

"Open your eyes and look at me fucking you, Little Pet," I command as a watch her gaze drop to the space between our sweaty bodies.

My thick dick plunges in and out from my tip to my root as her greedy pussy grips it. The sight spurs both of us on and we buck as Lola cums again with a throaty moan.

"Oh... Oh... Oh... Oh..." she pants with each well-placed thrust of my throbbing cock.

"This pussy is mine, Little Pet. Mine to fill with my seed. Mine to put my baby inside of you. Do you want that? Do you want me to put my baby inside of your womb, Little Pet," I growl like the feral beast I've become as I fuck my mate raw.

Lola squeezes my dick so hard I howl.

"Yeeessss... Sir!" She screams from my dominant possession as another orgasm rips through her pulsating pussy.

"Then take it. Take… every… fucking… drop!" I roar as my cock jerks and my seed coats her womb.

Lola writhes beneath me as I wring one last orgasm from her wrecked pussy.

I collapse on top of her, spent from my mind-blowing release, and she wraps her arms and legs around my shuddering body.

"Thank you, Baz. I needed your passionate dominance, my love," Lola says in a voice filled with sated desire.

On a groan, I roll us over and bury my face in her damp hair. My lips brush her ear, and she trembles.

"Feel better?" I ask.

"Mmm mmm good," she purrs and squeezes my cock still buried within her folds.

It thumps, and I grind up into her as I circle my hips.

"Excellent because we are just getting started, Little Pet," I growl.

SEBASTIAN

"*Sebastian, I need you to come to my doctor's office. Now. The address is—"*

As I race up the steps of the elegant townhouse off Fifth Avenue on Sixty-fourth Street, I can't hold back my panic.

Over the last few weeks Lola's suffered from nausea, extra tender tits and nipples, food repulsion, and tiredness. She refused to admit she may be pregnant and wouldn't take an at-home test despite the six packs of two I brought home. She blamed her symptoms on coming off of the birth control injections.

When I asked her about her period not coming, she claimed it was never regular before the injections. I tried to cajole her into at least seeing the doctor in case she had a stomach virus or the flu. But no…

Now she's at the doctor and asking me to come. I don't even know what type of doctor he is, general practician or gynecologist.

God forbid it's bad news. I'll lose my damn mind.

Edgar weaves my Mercedes-Maybach S 650 Sedan through the congestion of New York City midday traffic like a pro. The doctor's office is only seven blocks north of The STEELE Tower, but it takes longer to drive than if I had just jogged over.

Visions of Lola's belly round with my baby, then of her holding my child appear before my eyes. As much sex as we've had since she woke me with a blow job on her return from Paris, she should be pregnant with a brood!

I chuckle to myself at the thought.

The other morning I caught Lola in front of the full-length mirror in her dressing room, staring at her profile with her hand on her belly. I started to enter, but hesitated when she sighed and rubbed her eyes. From the distance, I could see her hazel orbs glistened with unshed tears.

Not wanting to intrude on her private moment, I backed away.

I guess part of her hesitancy in finding out the truth is her fear. I do know Lola wants a baby as much as I do. She's been pretty damn gung ho with our efforts, often starting the sex and not stopping until we're both too sore to move.

It dawns on me to Google the doctor to find out his specialty. Just as the results populate, Edgar opens my door. So absorbed in my thoughts, I didn't notice we arrived at the address Lola gave to me.

Since I'm a second from seeing with my own eyes, I put my mobile away and hop out. In my haste, I take the steps three at a time and burst through the front door. A second door leads to the foyer where a receptionist sits behind an ornate wooden desk.

"Hello, may I help you?" She asks as her gaze travels from my face down my body back up to my eyes.

I shake my head at the reaction women have when they see me—or my brothers for that matter, The STEELE Quaternity of multibillion-dollar bachelors, now only two single ones.

I ignore her lust-filled expression and reply, "Yes, my wife Mrs. Sebastian Steele is with Dr. Rice. Kindly take me to her."

The receptionist's shoulders droop at the mention of my wife, but she rises and gestures for me to follow her.

I don't bother to shake my head; I just ignore the exaggerated sway of her curvy hips as she sashays ahead of me. I avert my eyes and notice the walls display multiple photos of newborn babies.

Well, that answers my question: Dr. Rice is an OB-GYN and Lola is here. Ding, ding, ding! We have a winner, folks!

YES!

I feel like Lola and want to break out in a happy shimmy dance, except the receptionist might think I'm a nutcase. So I do a discreet victorious fist pump behind her back.

"Right this way, Mr. Steele," she says as she points to a closed door and steps aside.

"Thank you," I nod and knock on the door, then walk in after the doctor calls out to enter.

Immediately, my eyes seek Lola. She's sitting on the examination table in a gown. The shocked expression on her face makes my heart flutter with hope of a positive outcome. I hasten to her side and take her hand.

"Are you all right?" I ask, brushing my thumb over her knuckles. Her hand is icy, so I rub both of them between mine to give her some warmth.

My eyes dart to the doctor for answers.

"Mrs. Steele is perfectly fine, Mr. Steele. Or shall I call you Papa?" Dr. Rice smiles, the corners of his brown eyes crinkling.

Despite having an inkling of the situation, my mind blanks, and I freeze.

Lola squeezes my hands when I fail to respond.

"Baz?" She asks hesitantly. "Did you hear Dr. Rice? Are you okay?"

Slowly the cogs churn again, and I come back online.

"WHOOHOO!!!!!" I shout as I fist pump both hands in the air above my head and gyrate my hips in my version of a happy shimmy dance. "Call me Big Poppa, baby!!!"

Lola and the doctor laugh uproariously as I strut around the room handing out imaginary cigars to imaginary people.

Once I make my way back to my glowing wife, I swoop her off the table and swing her high. Then hold her close against the length of my body as I kiss her until her toes curl.

We don't realize Dr. Rice rose from his stool until we hear a soft click of the door.

"How do you feel, Sexy Mama?" I ask Lola as I sit on the visitor's chair with her snuggled in my lap. "How is my baby?"

I rub her belly and kiss her hair. My heart soars.

"We're good, Big Poppa," Lola laughs. "I was so nervous, though. I really didn't want to know, but I didn't want to do anything to harm our baby just in case I was pregnant. Holy cow, can you believe it? I didn't expect it to happen so—"

I cut off Lola's nervous rambling with another breath-taking kiss.

Her fingers dive into my hair and tug on my scalp as we devour one another. Soft moans slip from her mouth into mine. Lola's round ass squirms against my cock, and it begins to lengthen and thicken in response to her gyrations.

"Fuck, Naughty Pet, if you do not stop, I will take you right here, right now," I chastise her with a smack to the top curve of her ass.

Lola hums in delight and attempts to move again.

"Not now, I want to talk to Dr. Rice," I tell her and carry Lola to the examination table. "I'll get him now. Behave!"

I chuckle when Lola pouts. Roger told me how horny Leonie was all throughout their pregnancy. I should have known Lola was preggie from her increased carnal appetite.

Dr. Rice was waiting outside of the room and returns to show us our baby on the ultrasound.

"You see, from the imaging, all looks good. Based on the

timing of Lola's last birth control injection, lack of her monthly menses, and her levels, I place Lola at twelve weeks," he says. "At eighteen weeks, we'll perform another scan to detect your baby's gender, if you wish to know in advance."

"Absolutely!"

"Yes!"

Lola and I exclaim at the same time, then laugh.

Dr. Rice smiles and tells us to meet him in his office to discuss care, plans for birth, and a pediatrician. Before we leave, we'll schedule each of Lola's appointments for follow-up visits.

"Lola, you're so beautiful. The glow you have is even more resplendent now that Dr. Rice confirmed your pregnancy. I love you, sweetheart," I say as I watch her dress.

She bows her head, and I hear her sniffle.

Right away, I rush over to her and pull Lola close as I bend my knees to press my forehead to hers. The golden flecks in her hazel eyes shine as her tears spill down her rosy cheeks.

I kiss each one and murmur words of love.

We hold one another for a few moments, then I step back and put her stilettos on her feet. My fingers caress her calves, the backs of her legs, her hips, and across her lower belly as I rise to tower over her. Lola moans softly and wraps her arms around my neck.

"When we get home, I will show you just how much I thank you for giving me the gift of a child, Mrs. Steele," I say huskily.

Lola's eyes flare with lust, and she rises to her toes for one more sultry kiss.

Lola

"Congratulations! You're pregnant, Mrs. Steele."

Dr. Oscar Rice has been my gynecologist since I moved to New York permanently. I chose him based on friends' recommendations and since he's an obstetrician, too. I knew eventually Baz and I would have children, so I didn't want to have to change doctors.

It scared me to death something was wrong when I was sick every morning and had a major headache. Instead of addressing the issues, I put my head in the sand... The possibility of me being pregnant wasn't my first thought. I figured I experienced side effects from having the birth control injections for so many years.

In a roundabout way, I asked Leonie questions about the early stages of her pregnancy with The Twins. Being the BFF she's always been to me, Leonie didn't make any judgments or ask me any specifics. She did urge me to see the doctor to rule out any sickness.

So this morning, I gave in and scheduled an appointment. Luckily, Dr. Rice had an opening. When he told me those words, I became dizzy and had to lie down on the exam table to let the wave pass.

He assured me all was well, and dizziness was another symptom.

I knew I had to call Baz and have him come right away. I didn't want to face it alone. And he'd want to be here.

My heart swelled with happiness when he reacted the way he did. Even though my heart stopped when he didn't respond at first. Whew!

Baz is so cute. He put each of my appointments in his calendar before we left the doctor's office. He insisted I get the same date and time as the first patient of the day. *"Bright and early, so Dr. Rice is sharp."*

The administrative assistants and receptionist were in awe of him, so whatever he wanted he got…

It didn't bother me in the least. Baz is mine and now that I'm carrying his baby, it sealed our deal!

I giggle remembering how our relationship started with a deal, his proposal was a deal, and now our first baby is the consummation of our deal.

"What's so funny, babe?" Baz asks as he kisses my knuckles.

We're on our way home, and I cannot wait to jump his bones. I squeeze my thighs together to ease some ache. Damn, pregnancy makes me horny AF.

"Oh, I see, Naughty Pet has an ache that her Dom needs to take care of for her. Is that correct, Naughty Pet?" He asks with his gray eyes shining like molten platinum.

I whimper in response and peek at him from beneath my eyelashes. Ever the sexual submissive.

"Yes, Sir," I reply.

Baz chuckles darkly, and his eyes spark with carnal lust.

I glance out the window and smile when I see The STEELE Tower across Fifty-seventh Street.

YES!

Baz and I nearly race through the lobby, so eager to get butt naked and fuck as Ice-T raps. Once in the hallway of our duplex's second floor, we strip the clothes off of each other.

I barely have him free of his jacket before Baz slams me against the wall and thrusts his ginormous dick in my throbbing slick pussy. Guttural groans fall from our mouths upon penetration.

Thankfully Baz takes Dr. Rice's assurance we can have as much sex-wild and gentle-as we want, barring any discomfort on my part.

None whatsoever, I think as Baz jackhammers deep inside my welcoming pussy. His tip hits my G-spot, then his length strokes it as he pistons inside of me. His girth stretches me to the point of pleasurable pain.

"Uh… Uh… Uh… Nnh…" I gasp with each feral plunge.

Baz growls and grunts indecipherable words as he takes us higher and higher to the pinnacle of erotic ecstasy.

I squeeze my eyes shut and dig my heels into his firm ass when a powerful orgasm takes hold of me. I feel it from my lower belly to my pulsating pussy to my sensitive clit, all the way to my curled toes. A bolt of lightning zings through every cell of my body to set me ablaze.

"Ooooooooo!" I cry out as I explode.

My body convulses from the waves of pleasure.

"MINE! MINE! MINE!" Baz roars as he rises on the

balls of his feet and lifts my leg to his shoulder, driving deeper inside of my spasming pussy.

Even as his dick unleashes a torrent of cum inside of me, Baz continues to pummel my pussy. He grinds his pelvis into mine, leaving not a millimeter of space between us. His body quakes from his release. Then his knees buckle, and we slide down the wall to settle on the floor, where he pulls me into his lap as his big dick pops out of my well-fucked core.

"Did I thank you sufficiently, Little Pet?" Baz pants.

"Yes, Sir, more than I could ever desire," I sigh as I nuzzle against his heaving damp chest contentedly.

He chuckles and kisses the top of my head. His warm breath tickles my scalp as he trails his lips along my hair.

"Excellent," he murmurs.

"WHEN SHOULD WE TELL EVERYONE?"

After we returned to our right minds, Baz carried me to our bathroom and filled the massive marble tub with warm water and fragrant oils for us to soak our sore muscles.

Leaning my back against his chest, I consider his question. We're meeting everyone in Capri for Thanksgiving in a couple of weeks, then Verbier for Christmas. I'm torn between the two occasions. I'd rather wait and give us more time to make sure everything is fine with the baby.

I voice my concerns to Baz, and he agrees with his usual "Whatever Lola Wants" response. He's beyond happy and will give me the world if I ask for it.

We decide to tell everyone at Christmas and make the announcement one of our presents. Shelley and Morgan will be so excited. I remember the many times she hinted or outright asked when Baz and I will have a baby like Roger and Leonie.

I can't blame her. She had five children and loves to have kids around. Even after over two years of being married to Baz, the size of his family and extended family with the Jacksons and close friends awes me coming from a family of only three.

But I love it and can now contribute to the Steele ranks with a baby of our own!

I turn around to face Baz and place my palms on his cheeks.

"Thank you, my love, for giving me a loving family and now a baby of our own," I say.

Tears sparkle in his gray eyes, and he kisses me silly once again.

LOLA

"*L*ola honey, are you all right? You look a bit peaked."

Baz and I ride in the Sikorsky with Morgan, Shelley, Malcolm, Starr, Harris, and Haley en route to Roger and Leonie's Villa dei Fiori in Capri for Thanksgiving.

We flew to Naples on the Gulfstream G650 an hour ago. The move from one aircraft to the other doesn't sit well with my queasy stomach. I drank ginger tea with lemon on the private jet to settle my nausea, but didn't have time for a cuppa on the helicopter.

Ugh…

I smile wanly at Shelley, but can't risk opening my mouth to vocalize an answer. Fortunately, Baz chimes in.

"Yes, Lola had a touch of food poisoning last night from the Thai takeout we ate for dinner"—he rubs my hand and continues—"She'll settle down once we get situated at the villa."

Shelley eyes me for a moment, and Haley and Starr watch on in silent observation.

I smile and use Baz's tactic: don't avoid, admit a partial truth.

"Yes, ignore me," I say with a grimace dramatically.

They nod, and I turn to glance out of the window. How the hell much longer until we land??

Moments later, the Sikorsky touches down on the helipad at the rear of the villa. Leonie and Roger stand holding The Twins, waving at us.

Morgan and Shelley alight from the back of the helicopter first, followed by Baz and me. Malcolm and Starr, then Harris and Haley disembark next. We wave and troop over.

"Hey, Little Pumpkins! Did you miss your favorite auntie?" I ask as Baz scoops Gaspard out of Roger's arms.

"And your very favorite uncle?" He adds giving Malcolm and Harris the side eye with a grin.

We make our way around to the terrace where Guy and Josy sit. They flew in this morning. Everyone exchanges greetings before Leonie and Roger show us to our sumptuous bedroom suites.

Villa dei Fiori has fast become one of their most cherished homes. It's where they had their babymoon when Leonie was nineteen weeks pregnant and they'd been back together for nine months. She fell in love with Lucien's former home the moment she set eyes on it. So, of course, Roger bought it for her.

The salmon-colored stucco exterior with white trim around the windows, columns, and roof lines blend beautifully with the lush greenery and stunning sea views from all sides. The sea-edge gardens, bountiful with camellias, magnolias, and palm trees prove as captivating as the impressive views of Mount Vesuvius, the Peninsula of Sorrento, the entire Gulf of Naples, and Anacapri. Its private swimming pool set in the side garden's grass and its exclusive sea access with a second plunge pool below makes it a unique property.

Baz and I, the siblings, and Guy and Josy take advantage and stay on different occasions. Since Morgan and Shelley have Villa Sogno across the Tyrrhenian Sea in Positano, this is their first visit.

"Oh! This is a stunning villa! I love the gardens with all the fragrant flowers," Shelley gushes as we walk to their suite first. "I'm surprised Lucien gave it up."

Roger chuckles and responds, "He drove a hard bargain. But it was worth it to see the smile on Leonie's face when I gave it to her."

Morgan nods, then adds, "I know the feeling, son. Nothing is better than your wife's happiness. Remember my words well."

As we pass through the villa, Roger points out the rooms for a mini tour. The antique furnishings, Murano glass fixtures, and unobstructed views charm everyone.

However, Morgan and Shelley are even more pleased

with their enormous corner suite and balcony overlooking the sea. The cobalt blue, champagne, and gold color scheme with crystal chandeliers and wall sconces, silk fabrics, plus a bathroom in floor-to-ceiling travertine slabs make for a lavish set of rooms.

"Very nice indeed," Morgan says as he takes in the suite.

Baz and I head to our plush suite. I can't take another moment without giving in to the need to throw up. Yuck!

We make it just in time. Baz kneels beside me to hold my hair out of my face and rubs circles on my back to soothe me. I groan and sit beside the toilet.

He goes to the sink and brings back a glass of cool water.

I take some sips and close my eyes as I rest it against the marble wall. My stomach rumbles, but doesn't explode again. I open one eye to peer at Baz.

His expression is one of concern and guilt.

"Help a preggie lady up, would you?" I smile, not wanting him to feel bad. It's not his fault. Blasted hormones!

Baz lifts me to my feet and helps me to the sink where I brush my teeth. He leans his sexy butt on the edge of the vanity with his muscular arms folded over his broad chest and watches over me.

"Do you want to join the others for lunch or stay here and rest? Either way, I'm with you," he says.

I shake my head and respond, "No, no. Let's go down. Some toast and tea will do me wonders."

On our way back outside for an alfresco lunch in the seaside garden, Harris catches up with us.

"How're you feeling, Sis?" He asks, concern etched on his handsome face.

"I'll feel much better once I get something in my stomach. Thanks for asking," I respond with a smile as I loop my arm through his.

We find Leonie, Roger, The Twins, Malcolm, Starr, and Haley seated on blankets in the grass near the lunch table. As we reach them, Leonie bursts out laughing, then starts to snort uncontrollably.

"What's so funny?"

They glance up to find us behind them.

"Oh, just the rigors and demands of travel," Starr deadpans.

Malcolm sits back on his hands, all smug with a cocky grin on his face. The Alpha Dom took his carnal tastes to the skies for fifteen hours.

Sebastian snickers and I snort.

"No comment..." Haley says, rolling her eyes, disgusted as usual with hearing about her brothers' sex lives, even as innuendos.

She glances down at her mobile and smiles. Then types a response at lightning speed. When she raises her head, her cheeks flush and her eyes shine. No longer wearing her glasses makes the dove gray orbs more expressive. Happy Haley, hmmm interesting.

"What's up, Baby Girl?" Roger asks, knowing the nickname drives her crazy.

Still in la-la land, Haley startles, then responds rushed, "Oh, uh… Callum's over in Sorrento."

When she doesn't continue, Roger prods her. He wants to take Haley to dinner. So Roger tells her he can come here if they want. He's more than welcome. They agree, and Roger arranges for the helicopter to pick him up in an hour.

As it turns out, her brothers think Callum could be an excellent match for their little sister. He proved himself during Labor Day weekend as a guy who's worthy of Haley, has his own fortune, and blends well with the Steele clan. The girls and I love he's a Scottish duke, but the guys couldn't care less. Baz hired his guy to conduct an extensive background check on Callum as soon as they met him while we were in Verbier for Christmas last year. Nothing in it caused concern.

Haley being with Callum and not with Lachlan sits better with Sebastian and with the rest of the guys. Baz can't get past his best friend with his younger sister. Baz had been suspicious since we were at Villa Sogno when he proposed to me. Then at our Labor Day party, he argued with Lach after he saw him in an intense conversation with Haley. It has strained things with the friends since.

Leonie's parents and my in-laws appear. We gather around the table for a delicious lunch of flavorful local dishes prepared by the chef and served by the staff with wines from the villa's prized cellar.

The chef prepared a simple meal for me with toast,

meats, and ginger tea with lemon. My stomach calms, and Baz rubs my thigh under the table.

Fortunately, no one comments on my requests. Leonie just peeps at me, then smiles to herself.

Shortly after we finish eating, Callum touches down. Haley goes to greet him, and some time later they join us for Limoncello Gin Collins on the lawn furniture. Her lips appear swollen, and his eyes gleam.

Mmhmmm.

"How are things with you, Callum?" Morgan asks as he sips his digestif. "I read in the *Financial Times* renewable energy is on the rise for another year in a row for Scotland."

They get into a discussion on Callum's family's business, Graham Energy, Oil & Gas Company, based in Aberdeen, Scotland. His father still leads the company as CEO, but he's in the process of grooming Callum for the role in five years. His younger brother and sister hold positions, too.

The conversation flows easily with everyone's participation.

The siblings grew up discussing business to prepare for joining their family's legacy while I worked hard from a teenager to grow Lola's Coterie. All of us volunteer in some way to help others, so we're a well-rounded group. All of our perspectives add to the conversation.

As we continue to chat, Baz reaches over and pulls me onto his lap. Content to relax in his arms, I snuggle against him and drift off, exhausted from the travel.

* * *

"Let's begin with some breathwork."

Each morning Starr starts our day with yoga in the sunroom facing the sea. Aside from the girls, the guys join us. Starr's influence runs deep.

I admitted my pregnancy to her so I did nothing to harm my baby. Since Starr taught Leonie during her pregnancy via Skype and served as her doula, I asked her to do the same for me.

After Starr suggested we meet for morning yoga on our first night here, I pulled her aside to let her know. She was so excited for me, but kept it hush-hush.

I haven't even told my BFF yet. So I don't want anyone else to find out before Leonie.

Baz thought it was a good idea to let Starr know, especially since she's been my yoga teacher all these years and would know prenatal modifications. He agreed she'd be perfect as my doula, too.

So far, I've avoided showing my baby bump. Instead of a bikini, I opted for cut-out maillots and flowy dresses. Even when we do our yoga sessions, I wear a tank top with loose-fitting pants. My petite frame carries my pregnancy well.

Baz of course noticed—and relishes—my bigger boobs.

Even though we welcomed the guys to yoga, we're kicking them out so we can have some much needed Girls' Time. We have a lot to catch up on and only two days left before we go our separate ways until Christmas.

After a peaceful Savasana and light sharing namaste, we kick Baz, Roger, Malcolm, Harris, and Callum out of the sunroom.

"So, spill with Callum and Lachlan, Haley," Starr says as soon as she shuts the door behind them.

Haley turns scarlet and reaches to push her glasses up the bridge of her nose. It's her nervous tell she can't stop even after wearing contact lenses for the last couple of years.

"What do you mean?" She asks, not realizing we know she's bluffing.

We giggle at her gaffe.

"Oh, don't play the innocent, Ms. Kiss Me Until My Lips Swell Steele!" Leonie laughs.

On a breathy sigh, Haley fills us in on the last couple of months since she saw Lachlan at the Labor Day fundraiser. The drama of her love triangle with one man who's her brother's best friend and one man who's had his eye on her since Harvard Business School proves more intriguing than any telenovela I've seen!

"Well then, what about you, Ms. Comfy on Malcolm's Jet Knight?" I add to avoid the teasing coming around to me and my hormone-induced nausea.

Now it's Starr's turn to blush. Her chestnut-colored skin adds a crimson hue to her cheeks.

Haley smirks.

"Fine! He's a monster!" Starr laughs as she holds her hands two feet apart in front of her.

We fall onto our mats, snorting as Haley sings at the top of her lungs with her fingers in her ears.

Once we catch our breath, Starr fills us in on how Malcolm fills her and not just with his "monster" dick. It's obvious they're really into each other. I'm happy for my good buddy and brother-in-law.

By the time Starr finishes her tales, Shelley and Josy come in the sunroom to invite us on a shopping trip to Capri town between the Piazzetta and Via Camerelle. It's one of the most fashionable centers in the world, with high-end boutiques and jewelry stores.

Grateful for the distraction, I'm the first one to agree.

Less than an hour later, we're strolling along the streets, popping in and out of the boutiques filled with designer pieces and handcrafted items by local artisans.

Most of the people in the shops and on the streets recognize Leonie. She takes it in stride when they ask for her autograph or a selfie. Our security detail keeps any overzealous fans at bay—precautions Baz and Roger implemented after the Labor Day situation.

My shopping spree is complete when I order two pairs of bespoke Canfora Sandals, my favorite, purchase some hand-painted silk scarves, including three ties for Baz, and perfume that reminds me of the island's natural scent.

"Lola, honey, the sun did you some good. You're glowing."

I glance up into Shelley's smiling face as she loops her arm through mine. Her expression of genuine joy makes me wonder if she can tell I'm pregnant. I feel horrible not admitting it yet, but it's only a few more weeks before Christmas.

"Yes, the fresh sea air and warm sun make a tremendous difference," I grin using Baz's tactic once again. "Plus, your son makes sure I eat properly and rest."

Shelley throws her head back and laughs. Her brown eyes shine with mirth.

"I'm sure he does! My boys better treat their women well. Right, Starr and Leonie?" Shelley adds with a wink at the girls.

They giggle and nod their agreement.

Maman Josy cups Leonie's face and says, "And you treat those boys well, *non?*"

"*Oui, Maman, absolument!*" Leonie smiles lovingly at her mom.

I sigh and swallow back my tears as I unconsciously place my hand on my belly. I wish my mother were here with me.

How in the world am I going to raise my baby without my mother's guidance? Who's going to give me tips for teething pains? Or just listen as I share my thoughts on motherhood?

I bite my lip to hold back a cry and glance away from Leonie and *Maman* Josy. It hurts too much, and my hormones are making me overly sensitive and emotional.

"You know Josy and I are here for you, Lola, honey. We may never replace your mother. But know we love you dearly and will help you in any way."

Shelley's kind words break the dam, and I sob.

She pulls me into her arms and rocks me gently as she hums a soothing tune.

"*Chérie!* What's the matter?!" Leonie cries as she rubs my back.

Shelley answers for me, just as her son did before. "She's fine, just a bit overwhelmed. Let's head back to your villa, shall we?"

Leonie agrees and takes my arm while Shelley holds the other. Josy, Haley, and Starr gather around us, and we make our way back to the Mercedes-Benz G-Wagens. The security detail follows, then drives us to the villa.

Determined not to upset anyone, I put a smile on my face and tell them I'm fine. Since we had lunch in town, I go to my suite and curl in the bed for a nap. Baz and the boys went boating with friends. So I have time to get myself together before Thanksgiving dinner tonight.

"This is fantastic! I agree we should have an opulent Edwardian-themed-*Gigi* party!"

Leonie and Roger finished giving everyone a tour of the vintage steam yacht he bought for her. She named it *Gigi* after her favorite film.

I can't wait to plan the soiree.

Leonie and I do our happy shimmy dance, then continue on to the bow where we'll have cocktails before Thanksgiving dinner begins.

The last few days have been full of swimming at our private beach or in the pool and excursions to the Blue

Grotto, Monte Solaro, and Villa di Tiberio. The Blue Grotto thrilled The Twins when their laughter echoed inside of the water-filled cavern.

Leonie wanted to save *Gigi* for last as the highlight and setting for our Thanksgiving dinner as we cruise around Capri for three hours. They time it for cocktails at sunset and dinner by torchlight—electric since they don't want to risk damage to the boat.

We dress in semi-formal attire with the guys in suits and the women in dresses. The Twins wear shirt and shorts one-piece sets with socks that mimic shoes and outdo us all.

Once we're gathered at the bow with drinks in hand, Morgan leads us in expressing his thanks over the past year. Each of us takes a turn ending with Roger. It's obvious he's already emotional after Leonie's heartfelt words of gratitude for their lives together and most of all for the safety of their sons.

Coming on the end of her touching speech and tears, he holds her close in his arms and address us.

"Thanks can never express the depth of my feelings for all of you and others who are not present. Your love and support from the start of that fiasco to the joy of our wedding with the addition of my in-laws and the wonderful holidays we shared to the return of our sons mean more than you can imagine. Mom, Dad, all of our lives you raised us to be a close-knit clan. This past year proves you succeeded. I love you all beyond measure."

Roger lifts his glass and proclaims, "Now let us enjoy this Thanksgiving dinner and here's to many, many more!"

"Hear, hear!!"

"Bravo, Roger! We love you, too!!"

"Happy Thanksgiving, everyone!!"

Baz nuzzles my neck and whispers, "Happy Thanksgiving to my babies. I love you with all my heart."

SEBASTIAN

I glue my eyes to the monitor where the screen shows an alien-looking world of red clouds and swirls, much like Mars. In the center floats my baby, my son.

He's the size of a cucumber, but looks like a mini human—no martian features. His facial expression appears peaceful with closed eyes. Tiny fingers of one hand wrap around the umbilical cord while he sucks the thumb of the other.

Dr. Rice tells us our baby boy can hear our voices in utero with studies proving he can recognize us once he's born.

Yeah, I made a super baby!

"A boy for you, Mr. Steele," Lola says as she squeezes my hand and smiles at me. "Are you pleased?"

I cup her beautiful face between my palms and brush

my lips over hers before I kiss her softly. With my forehead pressed to hers, I whisper words of love.

This woman carries my child, the next generation of the Steele clan, the son of the eldest son. Lola probably doesn't comprehend the magnitude of her pregnancy.

Each first son before me laid the groundwork for the following generations to grow STEELE International, Inc. into a multibillion-dollar corporation. The subsequent generation added to our family business' success. As the head of this generation, it is my duty to continue that upward trajectory set by those before me and will be the responsibility of my son. My heir.

I take a deep calming breath to re-center myself, then kiss the tip of Lola's nose before my gaze returns to the monitor.

"I'll print some images for you," Dr. Rice offers.

"Oh, wonderful! We can show everyone when we arrive in Verbier next week," Lola says full of excitement.

My face nearly splits as I grin and respond, "Yes, the perfect present!"

"Hey, hey, hey! The gang's all here!! Merry Christmas Eve!"

Roger and Leonie laugh as Harris makes his way through the front door after Lola and me, arms laden with gifts. They tease he looks like a young Santa Claus.

He rejoins with, "A sexy AF one, no doubt! And no last-minute presents for me, Roger dear! Let's see if you get coal in your stocking this year…"

Malcolm and Starr enter behind him, and the girls hug while Malcolm and Roger bro hug.

"Good to see you, man!" Roger tells him.

"Still looking goofy, bro!" Malcolm teases.

Haley walks in looking glum, and Roger pulls her into a bear hug, lifting her off her feet.

As per Lola's intel, Haley was going through some relationship issues, so he tries to cheer his baby sister up posthaste. *Duke* Callum will rue the day if he hurts our little sister. I'll *duke* his ass.

"You better have brought your, A game or I'm going to leave you in the powder tomorrow morning for our Christmas Day run!" Roger teases Haley. "Don't blame me when your googles get covered in snow!"

She rolls her eyes and retorts, "Even on my worse day, I can outrace you, Roger!"

Guy and Josy enter carrying The Twins. They cared for Rodolphe and Gaspard while Roger and Leonie enjoyed their first wedding anniversary.

They scoop The Twins up and hold them close. These past few days are the longest they've been apart from them. They laugh at their parents' overzealous kisses and pat their faces with their chubby hands.

I smile to myself at the thought of my parents taking care of our baby while Lola and I spend quality time together. I cannot wait for our baby to be born!

Speaking of my parents, they're last to enter, and they greet Roger and Leonie warmly.

"This tree is even bigger than last year's," my mother says, smiling as she takes a glass of hot mulled wine. "I love the new decorations!"

Everyone makes their way to their suites while Leonie and Roger tend to The Twins.

"I can't wait to tell them!" Lola exclaims as she rubs her belly. "This sweater is warm even if it hides my baby bump."

I walk back out of the bathroom to slip my arms around Lola from behind. My sizable hands cradle her belly that reminds me of a basketball, though I would never tell Lola. She's still getting used to her body changes.

"Then you should take the sweater off, babe. You don't want to overheat," I tell her.

She switches out of the turtleneck into a silk camisole, not wanting to give away her baby bump before we make the announcement after dinner.

Lola and I head back downstairs to the dining room where Josy chats with the chef she favored last Christmas about tonight's dinner. It's like the holiday before, in honor of the French tradition of le *Réveillon de Noël* for the Christmas meal.

We relish in each other's company as we dine on fine dishes and excellent wines. The conversation flows easily.

Once we're gathered in the great room and exchanged our first gifts as our tradition for Christmas Eve, Roger stands and pulls Leonie to her feet with him. The two female Bichon Frise puppies Roger gifted Leonie and The Twins scamper around their feet, playing with a toy.

"Well everyone, Leonie and I have some news to share with you," Roger gazes from one smiling face to the other before his eyes turn to his wife's gorgeous face.

"We're twenty weeks pregnant with a baby girl!!" Leonie announces, grinning like the Cheshire Cat.

Everyone whoops and hollers.

"Congratulations!!"

"*Oh, Mon Dieu!*"

"Awesome news, Roger and Leonie!!"

"*Fantastique, Mon Trésor!*"

When the well-wishing ends, I clear my throat and stand, too.

"Roger and Leonie, Lola and I are so thrilled for you! Once again you'll make us an aunt and an uncle—the most favorites, of course," I pause to pull Lola into my side. "And we will make you an aunt and uncle, too. The most favorite is up to the others."

At first everyone smiles and nods. Then the room erupts when they realize what I mean about us expecting a baby, too.

"We're twenty weeks, too!" Lola gushes as she rubs her belly covered by an oversized sweater. "Can you believe it, BFF?!"

"Oh, Lola, Sebastian! We're so happy for you, too!!" Leonie exclaims as she hugs a beaming Lola and they start to cry, overcome with hormonal emotions.

Undoubtedly Leonie remembers Lola being upset this

time last year as she sat in the windowed walkway in the early morning debating having children with me then or later.

Now here we are a year later, and we're both expecting. This Christmas is going to be even more special than the last!

The doorbell chimes, and Shelley waves Roger off as she heads to the entryway to answer. Everyone is present, so we're not sure who it could be.

Roger glances down at Leonie, and she shrugs her shoulders.

Everyone turns to the entry, wondering who has arrived at this late hour.

Shelley returns to the great room with Lachlan behind her. She glances at Haley questioningly, then at me worriedly.

Lachlan strides right in and stops in front of Haley, clasping her hands in his. Without his emerald green eyes leaving her dove gray ones, he addresses Morgan and Baz.

"No disrespect, Uncle Morgan. We're like brothers, Sebastian. But Haley is mine, and I won't go another day without her for anyone."

Silence descends on the great room. Talk about the other shoe drops, rather the third…

"What the fuck, Lachlan?!" I growl as I advance on my best friend. "What do you mean Haley is yours?"

Lola puts both of her hands on my arm to hold me back. She knows I won't pull away and risk hurting her and our son.

"Baz, babe, let them be. It's Haley's decision, not yours," Lola says calmly.

"*Oui*, give them some privacy," Leonie adds, then turns to Haley and Lachlan. "Haley, go to the library. No one will disturb you, *Chérie*."

"Leonie—" Roger pins her with his intense stare.

"*Non*! Enough of the big brother meddling! Let Haley live her life," Leonie demands, her fierce feline gaze sparking golden amber.

Haley nods, and she leaves the great room with Lachlan in tow.

Malcolm, Roger, Harris, and I glare after them. I swear I hear Harris growl. He's the most easygoing of us, but he's extremely protective of his twin.

"Now, Sebastian, Lola, boy or girl?" Josy asks, clapping her hands to diffuse the situation. "We must know how to prepare, *non?*"

Lola jumps right in and tugs me to the sofa.

"We're having a… baby… BOY!!" She shouts as she shimmies in her seat beside me.

Her exuberance melts the arctic chill from the air in the room. No one can resist her joy, especially me.

I wrap my arm around her shoulders and lean over to kiss her temple. Then I face our family.

"Yes, a son! A healthy baby boy! See for yourselves," I say as I stand to pass out color copies of the ultrasound images I had in an envelope.

"Fantastic! You're right, Josy, we have so much to

prepare!" My mother gushes. "June will be here before you know it."

"A girl and a boy at the same time! Busy, busy, busy!" Starr laughs.

I notice how Malcolm watches her with what appears to express longing. Could he have the baby bug, too? Starr doesn't catch his look since she's chatting with Lola and Leonie.

Malcolm must sense my stare and shifts his gaze to me. He purses his lips and crosses his arms over his chest when I raise an eyebrow questioningly.

I chuckle. Yeah, right. He's smitten.

"I know you'll be busy with your pregnancy, your work with Lola's Coterie and STEELE, and your volunteering with the girls. But... I'd love if you'd design my nurseries... Please, bestie?"

Leonie, Haley, Blair, Billie, Starr, and I sit in my chill room on the first floor of my New York City penthouse while The Twins play with their Bichon Frise puppies and toys on a blanket. The boys including Morgan, Luc, Patrick, and Lachlan went to the STEELE box at Madison Square Garden for the Knicks versus the Los Angeles Lakers basketball game.

The girls and I take advantage of some time alone. It's been a month since we left Verbs and the first time we've all been together.

As the Head of STEELE Children and Young Adults Division and since she did a fantastic job with my Sutton Place penthouse, Leonie would be perfect to help me. The last few weeks I tried with Shelley's assistance, but Leonie just has that special touch.

The Twins' nurseries—nine in total, no less—are spectacular and suit each of Leonie and Roger's and their grandparents' residences. We need eight: our and Morgan and Shelley's New York City penthouses; our and their Southampton Village beach houses; our and their Paris penthouses; Josy and Guy's Paris mansion; our London mansion.

It's a Herculean task. I give Leonie my puppy dog eyes.

"Of course, *Chérie*! I was hoping you'd ask!" She says clapping her hands as her amber eyes twinkle in delight.

Leonie has always had an eye for design. The combination of being the world-renowned megamodel *The Lion* for almost nineteen years and as the daughter of an old, wealthy Parisian merchant family that travels seeking antiques, antiquities, and fabrics instilled in her a love for the aesthetics. Transitioning into interior design was her dream for years.

"*Merci! Merci beaucoup, mon amie!*" I thank her with a huge sideways hug to avoid bumping our bellies. "We must start with the nurseries here and in Southampton Village. The ones in Paris and London can wait since we won't travel abroad until after the summer season."

Since Baby Boy is due in June, Baz and I decided to stay out in The Hamptons after they're born. Time away from the city during the sultry New York summer proves just the solution. Who wouldn't prefer to be on the beach?

Shelley already told us she and Morgan will stay out

there and not go to Positano for the summer. So Baz and I will have plenty of support.

"Do you want to remain true to your interiors or go with unique designs? Have you decided which rooms you want to convert? Oh, and Shelley showed me some incredible heirloom pieces from their family we can incorporate like we did for The Twins. Not to mention antiques from mine and pieces from the collections of Beaulieu Enterprises. I know just the ones…"

We jump right in on ideas. Leonie sketches on a pad I pull from my secretary desk as her creative juices flow from her head to her fingers. In no time at all she has several options from themed to traditional, down to the layouts and the color palettes.

I love them!

"Do you think Nanny Grace would make a blanket for Baby Boy? Rodolphe and Gaspard's are beautiful," Haley says. "They'll treasure them forever."

Nanny Grace hand-crocheted two navy blue cashmere blankets. Everyone admired the fine stitchwork of the intricate design. The center panels have entwined B and S for Beaulieu and Steele, surrounded by a twelve-inch border of swirls and whorls. She made matching beanies and booties to complete the sets.

I clap my hands together and lace my fingers as I bounce on the sofa.

"Ooooh! That would be phenomenal! Will you ask her for me, Leonie?" I say. "I'd love to combine Baby Boy's initials."

"Have you chosen a name, yet?" Starr asks.

Baz and I thought of some options and narrowed it down to two. We want to wait until the day he's born to pick based on which feels best once we set eyes on Baby Boy.

I share our decision with the girls, and they understand.

"Being that you and Lola are due at the same time, I spoke with Anita since she's a doula now. She can help you, Leonie, while I help Lola. It's better for you both with me in the States and Anita in Paris. We can give you the attention you need without concern for distance," Starr says.

I smile at her for such a brilliant suggestion.

After Baz and I made the official announcement, I told Leonie about admitting my pregnancy to Starr first since the yoga sessions concerned me in my prenatal state. And how I asked her to be my doula. I did not know when I asked Leonie was expecting too and would want to have Starr help her again.

Of course, my easygoing BFF took it in stride. Leonie rarely allows situations to become problems. It reminded me of her favorite saying: *"Only solutions, Lola!"* She figured she'd make do with a referral from Dr. Berger, her OB-GYN.

Now Starr offers the perfect solution!

Anita Green is the wife of Norman Green, Roger's boxing coach and personal trainer and the former world heavyweight champion nine years straight—eight by knockout. At Roger's suggestion, Norman opened eponymous chains of branded gyms through STEELE's Entertainment Properties Division when he retired. One for underprivileged youth and another as exclusive elite training facilities for the überwealthy and star athletes.

In her own right, Anita is a star yoga instructor with a flourishing global practice and with her degree from the culinary school at Le Cordon Bleu started a meal plan delivery service. Norman added her customized plans to the paid offerings of the elite facilities and complimentary healthy snacks to the youth. She also took over the food services in both chains. They're a dynamic couple who raise the bar in the fitness industry.

Anita became Leonie's yoga instructor once she was further along in her pregnancy, and Starr wanted her to have hands-on attention not possible through their Skype sessions. Over the years, Anita and Leonie, then with the other girls, became close. She's now a part of our clique.

"Wonderful, *Chérie*! I remember when Anita completed her doula training. She'll be perfect, *merci!*" Leonie gushes. "I'll send a text message to her now."

"While we're on the topic of baby plans… Leonie, Sebastian and I want to meet with Nanny Grace's agency for selecting a nanny and a nurse," I say, remembering the conversation we had a few nights ago. "Baz and I figure you can speak with the owners since they're based in Paris before we meet with their New York City office."

Grace Hart is one of their stellar nannies who's also a trained nurse. The überwealthy and celebrities use her agency to hire their nannies, nurses, and governesses. Their training is top-notch in everything from changing a diaper to language lessons to disarming a would-be kidnapper. Even though Baz has a security detail for me, it's good for the nanny to have training.

"*Absolument!* Nanny Grace is the best! Roger and I will call them tomorrow morning Paris time. Perhaps we can video conference into the call the head of this office," Leonie responds.

The house intercom rings, and I answer it to Shelley on the line. The spa day with her best friend and the Jackson Matriarch Lucie ended early. Shelley asks what we're up to, and I tell her to come down since we're talking baby plans.

When she arrives, we fill her in on the latest. She's just as excited as we are about the developments.

"More grandchildren to spoil," she laughs, clapping her hands. "I cannot wait!"

My heart fills with joy. I may not have my mother here, but Shelley and Josy have lived up to their word and helped me in every way. I know my mother would be happy for me. And I send a silent prayer to her.

"Excuse me, everyone. May I have your attention? I have an announcement to make."

We're in the private East Room of Per Se, my favorite restaurant in New York City. It's also where we celebrated the deal between Lola's Coterie and STEELE over three years ago.

I smiled to myself as we walked in, and my gaze went to the stunning views of the Manhattan skyline and Central

Park clear across Columbus Circle to Fifth Avenue. The other side of the East Room is a glass panel that overlooks the restaurant's main dining room. But prior to our arrival, the staff closed the silk drapes for privacy.

Then my thoughts shift to the feral way Baz fucked me in the ladies' room against the vanity after he spanked my ass until it was on fire. He pounded into me from behind like a man possessed until he came with an explosive roar. The shock on Baz's face when he realized he lost control and took me bareback was priceless.

Even though I was pissed with him, I returned to his penthouse right after we straightened our clothing. His declaration to take my last hole proved more tempting than my anger. My pussy and ass clench with the memory.

Now my gaze travels around the circular table to Luc, who smiles encouragingly. He and Baz agreed with my newest business decision. It's a long time coming.

With a nod, I stand and smile at Blair.

"Years ago I thought I was Wonder Woman and could do every aspect of Lola's Coterie by myself. From the design to the marketing to the management of the Paris flagship and the London boutique. My wise mentor told me to focus on the creative design side and let an assistant handle the day-to-day tasks. In came Blair and she blew me away with her efficiency, dependability, and cleverness when balancing the activities that didn't need my constant or immediate attention."

Then I turn to Billie seated beside Patrick and smile.

"I learned from my experience with Blair to find

someone I can rely on to handle my business affairs long distance for Lola's Coterie Las Vegas. Thanks to Baz's director of STEELE's West Coast retail properties, I met Billie. I needed someone who could handle the contractors, staff, and clients who like me could charm the best of them, but can turn into a spitfire when necessary."

Everyone laughs when I waggle my eyebrows.

"Over the years, you've proven yourselves to be incredible in your jobs, but also wonderful friends. With Baby Boy on the way, I realize once again, I cannot do it all"—I raise my glass of iced lemon ginger tea—"So this decision was a no-brainer. Blair I would like to offer you the position of my chief marketing officer and Billie my chief operating officer!"

Blair and Billie gasp while the others stand and clap, then raise their glasses in a toast.

"So deserved, *Chéries*!"

"Whoohoo! Congratulations!"

"*Félicitations!*"

"Cheers!"

After a few moments, I quiet everyone down and turn back to Blair and Billie.

"Do you accept?" I ask, hoping they answer in the affirmative. "I mean, just don't leave a preggie lady hanging, no pressure!"

Billie jumps up and gives me a hug, and Blair does the same. They agree wholeheartedly. And the servers appear with chilled bottles of Dom Pérignon Rosé Vintage 2005 and a variety of desserts.

"We'll drink for you, Leonie and Lola!" Malcolm teases.

Lachlan adds, "We know it's your favorite bubbly, Lola!"

"Awww… Don't tease my sisters. Although I must say you are missing out, ladies!" Harris chuckles.

Leonie laughs, and Roger pops Harris on the back of his head good-naturedly.

We spend the rest of the time chatting and enjoying one another. The boys rehash the basketball game, including the "incredible last second three-pointer by LeBron *King* James." Billie jokes about her date with another basketball superstar. But Patrick whispers in her ear, and her eyes widen as she turns bright pink. He sits back and smirks.

I giggle knowing Patrick being an Alpha Dom must have told her just how he feels about her date with another man. Baz squeezes my thigh under the table, and I can't help but snort.

Starr who sits next to me covers her mouth with her linen napkin to hide her laughter. Then Malcolm silences her with words said in her ear.

It cracks me up further to realize how each of my friends—who despite being Independent Women—find themselves attracted to Alpha males, Doms or not. Some-times when you're in control of your business, career, life… it's a relief to turn over control to your lover. No need to think, just feel as Baz tells me.

"What is going on in that busy mind of yours, Little Pet?"

Baz's warm breath tickles my neck as he leans over to murmur in my ear. His lips trail along the side of my neck, making my nipples pucker against the silk of my blouse and my pussy clench with need. My mind was already on lascivious thoughts. He just drove me closer to the edge.

"Well, Sir, since you asked… A vision of my wrists bound by red silks to the corners of our bed with my ankles in the spreader bar. My legs thrown over your shoulders as you kneel above me, pounding your ginormous dick into my dripping, tight pussy. The bed creaks from your powerful thrusts as though the frame may crack at any moment. I scream your name—hoarse from my previous carnal cries—as you wring a fourth orgasm from my wrecked pussy. Sweat drips from your chin to land between my bouncing breasts. You bow your head to lap it up, then suckle my peaked nipples voraciously until I cum again. Head thrown back, eyes shut, a roar rips from your throat as you blow your load deep inside my pussy. It squeezes every drop from your cock."

I lift my lowered gaze to his and smile in triumph when I see his pupils blown and his mouth slack.

Baz flares his nostrils and smirks, "Well my Petite Seductress, let us return home to make your vision our reality."

My grin widens, "Yes, Sir. Thank you, Sir."

"Where are we going? The water has the most beautiful shades of blue and green! Look! Are those dolphins over there?"

Lola's excitement as she peers out the window in her seat beside me on our Gulfstream 650 makes me chuckle.

At twenty-six weeks pregnant, she's two-thirds of the way through our pregnancy. It's month six with only three months left to go. I'll be a father in no time. Holy shit!

Roger reminded me I need to take Lola on our baby-moon before she's twenty-eight weeks. Leonie had the great idea of taking Lola to the Caribbean since it's less than three hours from New York City or an hour from Miami by plane just in case we need a doctor.

That was a few weeks ago, and it gave me time to decide to stay at a STEELE beach resort or to rent a private villa. In the end, I chose to invest for our family—the three of us and the rest of the Steele clan.

What can I say? It's the big brother in me to care for my siblings.

I researched private islands instead of giving money away to an owner for a villa rental and not doing our usual of a STEELE property stay.

The private island realtor suggested by a business associate helped me to narrow down the location to the Exumas. More specifically to an island within the chain of the Exuma Cays known as the yachting, sailing, and fishing paradise of the Bahamas. The location offers an ideal spot for relaxation and fun activities.

The forty-million-dollar investment of Bougainvillea Cay lies in one of the most beautiful parts of the Bahamas. It features over five hundred acres of lush, tropical land with a network of paths and walkways. Surrounded by crystal clear turquoise waters, it boasts many white sandy beaches, three inner lakes, and different elevations for stunning views. An airstrip for us to fly in and out with ease makes it perfect for quick getaways. Another plus is its proximity to STEELE Exumas should we wish to use the recreational, spa, or dining facilities.

Two properties round out the island. A palatial two-story, ten-bedroom beachfront villa with saltwater pool, four guest cabanas, and a caretaker's house and an actual castle built by an Englishman in the 1930s. We can rebuild it into a spot for the kids to take over, especially as they grow into teenagers and want their space apart from the adults. I'll leave it to Leonie to design through her STEELE division.

My parents and siblings can build their villas along the coastline that features natural coves for privacy. With his STEELE division, Roger can create a clubhouse on the largest beach for our family to gather. We'll add docks with lifts for sailboats, Jetskis, and other water toys.

Bougainvillea Cay will be the Steele Caribbean retreat. A spectacular place for our family to gather for the winters, as we do at Steele Southampton in the summers and *Chalet de la Joie* for the holidays.

I reach over and place my palm on Lola's round belly. Now it's bigger than basketball, but smaller than a beach ball. My fingers caress her baby bump and tweak her newly outie belly button.

Lola giggles and slaps my hand away.

"Tell me! Why and where have you kidnapped me?" She demands. "At least you didn't blindfold and gag me. Well… Not that I would have minded!"

"Naughty Pet. You will soon find out," I respond as I sweep her much longer hair aside to nuzzle the side of her elegant neck. "Patience, Pet. Patience."

Lola gasps when I nip her soft skin between my teeth and suck hard. Once satisfied a mark will appear, I lick and kiss the area to soothe her.

My Petite Seductress drives me crazy with need. Her pregnancy body is a whole new world for me to explore and to delight in. From her sensitive oversized nipples to her Double-D tits to her ample ass and grip-worthy hips.

Mine!

Our pilot announces we'll land in fifteen minutes.

I grin at Lola when she looks from me to the window and back again. I'm sure she can see the cays and from our flight time guess we're in the Bahamas.

She just smiles and takes my left hand in hers to kiss my platinum wedding band. Then she lifts her hazel gaze to my dove gray one.

"Wherever we may be and why, you captured me the moment I first saw you at LEVELS New York. My vision locked on your magnetic gray eyes and a thrill rushed through me as if a jolt of electricity shocked my very soul. I love and trust you, Mr. Steele," Lola says with a twinkle in her eyes.

My heart beats wildly. This woman is the best thing to happen to me in my life, ever. Never afraid to show my true self to her, my eyes glisten with tears.

"Thank you, my love," I murmur as I slant my mouth over hers for a soul-shocking kiss.

BEFORE WE LANDED, I pointed out the window for Lola to take in the majesty of our private island. I didn't tell her it was ours. I wanted to wait until we were at the villa.

When I finished giving her a tour of the primary residence, we changed into bathing suits and headed to the beach for lunch at a table set on the warm white sand. Staff stand at the ready to serve us.

I help Lola into her chair after I place a bougainvillea flower behind her ear, then sit across from her. Once they place our appetizers before us and pour our beverages, they depart. They'll return for our entrees.

"How do you like Bougainvillea Cay?" I ask as Lola takes in the turquoise water, clear blue sky, and endless sand.

She turns her gaze to me and grins, "I love it! I've never seen such a picturesque private island. The flowers intoxicate me. Thank you, baby!"

My chest swells with pride.

"Do you like it enough to make it our new Caribbean retreat?" I ask nonchalantly as I pop a delectable grilled shrimp in my mouth.

No sound comes from across the table. So I glance up to see Lola's eyes wide, and her mouth hanging open in shock.

I laugh so hard I nearly choke on my morsel of conch fritters.

"Welcome to Paradise, baby," I grin.

Lola rushes over to me, and I pull her onto my lap as she flings her arms around my neck and kisses me until we're breathless. She pulls back and rubs her nose against mine.

"Thank you, so much," she whispers. "It's perfect, my love."

I tighten my arms around her and brush my lips on hers.

"I would take all the credit if I could. But Roger reminded me to take you on a babymoon so we could spend time as a couple before Baby Boy comes. Then

Leonie suggested the Bahamas. So here we are," I respond.

Lola beams and kisses me again. Then laughs, "So you bought an island?"

I chuckle, embarrassed by my enthusiasm. But when I explain its use as a family getaway like Southampton and Verbier, Lola agrees wholeheartedly.

We discuss plans for making the island our own as we enjoy a delicious meal of fresh fish prepared with local flavors and tasty sides, including pigeon peas and rice. Virgin Bahamas Mama Punch and cool water keep us refreshed in the warm sun. A delicious guava duff dessert completes our meal.

The staff leaves us after they clear the table. They return to the caretaker's house until we request their service.

Total privacy on our private island.

I take Lola's hand and lead her to the sunbed with a double umbrella, the only other item on the expanse of powdery white sand. We stretch out and lean back to gaze at the Bahama Blue water of the Atlantic Ocean.

Lola shifts on the sunbed to face me.

My eyes travel from her messy bun to her luscious tits in the triangle bikini top to her round belly, past her bikini-bottom-clad mound, down her toned legs to her red-painted toenails.

Sexy Mama Alert.

"You know bougainvillea is symbolic of abundance, prosperity, and passion. But most of all of fertility. How apropos, Mr. Steele?" Lola says as she touches her fingers to the vibrant pink flower in her raven hair.

A feral grin forms on my face. It pleases my caveman to provide for my mate, give her pleasure, and fill her belly with my baby. A growl rumbles from low in my chest.

Lola purrs in response and drags a fingertip from her ear down her throat to circle a beaded nipple. Her lust-filled eyes never leave mine. Instead, they spark with a carnal inner fire that threatens to consume me.

"Spread your thighs for me and present your pretty pink pussy, Little Pet," I command in my deep Alpha Dom baritone.

I smirk when Lola shivers visibly, and a soft cry falls from her mouth. She loves it when I control her sexually.

Being the vixen as always, Lola pulls the strings on her white bikini bottom slowly. Her heated gaze warms me more than the Bahamas sun. Just as unrushed, she slips the bottoms from her bare mound. She takes my request a step further and places two fingers on either side of her pussy seam to pull her juicy lips apart.

My cock jumps and my mouth waters at the sight of her glistening, pink folds.

"Are you satisfied with the view, Sir?" Lola asks seductively as she stares at my growing bulge pressing against my sky-blue trunks.

The clear outline of my mushroom head leaves no question of my arousal.

I mimic her moves and lift my hips to peel my trunks down my muscular legs unhurriedly. My ten inches spring free and slap my eight-pack abs. It aligns with my happy trail of dark hair as it reaches my belly button.

Lola licks her lips, dragging her little pink tongue from one corner of her mouth to the other. Her hooded eyes rake over my hard pecs, abs, and rod as I stroke my chest down to grip the base of my cock.

"Are you satisfied with the view, Little Pet?" I ask, repeating her question.

Lola smirks and raises her hands behind her neck.

When she pulls the string loose of her bikini top and it falls down to reveal her delectable tits, I nearly blow my load. I have to pinch the tip of my dick to distract myself.

"Tit for tat, Naughty Pet?" I rumble, and she quakes. "Hands and knees. I want to mount you from behind."

Lola hastens into position. She tosses her hair over her right shoulder to peer back at me over her left one. She bites her plump lower lip when her gaze lands on my fisted cock as I advance on her.

I lean forward and bury my face between her thighs.

Her cries of ecstasy drive me to increase the intensity of my licking inside her pussy and sucking her engorged clit. Lola squeals and drops to her forearms when I smack her dripping folds.

I slip one finger inside of her pussy, then flex and curl it to stretch her walls and stroke the rough textured nugget on top. She needs to be soaked and ready for my invasion.

"Cum for me, Little Pet," I command, adding a second thick digit and increasing the rhythm. "Cum now!"

Lola bows her back in a deep arc, throwing her head back as she keens. Her body shakes from her climax.

Just as her greedy pussy grasps my fingers, I pull out and jam my throbbing cock inside. I grunt and Lola yowls.

Her pussy still flutters from her orgasm around my dick as I pound into her. Barbaric growls and grunts fill the air in opposition to the calm lapping of the ocean waves on the sand. The scent of our fucking mingles with the salty air. Sweat drips down my spine and a sheen forms on Lola's back. Erotic energy surrounds us.

I grip her hips harder as she writhes on my dick, pushing back to meet each of my thrusts with vigor. She clenches her pussy walls, and I groan.

"So fucking good, Little Pet... So tight... So wet..." I grunt, then spank her jiggling ass cheeks one after the other.

"More, Sir! Harder!" Lola cries out in wild abandon as she slaps the sunbed.

I give her what she wants; what she needs. The sound of flesh on flesh—groin to ass, balls to clit, palm to ass—fills our ears.

"Right there! Oh... My... Go—" Lola screams as her body shudders from another carnal climax "Yeeessssss!!"

Caught in her sexual thrall, I lose my mind as I bury myself in her wet heat. Lola's last orgasm makes my rhythm falter as she clamps down on my cock.

I have to shut my eyes from the sight of her writhing beneath me to regain control. My left hand reaches under

Lola to wrap around her throat and pull her upright, her back flush with my front.

She mewls still in the midst of her orgasm.

It's time for my release. My hips grind in circles to allow my dick to hit every inch of her pussy. Shallow thrusts followed by deep strokes until the tingle of my orgasm turns into a mind-blowing tsunami.

I throw my head back and howl to the heavens.

We collapse in a state of sheer euphoria.

"Happy Valentine's Day, Mr. Steele." Lola whispers throatily when I spoon her in front of me.

I rasp, "Happy Valentine's Day, Mrs. Steele."

LOLA

"*Mon amie,* I have to thank you for two weeks of sheer bliss in Paradise! If Baz didn't have to go to Australia for business in Sydney and Melbourne, we would have stayed for a month instead of only two weeks!"

I tell Leonie as we sit on sofas wrapped in oversized cashmere throws in her living room in Paris.

Baz and I left the Exumas a few hours ago. He took the larger G700 private jet to Australia and I flew to Paris on the G650. Baz wasn't pleased I wasn't returning to New York City while he was away for ten days. He worries about me being further along in my pregnancy.

I'm sure the idea of me being in Paris without him—the same city as Simon—weighed on Baz's mind, too. He does not need to fear at all. That page turned months ago!

But I explained I won't be able to fly much longer and

190

want to see Leonie before neither of us can travel. Since she has The Twins, it's easier for me to go to her.

He relented after he spoke with Roger. He assured Baz he wouldn't let me out of his sight. Even the security detail isn't enough for them. The Cavemen are super protective of Leonie and me with us being pregnant.

I could only smile at their possessiveness. Once I agreed to limit my activities to Lola's Coterie Paris, The STEELE Tower Paris, *Le Beaulieu Manoir*, and shopping, Baz relaxed.

Roger even said he'd accompany Leonie and me when venture out to buy baby items. He's going to stay true to his word, traipsing around stores with two preggies and all. Good luck with that, brother!

While I'm here, I'll work out of my flagship and take care of some baby prep needs. I arrived on a Saturday, so today we'll hang out in order for me to get some rest, then tomorrow go over the nurseries' status. We're enjoying some tea and cookies while Rodolphe and Gaspard nap in their rooms. The puppies chase each other, gamboling with a chew toy.

"No need to thank me, *Chérie*! I'm sure you would do the same for me. I don't blame you for wanting to stay. When you sent the photos, Roger teased we'd crash your babymoon and move into a guest cabana!" Leonie's laughter fills the room.

Then she claps her hands in glee as her amber eyes sparkle.

"I cannot wait to get started on the castle! It's gigantic. *Les petits enfants* will love pretending they're storming the castle or are princes and a princess. Baz is right, the castle will make the perfect spot just for them, especially as they get older and want time away from us," Leonie adds.

I nod, "It definitely will let their imaginations run wild. Baz and I role-played an erotic *Sleeping Beauty…*"

Leonie bursts out in a fit of giggles, then clutches her belly and grimaces.

"Daphne didn't appreciate being shaken. She just jabbed me!" Leonie says wide-eyed as she rubs the painful area. "*C'est la vie.* At least it's just one foot or hand and not two like with The Twins!"

I agree and rub my belly, remembering the boxing match Baby Boy had on the jet. His pokes were so intense I had to lie down in the bedroom for the last part of the flight. The thought of two babies at once makes me shudder. How the heck did Leonie do it? I muse as I shake my head in awe.

"You thrilled Roger with the idea of a family retreat in the Bahamas. The Beaulieus have a private island in Greece, but my father leased it in perpetuity to a luxury resort. We would stay, but it's not the same with other guests around. I can't wait to go to Bougainvillea Cay!" Leonie says smiling again.

We talk some more about the changes we want to make and the type of villa she and Roger prefer for their home. First on the list are the clubhouse and the docks, since there's room in the primary residence and the guest cabanas for everyone until they complete their villas.

Roger promised to share some of his ideas after dinner. He wanted to give Leonie and me time to catch up.

"And Malcolm is excited about selecting the boats. You know Mr. Fast Cars and Motorcycles! He's investigating sailboats and other water toys," I giggle mimicking him riding his Harley-Davidson at top speed. "Starr teases him all the time about a boy and his toys!"

"Well, she'll go gaga over the endless stretches of beach for yoga and the trails throughout the island for hikes. Not to mention swimming in the interior lakes," I say envisioning the exercise sessions Starr would come up with while we're on island.

My mobile rings, and Starr's name appears on the screen. I laugh and tell Leonie guess who as I answer on speaker audio.

"Hi, honey! How was your flight? Do you and Baby Boy fell all right?" Starr asks.

I tell her all is good, and I didn't return home. Instead I went to Paris to visit Leonie and to take care of some European business before I'm too far along.

Of course Starr already knows. As it so happens, Baz told Malcolm, who in turn told her. She and Malcolm want to make sure I made it in safely, and Baby Boy is fine.

In the background, I hear Malcolm ask if I'm okay, and Starr relays our conversation.

"Okay, well, other Hot Mama, Malcolm says you better take care, too! We'll leave you guys to it. Have some Girls' Time fun for me!" She says. "Oh, and don't forget to do your Kegel exercises and breathwork."

Leonie and I promise to follow Starr's prenatal instructions and tell her to thank Malcolm for his concern, too. We end the call with plans to meet up when I fly to the West Coast to visit my Las Vegas and Beverly Hills boutiques before my travel time draws to a close.

My goal is to attend to as much work at each boutique as possible before I give birth in June. Despite witnessing Leonie's bounce back after The Twins, I can't be sure how my body will react and don't want to risk not being able to attend to Lola's Coterie. My original baby!

I say a silent thank you for Blair and Billie already rocking it out in their new roles. They'll be my saving grace in the coming months. Even more so than they were before. My mind is at ease.

Leonie and I get back to talking. But my mobile rings again, this time with a FaceTime call from Baz. She laughs and goes to the kitchen with the puppies on her heels.

"Tell my brother hi for me, *Chérie*. And not to worry!" She says over her shoulder.

I answer the video call with an enormous smile on my face. This man is the definition of an overprotective first-time father.

"Hi, my love. Baby Boy and I arrived safely, and we feel great! No need to worry. How's your flight going?" I ask in an attempt to answer his questions and to redirect his thoughts.

Knowing me so well, Baz raises his eyebrow and purses his lips.

With a shake of his head, he responds, "Oh, don't even

try it, babe. Deflection won't work. Your flight attendant told me you retired to the bedroom with a pained expression…"

I roll my eyes. Damn. Spies everywhere.

We talk some more, and I vow to take it easy for the next two days. Otherwise, Baz informed me he'll be here in no time and will cart me to Dr. Berger's office stat—Leonie's OB-GYN. Not wanting to go that route, I reaffirm my pledge.

Satisfied, Baz ends the video call with kisses for me and his son.

My heart flutters, and Baby Boy pokes my belly as though responding to his father.

Baz gets as big a kick out of it as I, although mine was physical…

When Leonie returns, Roger enters with her and gives me the once over with his intense dove-gray stare. With a nod, he leaves us and pulls his mobile from his jeans pocket. Undoubtedly he's calling his brother to make a report on his assessment of me.

Leonie and I watch him leave, then turn to each other. We bust out laughing and hold our bellies to keep our babies from rocking too hard. Tears pop out of the corners of our eyes when we try to come up for air.

It feels so good to spend quality alone time with my best friend. And even better to share our pregnancies with each other. It's a blessing I'm so grateful to experience.

* * *

"OH, *chérie*! You look so good and happy!"

Maman Josy pulls me into her warm embrace once Leonie, Roger, The Twins, and I stand in the magnificent entry foyer of *Le Beaulieu Manoir*. Their ancestral home never ceases to amaze me.

Leonie is right. I'll definitely find some jewels for Baby Boy's Parisian nursery amongst her family's collections. I love the idea he'll have true antiques to fit in with the history of the city.

I squeeze *Maman* Josy to infuse an extra burst of love and thanks.

"Come, let's have brunch, then we'll get into the goodies," she says as she takes Gaspard and Rodolphe's hands with the puppies in tow.

Roger offers Leonie and me his arms and we loop ours through his as he follows *Maman* Josy.

We walk past beautifully appointed salons to an all-glass solarium that overlooks the rear rose garden. They set a table for our Sunday brunch, a tradition *Maman* Josy enjoys preparing as proved by the sideboard arranged for a buffet-style service with an abundance of platters. The delicious aroma of savory and sweet dishes fills the air. Spices, meats, and baked goods blend to make my mouth water and my stomach to growl.

We just settle in our seats when *Papa* Guy's voice booms in the solarium.

"*Bonjour, mes filles et mon fils!* Rodolphe, Gaspard come to your Grand-père!"

We turn to find him striding into the room, ever the

man of the estate. He's impeccably dressed in bespoke blazer, shirt, and trousers with Gucci loafers. After he scoops up The Twins, he hugs us and gives us double kisses. Then plants a soft kiss on *Maman* Josy's upturned lips.

His obsidian eyes scan Leonie and me as he takes us in from our heads to our rounded bellies. With a satisfied nod, he takes his seat.

"Come, let us eat," *Papa* Guy commands.

And eat we do!

Maman Josy is an incredible cook. Her skill of combining traditional Tunisian delicacies with Parisian cuisine makes for delectable dishes. Add in her baking specialties, including double-chocolate soufflés, and one can't ask for anything more.

Yum-my!

Throughout brunch, we chat and enjoy one another's company. Bougainvillea Cay thrills *Maman* Josy when I show them photos. *Papa* Guy regales us with his deep-sea fishing tales from his trips to the best fishing waters around the world. He's looking forward to those of the Exumas. It's been a while, he says.

Roger tells them he and Leonie will design a villa with living quarters for them. They beam when I assure them they're welcome to come and go as they wish, whether Baz and I are on island.

"*Merci, mes enfants!*" *Papa* Guy says in his deep baritone.

"Now, let's go upstairs. I had the servants move some pieces I think will be perfect for Leonie and you to select from for your nurseries," *Maman* Josy says as she rises from the table.

Papa Guy helps her, and they smile at each other as she touches her hand to his cheek. Their love is palpable.

The relationship they and my in-laws have are couple goals for Sebastian and me. Love at first sight and happily married for over thirty years is what I want for us. I know Leonie agrees; I think as I watch her grinning at her parents.

"Oui, *Maman*! I can't wait to see what goodies we have. There are some pieces I remember from before I'd like to use for Daphne," Leonie says as she rubs her baby bump. "They were too girly for The Twins. Now… Yippee!"

We laugh.

Guy assures Roger their staff will help us so the two of them can watch the Real Madrid and Manchester United football match.

After Leonie and I swear to not move or lift a single thing, not even a sheet, Roger concedes. As we part at the elevator, he gives us another warning, including calling Sebastian if I don't listen.

Maman Josy shoos them away with a bubbly laugh that makes her amber eyes glow when the door opens.

"*Chéries*, you'll learn to let your husbands talk and worry, then let them have their way. But on your terms," she says with a wink as she nods her stylish curly ebony bob.

Her words remind me of the advice Shelley and Lucie gave to us at my bridesmaids' luncheon in Dubai. Particularly their counsel on handling possessive Alpha males, and I'm certain in both of their cases Doms.

"Always listen more than you talk so you can understand how to respond if you have a disagreement," offered Lucie.

Shelley nodded and added, "Don't lose yourself in their lives. Maintain your friendships, work, activities."

"Yes, and your personality. If you were feisty and independent when you met, don't change. That's what attracted them to you. Don't simper like women who clamor for their attention," Lucie said.

"Oh and most important, be a proper lady in public, but a sex kitten in the bedroom! Pleasure them in the way they love the most regularly without fail!"

Shelley and Lucie burst out laughing as they high fived each other. Shelley dabbed the corners of her eyes. She laughed so hard she cried. Lucie covered her mouth with her hand and giggled some more.

Clearly, they had private jokes.

But now, after being married to Baz for thirty-two months, I get them, too!

Maman Josy, Leonie, and I step off the elevator into the Beaulieu family collections.

They dedicated the entire fourth floor of the massive mansion to their family's archives of antiquities, antiques, paintings, furniture, and clothing in temperature-controlled and damage-proof rooms. Generations of goodies cataloged in books with photos and details on each room door for easy access.

I can guarantee no other home in the world has such an elaborate setup for their family's archives.

"*Ooohhh, fantastique, Maman!*" Leonie claps in glee when she spies a beautiful hand-painted wooden cradle Josy set aside. "This is just the one I was thinking about! It's from before the Revolution, *non?*"

She's unfazed completely by the wealth and history of her family.

I smile and walk amongst the selections in admiration. The pieces *Maman* Josy displays are more than fantastic. Now, I wonder whether it's appropriate for me to have any of them, removing them from the family. They're Beaulieu heirlooms.

Maman Josy must sense my hesitancy. She's as in tuned to me as her daughter. *Maman* Josy wraps her arm around my shoulder and places her other hand on my belly.

"*Ma fills*, Guy and I want you to have any pieces your heart desires. We are blessed Leonie brought you into our family. You are a true daughter to us," she says with a smile, her eyes full of sincerity. "Come, I thought of Baby Boy when I saw this cradle."

I place my hand over hers on my baby bump and return her smile with tears shining in my eyes—damn hormones. My throat too thick with emotion, so I can only nod.

Once again I say a silent prayer for the loving family I have with me in my life and for my parents who continue to watch over me and now their grandson.

. . .

"You didn't overexert yourself, did you, babe?"

I'm back at our penthouse in bed doing a FaceTime video call with Baz. His worried platinum eyes search my face for any sign of fatigue.

"No, my love, brunch as usual, was delicious. Then the staff helped us with the selections. Leonie and I never lifted one pinky finger. Scout's Honor," I respond with a smile and three upright fingers.

Baz nods, and I tell him all about the pieces for the nursery. He's just as excited as I am for the beautiful items.

When I yawn, he tells me to go to sleep and to stay in bed later tomorrow morning. Work can wait.

It's nine in the morning Baz's time in Melbourne. So he's up and already at the STEELE offices, ready to start his day, while I'm just in bed at eleven at night.

"Okay, I will," I promise as I burrow under the bedding and sigh. "We love you."

Baz smiles, "I love you both very much. I miss you. Sweet dreams, babe."

Before he ends the call, my eyes close.

Baz knows me so well, I think as I drift into a peaceful slumber.

SEBASTIAN

*B*eautiful.

My hungry gaze rakes over my Naughty Pet. Her glossy raven tresses cascade to the floor. The line of my Naughty Pet's slim back leads to her lush ass. She's bound by red silk ties around her wrists and ankles to the vamp red spanking bench padded with suede leather. Her belly full with my son, my heir, cradled in the soft suede and silk pouch beneath the bench.

Her comfort is of the utmost importance at this stage of her pregnancy—thirty-three weeks and counting.

But my Pet craves punishment.

I growl my pleasure at the sight of my mate presented to me for her punishment. A punishment she so rightly deserves for disobeying my command.

"Yes, yes, Sebastian, I promise already!" Lola says, her voice tinged with irritation.

I don't give a damn she's annoyed I want her to take it easy.

She's been traveling nonstop the last three weeks since we returned from Bougainvillea Cay: Paris, London, a brief stop in New York City, Las Vegas, Beverly Hills, back to New York City after a go-see in Dallas.

Now she wants to visit a STEELE row of retail stores on Main Street in Southampton Village for a Lola's Coterie pop-up shop this summer.

"Oh Baz, the helicopter ride is brief," Lola continues as she slams her Hermès attaché closed with a huff. "I'll be back this afternoon."

"Why can't you let Billie take care of the walk-through? Isn't that why you promoted her, so she can handle the 'operations' of Lola's Coterie?!" I retort.

She throws the stink eye at me over her shoulder as she bustles to our private elevator.

"I will see you later, Sebastian. Have a good day at work. I love you," she calls as she steps through the open doors.

I roll my eyes to the heavens for strength, then settle on her face—lit from within, from her mommy's glow.

"Make sure you go easy today. I'll call you to check in"—when Lola winks at me like a sassy vixen, my mood softens—"I love you, too."

Lola grins in victory, knowing she has me wrapped around her little pinky.

"Take care with my son!" I shout as the doors close.

She blows kisses at me and disappears from sight.

"SEBASTIAN! IT'S LOLA! SHE FAINT—"

When I saw Billie's name appear on the screen of my mobile, I knew it was bad news. I race out of the conference room on the Executive Floor of STEELE in the middle of a budget meeting with my Retail Divisions Team. All heads turn towards me as I run to the private elevator, yelling with my mobile to my ear.

"WHERE IS SHE?!?!"

"Mr. Steele! I called for Edgar to bring your car around to meet you in the building's front now."

I glance over my shoulder as I reach for the elevator call button. Then thank Tina with a quick nod. My PA is always on point and in tune with my needs after all of these years.

"She's resting in the back of the car. But she slipped to her knees before we could catch—"

"WHAAAAT?!?!?!?!" I scream, the word reverberating around the enclosed space.

Billie's voice chokes, startled by my ire.

"I'm so sorry, Sebastian!!" Billie cries. "Lola says she didn't hurt herself. But she should still see Dr. Rice. Blair called him, and he's meeting us at the hospital. We're landing on the roof, so you can meet us there—"

"Tell him not to worry... I'm fine... Please."

Lola's strained voice in the background makes my chest tighten as my heart clenches.

I don't want to stress her further, knowing it can cause her blood pressure to rise and harm our baby. We don't need any problems with him added to what's happened with Lola. So I tamp down on my anger with her for not heeding my request to rest.

FUCK. ME.

When I lay eyes on Lola as Dr. Rice and the nurses rush her from the Sikorsky to the hospital roof's door, I lose my control nearly. I have to bite down on my molars to keep from blowing my top.

Her eyes are closed in her pallid face—no longer glowing as it was this morning—covered partially by an oxygen mask. The lids flutter when the nurse calls me by my name to step out of the way.

Stormy gray orbs meet dull hazel ones.

Lola blinks, then grimaces.

"Is she all right?! How's our baby?!" I demand as the medical team hurries her past me into the hospital with me on their heels.

"She's stable. But we'll know more when we monitor her and the baby," Dr. Rice responds in between commands to the others.

I follow the team as far as they allow to the doors of an operating room on the obstetrics floor. A nurse turns to block my path and points towards a waiting room down the hall. Reluctantly, I head to it once again with my mobile to my ear to alert my parents.

That happened over a week ago. Fortunately, neither Lola nor Baby Boy suffered any repercussions from her fall. Not one test or observation revealed any harm to either of them. I said a prayer of thanks then and repeat one now.

Even as my erect cock twitches in my gray sweatpants, appreciative of the beauty spread before me.

Lola's round ass reddened by the spanking I gave her moments ago. The imprints of my palms and fingers leave my marks on her soft skin.

I trace my fingertips along the edges, then palm the heated flesh and squeeze.

Hard.

Lola hisses past the ball gag. Her body tenses, and she bows her back, seeking the pleasure from the pain.

"How do you feel, Naughty Pet?" I ask, not wanting her to sense any discomfort from the binds or the position. The spanking, well…

Lola glances over her shoulder in my direction and nods twice. A red silk mask on her face—a playtime one over her eyes and not one for oxygen atop her mouth. Instead, a cherry red ball gag parts her full lips.

"Excellent. Do you understand why you are being punished, Naughty Pet?" I ask as I pick up the next implement and run it through my fingers.

Time to step it up, I chuckle low in my throat darkly.

The fringes of the suede flogger glide along the soles of her feet, up the backs of her calves and thighs, then along her dripping pussy seam to between the crack of her rosy ass.

Lola whimpers around the gag and nods twice. She shivers from the erotic touch of the toy. The scent of her arousal—a carnal perfume—fills my nostrils.

I inhale deeply and close my eyes.

Mmmmmmm.

"Ten. One for each city you insisted upon traveling to, despite me asking you to take it easy. Plus two as encouragement to listen to your husband," I say as the flogger arcs through the air and lands on Lola's left ass cheek with a

THWACK. Then I follow it with another strike on her right ass cheek. THWACK!

"AAARGH!!!" Lola yowls past the gag as she pulls against the restraints.

I tsk and walk around standing before her.

Lola turns her head to track the feel of the flogger as I drag the fringes along her flank, over her shoulder, and place the butt beneath her chin. She shivers, and not from the cold.

"You forgot to count, Naughty Pet," I smirk. "Oh, well, we must start from one."

A mewl escapes her mouth, and she drops her head. The thick waves conceal her gorgeous face.

I lift the butt to raise her head on a level with my face as I squat before her.

"Naughty Pet, how do you feel?" I ask.

Without hesitation, Lola bobs her head and stretches her neck to reach closer to me. I stroke her cheek and purr in her ear.

She trembles.

Abruptly, I step away and reposition myself behind Lola. The flogger makes contact with her round rump again and again as she mumbles the count. The last strike has her keening, a combination of pain and pleasure.

My dick throbs and drips pre-cum from the mushroom tip.

Quickly, I release the silk ties and lift Lola's limp body into my arms. Lost in subspace, Lola's head lolls against my broad chest. Her breathing is strong, and her face flushed.

I stride over to the swing and strap Lola in the harness. With care, I remove the ball gag from her swollen lips and slant my mouth over hers.

The passionate kiss wakes my Sleeping Beauty. She returns it with a voracious one of her own, sighing in satisfaction.

Once we part, I lift the mask from her eyes.

Lola blinks to regain the sense I deprived her of from the moment we entered our new playroom. The original Valentine's Day gift I created for us. Lola thought I was Captain Caveman before, but now…

I refuse to allow others at LEVELS New York to see my mate's voluptuous body further enhanced by her pregnancy. No fucking way.

Not willing to give up our BDSM lifestyle, I hired a renowned designer to create a custom playroom on the second floor of our penthouse. Every toy, apparatus, and accessory Lola and I incorporate into our erotic delights dwell here.

The sex swing is the latest goody I insisted upon adding to our repertoire. It offers the perfect solution to fuck Lola inclined on her back while she's seven months pregnant and more. I love her baby belly, but it lessens our frontal connection.

Lola smiles when she realizes she's in the swing. It's fast become her favorite apparatus, even over the spanking bench, her top choice.

She reaches for the cords elongating her torso. Her newly grown double D-cups lift, pointing her beaded nipples towards me. Lola smirks when she notices me lick my lips.

Well…

I latch onto her nipple and suckle it until she writhes in the harness. My hot wet mouth moves from one tit to the other, planting open-mouthed kisses in the hollow between her mounds.

When Lola cries out, I grip her spread thighs, swing her back, then impale her on my engorged cock in one deep thrust.

Both of us groan upon entry.

I swing Lola back and forth, driving into her soaked pussy. In and out. In and out. In and out. The squelching sounds and the smell of sex fill the playroom.

"Oh fuuuck… Sir… Yes… Yes.. Yeeesss!" Lola screams in ecstasy, her head thrown back and her eyes squeezed shut.

"Open your eyes, Naughty Pet! Watch me fuck my pussy!" I growl.

She obeys, eyes widening at the erotic sight of my thick dick plunging into her swollen pussy and my balls slapping her ass. As another massive orgasm overtakes her sensibilities, her mouth goes slack. Her greedy pussy walls clamp on my thick invasion.

My pulse pounds in my ears. With a carnal roar, I release a torrent of cum, enough to impregnate my mate again.

"LOLAAA!!!" I growl barbarically, throwing my head back to roar for the heavens.

· · ·

"You were right, my love. I overextended myself… and put our baby at risk…"

Lola shakes her head sadly as she rests her back against my chest during our evening ritual of a bath. It's our time to reconnect after a day apart at work or with family or friends. Now, we recover from our scene.

I burrow my face into her silky hair as my fingertips cover her mouth. No. I will not allow Lola to dwell on what happened. Time to move on.

"Babe, don't. You're good. Baby Boy is good"—I shift her to face me, then cup her cheeks—"And I believe you learned your lesson. Correct, Naughty Pet?"

Lola peeks at me from beneath her eyelashes submissively. Then smirks, "Yes, Sir."

I laugh a deep belly laugh.

My Independent Woman-cum-sub will never learn.

SEBASTIAN

"**G**o Baz! Go! Don't lose them, bro! No one wants to listen to them gloat!"

Harris shouts over the crashing waves of the Atlantic Ocean as he trims the jib sheet of the new sailboat we're racing against Roger's team.

We're on a Guys' Getaway before Roger and I become dads for the second and first times in just over a month. Along with Roger, Lachlan, Lucien, Laurent, Borya, and my close friends Scott and Porter join us for the four-day getaway. The destination of choice is Bougainvillea Cay. The guys wanted to have time to try out the new toys Malcolm ordered for the island retreat.

The racing yachts are on top of the list. So now it's the United States against The Others. Malcolm, Harris, Scott, Borya, and I make up the US. Roger, Lachlan, Lucien, Laurent, and Porter—based in Paris, Aberdeen, and Dubai —comprise our opponents.

"Scott, adjust the mainsheet! Let's go, let's go!" I shout as I man the helm.

Exhilaration runs through me as we take to the open water at the top speed of fifteen knots. The balmy weather —clear of any rain—provides the best backdrop for being on the ocean. Salty spray flies back and lands on my face. I laugh as I lick it from my lips, not daring to move my hands from the wheel.

"Yeah, baby!! We're gaining on them!!" Malcolm whoops. "Let's get it, boys!"

Lucien chances a quick glance as we come abreast with their sailboat. Lucien shouts orders for Porter and Lucien. They rush to adjust their sheets for optimum performance.

Aside from being Alpha males, we're a super competitive group. Not one of us likes to lose. So it's balls to the walls on both yachts.

We round the regatta buoy for the return stretch with The Others ahead. But we're on their asses! Damn near our bow to their stern.

As we overtake them, Porter gives us the finger and Borya yells back curses in Russian. Both crews hustle to reach the finish line. The winner's buoy beckons to us.

With a burst of wind in our sails, we pass the marker less than a minute ahead of Roger's sailboat. The US crew hollers in victory as we head for shore.

"Yeah, yeah, yeah. Whoop it up all you want. Congratulations already…" Lachlan says as he claps me on the back when he steps onto the dock.

"Tomorrow it's the JetSki relay, so let's see who's bragging then!" Laurent adds as he grabs Harris in a headlock.

At thirty-one, they're the two youngest boys of the Steele and Jackson clans. Laurent's bottle-green eyes sparkle with mirth as he noogies Harris in the back of his head. Evenly matched in muscle although Laurent at six feet, three inches has two inches on Harris, they wrestle as they've always done—two wolf cubs angling for dominance.

They're close, like Lachlan and me. Although I'm still not that keen on him and Haley, I've let it go to avoid a distance between my baby sister and me. Not to mention sparking Lola's ire. Not worth it.

However, should Lachlan misstep, I'll beat his ass senseless. And he knows it.

"Fuck off, Laurent! Sore loser," Harris retorts as he flips him off the dock and into the water.

Everyone laughs. Then Borya hauls Laurent from the water.

"*Davay rybka,*" Borya rumbles as he pulls the little fish back onto the dock. "We'll do a training tomorrow so you can learn to defend yourself!"

Again, we crack up. While Laurent rolls his eyes and shakes his head, slinging water over us.

"Time for celebratory drinks, boys!" I chuckle as I stride back to the villa. "The winners will even pay!"

"Aw hell, dude! Pay what? We're at your place!" Porter responds.

I chuckle and nod, "True!"

. . .

WE SHOWER and change into swim trunks. Then lounge on the beach drinking local favorite Kalik beers. In the outdoor kitchen, the chef grills vegetables, fresh fish, lobster, and steaks to go along with the pigeon peas and rice.

The sun dances on the waves as they lap onto the beach before us. Other yachts dot the horizon, taking advantage of the glorious weather. The Exumas live up to their name as one of the best yachting areas in the world.

"Okay, Pops, how do you feel?" Lucien asks as he lifts his bottle to his mouth.

I can't help the grin that spreads across my face at the thought of my son making his debut in five weeks. To hold him in my arms close to my heart is the first thing I'll do after I thank his mother for my ultimate gift.

"Oh brother, man. He's grinning like the Cheshire Cat. Sebastian the Alpha Dom playboy turned faithful married man, soon-to-be father will complete his transition to domesticated chap," laughs Porter. "I can't bloody believe it!"

"Well, my friend, believe it. And I'm thankful for it!" I respond as I tip my bottle in his direction. "I pray you'll find a woman who will make an honest man out of you. Although I don't know how lucky she'll be. Bless the poor lass!"

Porter throws his head back and guffaws.

"What about you, Daddy of Three? What're your thoughts on fatherhood?" Laurent asks.

Roger grins wider than I did. His usually intense stare softens whenever he thinks of Leonie, The Twins, and now Baby Daphne.

"Enjoy every day with your children. Cherish each moment. They grow up in the blink of an eye," he answers, leaning forward with his elbows on his knees as he glances at each of us. "Don't waste a second of your time with them. And just as important with the woman who gave them to you."

"Amen, brother," I say as I stride over to him and tap my bottle to his beer. "And I will add, take the advice of those who have gone through it. Roger has been an invaluable resource for me. Thanks, bro."

Roger grins and inclines his head.

"You're more than welcome, brother. Based on the way you've cared for all of us from childhood to now, you'll be an incredible father," he says sincerely.

Malcolm and Harris along with Lachlan, Lucien, and Laurent nod in agreement.

Now it's my turn to bow my head. Roger's words strike a chord within me. I know being the eldest, I've always taken the lead to care for my siblings. Sometimes unwanted as with Haley and Lachlan and some requested like a bully harassing Roger.

To hear him praise me for taking care of them so well it prepped me for fatherhood makes my heart swell with love and pride. Then for the Jackson brothers to agree, chokes me up.

I take a swig of Kalik to give myself some time to control my emotions before I respond.

They sense it and give me a moment. A brief, but comfortable, silence descends on our group. The sizzle of the food on the grill amplifies. The aroma tantalizing.

With a nod, I rise.

"Thank you, my brother. Now, let us eat. Team The Others will need their strength for tomorrow's challenge!" I quip.

Boisterous claps, whistles, and denials fill the air.

* * *

"THE PERFECT WAY TO end our retreat: pumping music, fine liquor, and most of all hot babes! Here's to Harris for the fantastic idea!"

Laurent says with a flourish as he raises his crystal snifter of Jackson Reserve Scotch in salute.

"Hear, hear."

"*Za nashu druzjbu!*"

"Yes, Borya, to our friendship!"

After two more days of testosterone-filled macho challenges, we had a tiebreaker this afternoon for the best water jetpack acrobatics. Malcolm, the biggest daredevil of us all, won. So the US beat The Others with flying colors, literally.

To celebrate and to cap off our Guys' Getaway, we came

to STEELE Exumas Hotel and Resort for dinner at the restaurant run by Lucien. Afterwards, the singles—Harris, Lucien, Laurent, Porter, Borya—wanted to party at the resort's nightclub.

Everyone agrees to go.

Harris makes out with a leggy brunette in a micro dress damn near showing her ass cheeks. Borya sandwiched between two fashion models bumps and grinds on the center platform of the dance floor. Lucien has Miss Bahamas in a corner on his lap with his hand between her legs devouring her mouth.

While they flirt with the more than interested female guests, those of us in relationships hang out in our VIP section partaking in a rum tasting. Lachlan gained cool points when he declined an offer to dance from a Bahamian beauty with long curly hair and doe-shaped eyes in her sepia-colored face. Instead, he stayed seated at one booth in our area.

"You should have seen Scott's face when—"

"Excuse me, aren't you Sebastian Steele?"

Inwardly, I roll my eyes at the interruption. But in case it's someone who's business-related, I school my features and face the woman.

"Why do you ask?" I respond.

A stunning ash blonde woman stares at me with large turquoise blue eyes. She scans me from my head to my lap, her gaze lingering on my groin.

I have to hold back a scowl from her blatant scrutiny of my crotch.

"My friends don't believe me"—she points out a booth in another section of the VIP with three other attractive women staring in our direction—"And I hate to be wrong, especially when it involves a fine man. So… Yes?"

This time I don't hold back my annoyance.

"Lady, whoever I may be, the one thing I am not is interested in you," I respond, waggling my left hand to show my wedding band. The platinum glints in the light.

She narrows her eyes and launches into an angry rejoinder as she points her red-talon finger at me.

Who do I think I am? I don't have to be a major asshole. All I had to do was answer the question. Just because my name is on the resort doesn't give me the right to act like a dick. Blah, blah, blah.

I glance over at the security guard and nod. I don't have time for this dramatic shit. I have the woman of my dreams at home, pregnant with my son. I left the days of fucking for release and to sate my need to dominate with a random woman behind once I met Lola. So I give zero fucks this blonde hates to be wrong or I pissed her off with my dismissive attitude.

He strides to our section and asks the woman to return to her table. She takes the hint and throws a nasty glare at me before she leaves with no further comments.

"Good grief. That was the worse pickup line ever," Scott laughs.

"And equally ridiculous reaction," Lachlan adds with an eye roll as he sips his rum.

Malcolm and Roger agree and return to our tasting.

My mind drifts to Lola. I cannot wait to get home to her, my soul mate love.

* * *

THE FLOOR-TO-CEILING WINDOWS not covered by the blackout curtains allow the moonlight to fall across Lola's sleeping form as she lies in our bed at the duplex penthouse.

Like a man obsessed, I stand beside her, staring down. She's stunning. Her raven hair fans out on her pillow. The glossy tresses shine from the moon's glow. Her belly so close to her due date reminds me of a beach ball beneath the sheet. My son growing inside of her womb. Almost ready to make his debut.

Lola sighs in her sleep and reaches her small hand for my pillow. She draws it near her face and sighs contentedly.

Eager to hold her in my arms, I strip out of my tracksuit and boxer briefs. Then slip under the sheets and curve my body around Lola's. I nuzzle her neck to inhale her sweet scent and palm her swollen belly with my sizable hand.

"Baz?" Lola asks in a voice husky from sleep.

"Yes, babe, it's me. And better not be anyone else, either," I respond, as possessive of my mate as ever.

Lola snorts, "Chill, Captain Caveman."

She glances over her shoulder as she brings her left hand up to tangle in my hair. Her Skating Rink Ring along with her eternity band sparkle in the moonlight. A tug to my hair and I growl. A quick nip to the sensitive area where her neck meets her shoulder elicits a squeal from her.

"I am not teasing, Little Pet," I growl.

Lola snorts again and scoots back against my body. Her lush ass wiggles against my cock that's happy to feel her soft warmness through the silk of her negligee.

"Missed me?" She purrs. Then mewls when I lift her leg and slide my cock into her tight pussy that's always wet for me.

"What do you think, Mrs. Steele?" I smirk, rolling my hips to deepen my thrusts.

Until the sunrises, I show Lola just how much I missed her.

LOLA

"These onesies are just too cute! Look at the little giraffes doing cartwheels!"

Starr giggles as she holds the tiny outfit up.

"I love it!" Shelley exclaims. "And get a load of this one with teddy bears!"

We're in nursery one at the duplex penthouse. Baz and I decided to keep one close to our bedroom, so it's two doors down. After the summer, Baby Boy will move into his suite of rooms that includes nursery two, a bathroom, sitting room, playroom, and a room for Nanny Janice Smart when she's at the penthouse. We moved her into an apartment on the thirtieth floor so she can be near at all times.

She's the ideal choice for us since she's trained appropriately as a nurse and has a master's degree in early childhood education. She can dress a scrape, teach early academics and social, motor, and adaptive skills, and disarm assailants. She's a total Wonder Woman!

Nanny Janice never married and is a mature woman in her late forties. Equally as important, she has zero interest in Sebastian.

Also checked off my list is the completion of the nurseries here, Southampton Village, and Paris in our and Morgan and Shelley's and Guy and Josy's residences. Surprisingly, the London nursery only needs the furniture delivered. Leonie worked her magic and finished ahead of schedule.

Each nursery reflects our homes: the color palettes, and whether traditional, Parisian elegance, or beach chic interior design style. My favorite is the Southampton Village with its calming greens, blues, and tans. The bleached wood and hand-painted tiles keep with the nautical theme. I can't wait to stay at our home there.

The girls surprised Leonie and me with a dual virtual baby shower a week ago. It was so much fun to play the games and to open the many presents while we interacted on the giant screens in our respective media rooms.

Blair, Billie, Starr and Shelley decorated mine while Josy, Haley, Anita and Hettie Bailey—a friend of Leonie's from Paris married to Roger's good friend Joel—did Leonie's room. They decorated hers in shades of pink and cream and mine in blues and grays.

Lucien had our favorite dishes from his restaurants in both cities for our lunches. The only downside for me was not having *Maman* Josy's delectable desserts! Instead, Sylvia Weinstock the Cake Queen who made my wedding confectionery delight crafted a gorgeous and delicious cake in the shape of a cradle. It was an edible piece of art.

Instead of the baby showers being limited to women, they included the guys. Anita and Norman's daughter Antonia and Joel and Hettie's toddler son came, too. Rodolphe and Gaspard, almost two years old, helped to hand presents to Leonie.

The whole affair turned into a fun fete we enjoyed for hours.

Since that time, I've had the urge to nest. Hence reorganizing the gifts we received from the shower along with others delivered in the last few days from friends, fashion colleagues, and business associates. I've even reordered Baby Boy's supplies in his bathroom!

Dr. Rice says it's natural instinct to use the burst of energy I've gotten to prepare for the baby's arrival. It's no different from mama birds, cats, and other humans—male included.

I drive Baz nuts with moving his things into an order I think works best. The other morning while I was in the library reorganizing the books to make room for the first editions of *The Bobbsey Twins* and *Winnie The Pooh*, he came in asking where I put his ties.

He didn't quite understand why I moved them from their drawers to racks behind his suits. I figured he picked a suit, then would move down the row to pick a tie.

Well, no. So I spent an hour putting them all back.

I roll my eyes at the memory. Then straighten up to glance at the onsies Starr and Shelley hold.

"Oh, those came from Anna Wintour. A baby boutique in Londo—"

A sharp pain in my lower belly and lower back makes me double over with a cry. The pain radiates down my legs, making my knees buckle. I whimper and clutch my belly when I realize I'm falling.

But instead of hitting the floor, two sets of hands hold me up.

"We have you, Lola, sweetheart!" Shelley exclaims.

"Deep breaths, Lola," Starr tells me in a calm manner. "Focus on your breath."

They maneuver me to the glider, and I sit gingerly. The bracelet on my wrist beeps. A second later, my mobile rings.

Baz.

Harris—the tech wiz—created a monitor to track vitals, particularly for erratic or elevated heart rates that deviate from the norm. Plus, it has a fall detection and a GPS tracker for location of the wearer. He gave one to Leonie and one to me. The app connects to the monitor, then alerts Baz, Roger, Harris, Starr, Anita, and our doctors.

Shelley answers my mobile while Starr checks my vitals.

"Lola! What's happening?!" Baz asks over the speakerphone.

I start to speak, but another cramp hits me and knocks the breath from my lungs. Instead, a pitiful moan spills from my lips as I grimace.

All morning my back bothered me, but I just assumed it

was gas from the French onion soup I ate last night. I craved the crouton and broth. It was yummy then, but it repeated on me… So I ignored the pangs.

Wrong.

"I'm on my way up!!" Baz shouts and disconnects the call.

Starr asks me questions while Shelley answers a call from Dr. Rice's nurse. They relay my answers to her, and she advises we come to the hospital even though my water hasn't broken since my due date is tomorrow. Dr. Rice will meet us there.

Just as they stand me on my feet, Baz and Malcolm rush in the nursery room's door. Baz takes one glimpse at me and barks for his mother to call Eddie to bring the car around. He and Malcolm carry me between them. Starr grabs my hospital bag.

"Hold on, babe, we got you!" Baz says as we hurry down the hallway to our elevator. "Just breath like Starr taught you."

"Yeah, Little Sis. Don't worry, just focus!" Malcolm adds with a nod. "You and Baby Boy are all good!"

I smile at his words, so similar to Starr's. She's definitely rubbed off on him. The grin gets wiped off my face a moment later when I feel a popping sensation, along with a slow trickle of fluid between my thighs.

OMG!!! Did I just pee on myself???

Embarrassed, I peek at Malcolm, then Baz. Neither one seems to notice. Shelley talks to Harris, who called because of the alert on his mobile. However, Starr picks up on my discomfort.

She raises her eyebrows and cocks her head to the side. Her silent question hangs between us.

I glance down at my lap, then at Starr with wide eyes as we descend in the elevator. I'm wearing a white off the shoulder loose tunic and black leggings. At least the dark color will hide the evidence of my oopsie. Although I'm certain it ruined my silk thong.

She nods in understanding and turns to Malcolm.

"Honey, before you put Lola on the car's seat, let me place a towel down," she says as she rubs his back.

Malcolm nods, and Baz's gaze shifts from me to Starr to Malcolm.

"Did your water break?" He asks softly.

I flush bright red and nod.

"It's okay, babe. That's good! Baby Boy is on his way!" Baz says with a smile so full of love my heart flutters with joy.

"FUCK!!!!!! WHAT THE HELL DID YOU DO TO ME, SEBASTIAAAANNN STEEEEELE?!?!?!"

I scream at the top of my lungs as I glare at him. Daggers don't even come close to the dangerous weapons of mass destruction I'm throwing in Sebastian's direction.

He stares back at me wide-eyed with his mouth agape. My Alpha Dom, Captain Caveman is no longer in control. He's in shock.

I've been in active labor for almost seven hours. Seven. Fucking. Contraction-Filled. Hours…

"HOW MUCH LONGER DAMMIT?!?!?!?!" I screech.

The contractions come faster and last longer now. I want to bear down. I feel a lot of pressure in my lower back, worse than before and now in my rectum. I want to push, but the labor nurse says not yet.

When I first arrived at the hospital, the nurses settled me in my suite at New York's best hospital renowned for its OB-GYN department, of which Dr. Rice is the head. Moments later, he arrived with his team. An anesthesiologist, a pediatrician, labor and delivery nurses, an OB tech, and a nursery nurse followed him into my suite.

They went to work in prepping me for the first stage of pregnancy, pre-labor. Dr. Rice explained in first-time pregnancies, it can take six to eight hours for my body to be ready for the actual delivery. Once my cervix dilates to ten centimeters, he expected the second stage to be as short as 20 minutes or as long as a few hours.

Hell to the no, no, no! Not another minute, let alone a few fucking hours!

"Let's have the labor nurse check your cervix. Since the contractions are coming closer together and occur for ninety seconds, you may be ready," Starr suggests as she massages my calves.

Shelley agrees, and Starr steps out. Malcolm and Morgan wait in the anteroom of my suite. I hear them ask how I'm doing as the door shuts.

Since Leonie and I are due around the same day, the

family split between New York City and Paris. Haley and Harris flew to Leonie as support for her and Roger three days ago. I haven't had a chance to speak with my bestie today, so I don't know if she's in labor, too.

Right now, I can't think past this pain honestly.

FUCK!!!

"Let's have a peek, Mrs. Steele."

I raise my gaze to see the labor nurse and Starr walk through the door. She helps me to lean back against the pillows while the nurse peeks under the sheet.

"Well, well, well, Mrs. Steele, your cervix dilated to ten centimeters. I'll get Dr. Rice now," she says with a warm smile and a gentle pat to my knee.

"Oh, thank you, Lord!!!" I cry.

Baz takes my hand in his and smiles as he says, "Babe, you're doing so well. Soon it'll be over, and we'll have our Baby Bo—"

He yowls as I grip his hand with all my strength when an excruciating contraction rocks me to my core.

"FUUUCK!!!!!" I bellow, followed by a string of curses. I call Sebastian every name I can think of and then find some more.

The labor nurse chuckles as she leaves for Dr. Rice and the rest of the obstetrics team.

"Mr. Steele, would you like me to have a look at your hand?" She asks over her shoulder.

"No, thank you. That's all right," he grunts as he rubs his hand.

Shelley rises from the sofa and reaches for Baz's hand.

"Sweetheart, it's not the best idea to hold a woman's hand when she's in labor," she laughs as she massages his hand with her fingertips. "Ask your father and brother. I'm sure I broke one or two of your father's fingers over the years!"

Baz groans, "Lesson learned, Mom, thanks."

Dr. Rice enters, and I say a silent prayer.

"Sounds as though you're ready for me, Mrs. Steele!" He booms. "Let's have a look."

Baz growls softly when Dr. Rice takes a seat on the stool at my feet and lifts the sheet. He lowers his head and peers between my legs. My Captain Caveman is not pleased. I'm surprised he's lasted this long with the many exams Dr. Rice gave me over the months—at the end weekly.

"All right, Mrs. Steele, we're in the second stage of labor. The time to push is now," he says with a fatherly smile.

"Thank the good Lord!!!" I cry as another contraction hits me.

"He's crowning. Get ready to push, Mrs. Steele," Dr. Rice raises his eyes to mine and nods. "All right, now! Push!"

At once, I curse myself for not accepting the epidural when I had the chance. I feel as though I have a hundred of Baz's massive hard dicks battering my pussy for hours with no end.

"AAARRGGGHHH!!!" I growl as I bear down.

"Breathe with it, Lola. Breathe," Starr says as she stands

to my right just in my line of sight. "Focus on your breath."

I take a deep inhale in preparation to increase the pressure within my belly and contract my abs. Holding my breath before I let it go as I push Baby Boy out.

"That's it, my love. You're doing well," Baz murmurs as he strokes my hair that Starr put into one long braid down my back.

My mind knows it's not his fault. Well, not entirely. But I just can't think straight at a time such as now.

"SHUT UP STEEEELE!!!" I growl as I slap his hand away from me with a kyber crystal-powered super laser stare from the Death Star. It's strong enough to destroy an entire planet. Or a Steele.

Baz opens his mouth, then thinks better of it speaking and closes it. He glances at Starr and she shakes her head, suppressing a giggle.

It's rare one sees my powerful husband at a loss and not in charge of a situation.

More contractions, more choice words, more killer looks, more pushing, and our Baby Boy makes his debut.

Our Baby Boy is born!

Holy shit! I'm a father, a Dad, a Daddy.

"Mr. Steele, you may cut the umbilical cord now."

Dr. Rice's words pull me from my pleasant musings, and I glance at him. He hands a pair of sterile scissors to me with a broad smile and a nod of encouragement.

I shift my gaze to Lola, my sub, my love, my wife, the mother of my child. Her hazel eyes—softened by the miracle she achieved—stare back at me from a face flushed red and damp from the exertion of nine hours of labor.

My heart swells and my eyes well with tears. I lean over to kiss her on her lips, then press my forehead to hers as I close my eyes on a silent prayer of thanks.

"I love you, Mama Steele. Thank you," I murmur huskily as tears slip down my cheeks.

Lola reaches a small hand up to wipe the moisture

away. She brings her wet fingertips to her lips, then places them on mine.

"I love you, Papa Steele. Thank you, my love," she whispers in a hoarse voice. "Cut the umbilical cord so we can hold our son."

She pats my cheek and sighs, exhausted from the delivery.

With a nod, I turn to Dr. Rice and do the honor. The pediatrician, Dr. Samantha Woods, takes our son off to the side in order to care for him. I split my gaze between her actions and Lola, who's being comforted by Starr. I confirm she's fine, then turn my full attention to our son.

"How is he?" I ask as I watch possessively over the doctor's shoulder while she tends to him.

She smiles at me and responds, "He's in excellent health! All ten fingers and toes! He weighs 7.8 pounds. An acceptable size for a male newborn. Congratulations, Mr. Steele!"

Relief washes over me. Then anxiety sweeps in when she places our freshly cleaned son in my arms. When I look at her in a panic, Dr. Woods smiles encouragingly.

I glance down at his mottled face. He may be tiny, but the weight of responsibility hits me in that moment. My son, my heir, and next generation of Steeles; the fruit of my loins. I am his father. His safekeeping ranks as my utmost priority along with his mother.

"Baz? What's taking so long? Is he okay?"

Lola's soft voice filled with concern calls me back to the suite.

"He's perfect, my love. See for yourself," I respond as I stride over to her and place our son on her chest.

Lola's face lights up with such love and joy when she stares at our son. Tears stream down her cheeks. Her fingers tentatively touch his soft jet-black hair, and his eyes open slowly.

Gray eyes and black hair. The Steele family traits continue.

Lola peers up at me and smiles angelically.

"Your son, my love," she whispers. "He looks like you, like a true Steele. Are you pleased, Baz?"

I nod, overwhelmed, and I bury my face in her damp hair.

AN HOUR LATER, a freshly washed Lola holds our son to her breast as she feeds him for the first time. They're skin-to-skin to help him stay warm as he gets used to being outside of her womb. Dr. Rice explained it's a great way for parents and baby to get to know each other right away. Our baby welcomes our gentle touches, and this closeness can help us to bond with him.

I rub his back beneath the blanket, wanting him to recognize his father, too. My hand is so much larger than his narrow back. I smile and pull my mobile from my pocket to take a video and some photos.

Lola giggles, and pats the bed beside her.

"Come, sit, Daddy," she says with a twinkle in her hazel eyes.

I smirk when for a moment my mind drifts to the fetish. But that's not our thing. Although we'll try anything once…

"Stop it! Sir…" Lola laughs. "Sit with us before the family comes in."

Family.

Now I have my family of Lola, Baby Boy, and me. Our family unit that fits inside of the Steele clan. Now I know how Roger feels. To have my own is the most incredible sense of responsibility. Mine to care for, mine to protect, mine to love forever.

MINE!!!

"Tell me, did Leonie go into labor? We're due on the same day, remember?" Lola asks. Her eyes pop in concern for her best friend, even on the heels of her delivery.

I smile before I put my mobile in front of her to hold it as Baby Boy suckles at her breast. With a few swipes, I load the video Roger sent earlier.

"Here, see for yourself, babe," I say as the screen fills with a grinning Roger angling his mobile to capture Leonie, their baby, and himself.

"*Ciao, Chérie and Sebastian! Guess who made her debut right on time? Your niece Daphne Beaulieu Steele! She looks exactly like her father—gray eyes and ebony hair,*" *Leonie trills.*

Roger moves his mobile closer to Daphne's heart-shaped face. Her little rosebud mouth purses and she opens her eyes to reveal the Steele traits.

"*My sweet baby girl. Can you believe it, big bro?*" *Roger says in awe.*

Leonie gazes at him with such love. Then faces the mobile again, and her amber eyes shine.

"Now it's your turn to send a video message. Nous t'aimons!" She laughs.

"Yes! We love you! Ciao!" Roger adds as he waves before the video ends.

Their intimacy tugs at my heart. This is what Lola and I have now. I'm beyond pleased!

As I put my mobile down, it vibrates with a call. A glance at the screen shows my mother's name. Lola and I have been so focused on enjoying these first few moments with Baby Boy we hadn't communicated with my parents, Malcolm, and Starr.

"Hi, Mom! We're all good. Give us a minute before you come in to meet your newest grandson!" I exclaim.

Lola laughs as she puts Baby Boy on her shoulder.

I rub his back to help him burp. The greedy bugger. While Lola fixes her nightgown and robe, I cradle our son to my chest through the opening of my button-down shirt. He's warm from Lola and smells like a baby, just as I remember Harris and Haley.

"'I'm all set, Baz," Lola says on a yawn.

"You need to rest, babe," I respond and continue when she starts to object. "We'll announce his name, make the video, and take some more photos. Afterwards, everyone leaves. It's important you take care of yourself, Mommy."

She grins and nods in agreement.

I place Baby Boy back in her arms, and she nuzzles his

hair, inhaling his unique scent. Before I let the others in, I take a moment to stare at my little family.

All mine!

As soon as my parents walk in, my mother makes a beeline for Lola and Baby Boy. She coos softly as she strokes his little leg.

"How are you, Lola, sweetie?" My mother asks. "You look so happy. But you need to rest. We won't stay for long."

My father agrees, "No, we won't keep you, dear. Only a quick peek. You need your rest."

I chuckle to myself, thinking how alike my father and I behave. My goal has always been to have a loving relationship like my parents and now to be the best parent possible as they were with us.

"Congratulations, Little Sis, bro! You did it," Malcolm says as he fist bumps with me. "Now, what do we call Baby Boy officially?"

My face splits in two nearly as I wrap my arm around Lola's shoulders while I pat my son's back. Lola turns him around to rest against her big boobs so he can face everyone. I hand my mobile to Malcolm for him to take the video.

"Dad, Mom, Malcolm, Starr, Roger, Leonie, Harris, Haley, meet Slade Steele!" I announce, beaming.

"Slade! I love his name!" Exclaims Starr as she claps her hands. "It means valley."

"It sounds badass!" Malcolm grins, his eyes twinkle with mischief.

My father grips my shoulder and smiles. "Well done, son, daughter! A strong name for the next generation of Steeles. Your brother- and sister-in-law had Daphne, a beautiful baby girl. Today is a great day for our family!"

LOLA

"*Chérie!* Slade looks more and more like Sebastian every day! I don't see a drop of my bestie in your son!"

Leonie's laughter comes across the screen as we Face-Time streamed to the television in the pergola on the ocean-facing deck of Baz and my Steele Southampton Village beach house. She's holding adorable Daphne dressed in a pink leopard-print onesie on her lap while we have our daily Girls' Chat.

Shortly after she gave birth, they flew to their hillside villa in Monte Carlo for the summer. Guy and Josy along with Nanny Grace made the seasonal move with them down to the "glitterati" capital of Europe, as Leonie calls the Mediterranean gem. Her parents bought a villa in the same STEELE luxury gated community to be near their grandchildren when The Twins were born.

As a mother of three and my best friend, Leonie has a

wealth of knowledge she imparts on me. I relate more to her since she's only a year older than me at thirty-three. Her recent experiences from what to do about swollen ankles to having a doula for support before and during childbirth to the best oils for breast massages help me tremendously.

"I know right! Baz struts around like a proud peacock!" I giggle as I nuzzle against Slade's soft ebony curls.

It's been three weeks since he was born. Without a doubt, Baz is his father. As my mother used to say, "You have no nickel in that dime!" Slade is a miniature Baz.

Billie gave a set of beautiful leather-bound journals to me as one of her baby shower gifts. The first one has my notes, sketches, and my musings on nearly every page. Each day I update Slade's growth and development: when he first lifted his head; his sleep patterns; feeding schedule. I even doodle little drawings of him sleeping or with Baz.

I love to go back to the first page and read through. Baz teases me, but I don't care. Especially since he's become a professional photographer!

He's kitted out with the top-of-the-line digital camera, various lenses, flashes, you name it. During my pregnancy, he used his mobile to snap my monthly baby bump profile pic. Before Slade was born, Baz had a fashion photographer friend of mine advise him on "nothing but the best equipment." Now Baz takes so many shots of us, I feel as though we're at one of Lola's Coterie's photoshoots!

Not only still shots, but video, too. "It's important to

mark milestones and to record our family like my parents did with my siblings and me, babe!"

I have to admit I love his enthusiasm and the time we spend going through his many libraries categorized by theme. If I didn't have my family photos and videos, I wouldn't have any means to show Slade his maternal grandparents.

That's another reason I never miss my calls with Leonie. She, Luc, *Maman* Josy, and *Papa* Guy are my second family; the ones who helped me through the loss of my parents. Time spent with them is even more vital for me. And I'm beyond thankful for them.

Shelley and Morgan have been fantastic. Even before Slade was born, Shelley lived up to the promise she made to me in Capri. She and Morgan may not be my parents, but they certainly make every effort to care for me and to love me like one of their own.

From the moment we announced our pregnancy at Christmas to Slade's birth, my in-laws helped to ease the sadness that would creep up, compounded by my raging hormones. On the very rare occasion Baz couldn't make an appointment, Shelley would come with me. She and *Maman* Josy gave as much input in Slade's nurseries as Leonie did with her designs.

Morgan made sure I had the best suite at the hospital since he's the top donor. "You never know when you may need a quality hospital, Lola dear. Best to support one as much as financially possible," he told me with a chuckle and a wink.

Now we're all out at the beach compound for the summer. Normally they would go to the Mediterranean either to their Villa Sogno in Positano or aboard their megayacht *Serendipity*. Just like Leonie's parents, Shelley and Morgan want to be near their newest grandson.

They come by to check on Baz, Slade, and me regularly. But Shelley insists we spend this time to bond as a family. She says it's important for Slade to recognize his parents, and for us to acclimate to a newborn.

Which brings me to Baz.

Besides being a proud peacock photographer, he's an amazing father. He's taking a paternity leave from STEELE International through September. Just as Baz did for Roger when he had The Twins, Malcolm has stepped in to cover for both brothers. Harris and Haley will chip in since two divisions along with the CEO responsibilities will require all Steeles on deck. Morgan will assist as necessary.

My thoughts drift back to our first morning here.

The sunlight streaming through the windows glows like orange fire behind my closed eyelids, still heavy from sleep. For a moment, I lie there and listen to the squawks of the seagulls as they soar above the Atlantic Ocean in search of their breakfast. The breaking waves splash onto the private beach in a soothing rhythm that lulls me to sleep briefly.

I'm exhausted.

My attention returns to our bedroom as I listen for interior sounds. The first things I notice are the loss of Baz's warm body wrapped around mine and the lack of breathing from his side of the bed. I crack one eye open to glance towards his pillow. An indentation serves as proof he slept beside me. I reach my hand out to touch the rumpled bedding. Cold.

The sound of his gentle baritone over the latest version of the fancy-schmancy baby monitor Harris created for Leonie originally is the third thing I notice. I lift it off of the night table and place it on my breasts heavy with milk as I lean against the headboard with a contented sigh.

My man is with his son.

"—understand your situation... Absolutely... But your Mommy needs her rest, Slade... You kept us awake all of last night. But that's okay. You realize why?... Because we love you so very, very much, my son. You are a gift."

The rustle of material and the coos of Slade float over the monitor. He's in Slade's nursery.

I imagine Baz changing his son's diaper or getting him dressed for the day. He's better at coaxing his son into his diaper than I by a long shot!

"Now, you have to feel better, Stinky Binky..."

I giggle at the nickname Baz gave to Slade. When Baz changed our son's first diaper, he gagged and ran out of the room holding his hand over his mouth. I laugh harder and snort at the memory.

Not one to back done from a challenge, Baz now aces the diaper and dressing routine. The night prior, he selects the outfits for the next day and lays them out on Slade's dressing table. His attire varies based on the activity: walking on the beach or visiting his grandparents or resting at home.

Again, I crack up at my silly husband.

"I appreciate you're hungry, Slade... Yes, okay... We'll sit on

the window seat this morning and watch the seagulls eat their breakfast while you eat yours. Deal?... Good..."

Over the last three weeks, we found schedules and routines that work well—and some that were abysmal. The one I recognize Baz treasures the most is his morning time with Slade. A time father and son can bond alone.

And a time for Mommy to sleep in bed longer. I roll over to my side and place the monitor beside Baz's pillow. The hushed cadence of his voice lulls me back to slumber again. My eyes drift shut, and I rest just as my husband knows I need.

"—Daphne loves the carousel mobile Luc bought for her with the princesses and princes riding on the horses! It mesmerizes her. Are you even listening to me, *Chérie?*"

Leonie's question pulls me from my daydream.

"So sorry! I was thinking about Baz and his morning routine with Slade. They're just so cute!" I respond, giggling. "How's Roger with all three babies?"

Leonie's amber eyes glow with love for her man and children. The stories she tells me about their escapades make Baz and his shenanigans seem professional. Roger *The Responsible* lives up to his name truly and cannot wait to organize his little family. Leonie balances his intensity with her easygoing attitude. What I love the most is how well they make it all work.

"Hey Leonie! How's my sister doing? And of course, how're my nephews and baby niece? They do realize they'll see their most favorite uncle in a few weeks?"

I glance up to see Baz standing beside me, waving at Leonie and making faces at Daphne. We laugh at his antics and Daphne coos waving her chubby arms in the air.

"Bonjour, big brother!! We're doing well, *merci*. Roger made the arrangements for us, my parents, and Luc to fly over together. You know your brother!" Leonie snorts.

"Oh, we know!" Baz and I respond simultaneously, then join her in boisterous laughter.

Our family will gather here as tradition for Labor Day festivities and the fundraiser. It'll be even better this year since we'll have our newest additions, Slade and Daphne. Even though Leonie and I video chat every day, I can't wait to see her in person!

The three of us talk, then Roger joins us. He had taken Rodolphe and Gaspard to the clubhouse for a playdate with other kids in the villa community. He sits beside Leonie and puts Daphne on his lap while The Twins climb into Leonie's lap.

"Hey, guys!" Roger says. "You look fantastic, Lola! How's my little nephew? Tell Slade his favorite uncle says hi!"

We spend the next hour talking. Baz and Roger trade war stories as Leonie and I giggle. It's such a peaceful time. Our little families growing together.

I still can't believe how fortunate Leonie and I are to have married brothers. We can see one another regularly and not lose our best-friend connection like so many women do when men come into their lives. The bonus of our children bonding as we did makes me so elated. Not to mention being blood relatives.

Grateful doesn't describe how I feel for my life.

After my adamant refusal to have a baby—I can finally admit I dodged the baby situation—I'm beyond thrilled at the joys of motherhood!

I find the connection between Slade and me is unconditional. The endless hugs, kisses, and loving gestures from my son remind me every day of the love I shared before he was born—as he grew in my body. I learned being a mother changes my life completely. Yet I love every single part of it from the body aches and labor pain to staring in his eyes as he feeds to his unique scent tickling my nose.

Prior to Slade, Lola's Coterie was my baby, my be-all and end-all in life.

I made it my sole focus not only for success, but as a dedication to my parents. I envision each success as a kiss and a hug from them; each setback I hear my father whispering his favorite saying in my ear, "Lola, are you a wolf or super wolf? Because there are no sheep in this family."

As I harness the super wolf that they raised me to be, it pushes me to work harder to turn each setback around. At their funeral, I promised them I would never forget how much they loved and believed in me and that I would make them proud.

In my heart, I know that they're pleased with all that I've accomplished in such a scant time—graduated FIT at twenty; completed an apprenticeship here in Paris at twenty-four; opened my first boutique on the Champs-Élysées at twenty-five; the second location on London's Bond Street at twenty-eight; expansion to New York City,

Las Vegas, Abu Dhabi, Dubai, Beverly Hills at thirty; future locations in Dallas, Tokyo, and Milan.

As I watch my BFF and her husband, I understand just as Leonie I can have it all—the success of my company, the love of my husband, and the blessing of my son—without the loss of myself and my goals.

My gaze shifts to the man beside me. I watch Sebastian and smile as I recall our chance encounter at LEVELS New York and the serendipity of him being the president of the company I planned to meet with for Lola's Coterie. He brought out my sexual sub and taught me I can still be an Independent Woman—my body shudders with desire for my Alpha Dom. We've come so far and have so much more ahead of us. My soul mate.

Baz glances over at me and smiles. His strikingly handsome face makes my panties wet no matter the circumstances. He must glimpse my want because his gray eyes twinkle and he bites his full lower lip as his nostrils flare.

It's been too long since he had me beneath his powerful body. I cannot wait until July 27. I have the time marked on my calendar: BAZ AND I FUCK ALL WEEKEND LONG!!!

Shelley and Morgan offered to babysit Slade for the weekend at their residence in the compound. Shelleysmirked knowingly when I asked her to take care of Slade the other day. Not that she needs an excuse to keep her grandson.

"So what's the plan for the rest of your day? A stroll on the beach, or are you going into town to that cafe we like?"

Leonie asks as she bounces a laughing Rodolphe on her knees.

He speaks to her in French, then turns to the screen and asks in English when he'll see us.

Leonie and Roger want them to speak as many languages as they—French, English, Italian, German, and Spanish. It makes sense living in Europe with so many countries around them.

Baz and I plan the same for Slade since we speak English, French, Italian, and Russian. We want him fluent in multiple languages as a future leader at STEELE and to appreciate other cultures. Our children will be worldly and have broad educational backgrounds like us.

"Well, Ms. France, it's July 4. So we're having a clambake and watch the fireworks on the beach in front of Shelley and Morgan's house tonight," I tease.

Leonie laughs and nods her head.

"Oh, yes, of course. I forgot! Have fun for us!" She says.

Daphne wails, and Roger cuddles her on his lap as he turns to Leonie.

"Feeding time, *Maman*," he says with a wicked grin.

Leonie's face flushes bright red as she glances away from the screen. She shakes her head and giggles while she gathers The Twins.

"Talk to you tomorrow, *Chérie*!" She sings with a wave.

When the screen goes black, Baz turns to me.

"I'm with Roger… Feeding time, Mama!" He smirks as he licks his lips.

LOLA

"Good afternoon, Mrs. Steele. Welcome to Spa Bliss Southampton Village!"

The receptionist greets me cheerfully as I walk past other clients to her desk.

Shelley suggested their spa for my day of pampering. It's her favorite of all places available in the village. Their facility provides individual suites per client for the utmost in privacy and attention since all treatments occur within the suite, no need to move from one area to the other. Plus, they have decadent products and tasty spa meals.

Baz gifted me with the day. He told me to take some time for myself. Unwind and tune into me. He would take care of Slade so I could relax. It's a Mommy Day Off.

Although we both know he's gearing me up for our weekend of debauchery! YES!!!

I notice two of the female clients lift their gazes from magazines at the mention of my name. Their sharp eyes take me in from head to toe. Who knows whether they're former lovers or wannabes—Baz was a notorious playboy before we tied the knot.

Even after three years of marriage, women still have no shame in expressing their desire for my husband. They take his denial as a challenge and disregard me completely. As if I give a good goddamn…

"Good afternoon, thank you," I respond to the receptionist. Then wave my left hand glittering with my gigantic Ice Rink Ring and eternity band at the vultures, "Ladies."

They blanched at the sight of the massive diamonds. A few defeated nods and mumbles greet me in response.

Right! I thought so.

"Kindly follow me to your suite, Mrs. Steele. Your aesthetician awaits," the receptionist says pleasantly.

I'm so excited about my spa day! All of my preferred treatments: hot stone massage, steam facial, salt glow with body wrap, deep conditioning hair mask, manicure, pedicure, aromatherapy. Not to mention a full-body wax, so my skin is buttery soft for Baz to slide all over me this weekend!

We pass through a curtained archway to enter the foyer that leads to my suite. Soft instrumental music plays in the dimly lit hallway while lulling essential oils of bergamot, lavender, and ylang ylang waft around us. Immediately, I'm transported to a land of tranquility. I take a deep restorative inhale and exhale all stress and negativity as I prepare for a day solely focused on Lola.

.   .   .

WHEN BAZ CHASED me down to Luc's beachfront villa in St. Barth's after I broke up with Baz the first time, we soaked in the outdoor sunken tub. The air fragrant from the fresh, tropical flowers in the surrounding garden.

It was in that moment I wanted to verbalize my love for him, but held back for fear of exposing myself to more pain. Instead, I told him with my body when I melded us together. I connected with him in the only way that a woman and a man can. I covered his body with mine and put him inside of me like a key in a lock.

My blood pulses in my veins as my body heats from the memory of our lovemaking. Baz is such a talented lover and Dom. An ache grows in my pussy, and I squeeze my thighs together for a bit of relief. I cannot wait until he gets back from taking Slade to his grandparents…

Meanwhile, I luxuriate in the tub here in our home. We recreated our St. Barth's experience on the deck near the side garden overlooking the Atlantic Ocean. The flowers may not be tropical, but their fragrant aroma wafts around me as the wind blows off the water.

I close my eyes and sink deeper into the warm sudsy water scented with sandalwood, neroli, and jasmine essential oils. The seductive blend heightens my desire for my man. With a sigh, I trail one hand from the side of my neck along my collarbone over the top of my heavy breast past my peaked nipple across my flat belly to the apex of my thighs. My long middle finger brushes against my puffy pussy lips to breach my seam—

"What are you doing, Naughty Pet?"

I gasp and jump from the unexpected sound of Baz's voice, thick with lust and displeasure. Water splashes out of the tub onto the stones. My hair tumbles from the messy bun and whips into my eyes as I swing around in his direction wildly.

The breath catches in my throat when I take in the sight of Baz.

He stands naked, towering over me at his full height of six feet, four inches of pure muscle. His olive skin darkened by the sun's rays. Flinty gray eyes scan my body, alighting on my mounds as they skim the surface of the water, the nipples sharp points despite the heat.

A low growl makes my hooded eyes move from the v-cuts of his Adonis belt where his engorged veiny dick with its bulbous angry red tip shiny from pre-cum juts towards me.

Like a hungry animal, my mouth salivates, and I lick my lips. I follow his happy trail up his eight-pack abs to his pecs. His Adam's apple bobs as he swallows thickly, just as taken by the sight of my wet flesh glistening in the sunlight as I am of his masculine beauty.

When our eyes meet, a frisson of eroticism shoots through my core. It throbs and floods in anticipation of the pounding Baz will give to me. We're both too wound up for slow lovemaking.

I. Want. Him. To. Fuck. Me. Raw.

Baz raises his eyebrow and cocks his head to the side.

Too engrossed with ogling his body to answer his question, I drool. He waits patiently. The marble sculpture of David in the flesh.

"Nothing, Sir," I respond demurely as I lower my eyes in submission.

Another growl—louder this time—forces my eyes up to his again.

My core clenches.

"What I witnessed is far from the definition of nothing, Naughty Pet," Baz rumbles. "Hands and knees. Now."

My mouth drops open, then my eyes widen at Baz striding towards me. The thick muscles of his long legs flex with each step. Even his calves bunch as he prowls towards me. His eyes narrow on me as I sit dumfounded.

Oh my.

I scramble to get into position with a carnal cry. More water sloshes out of the tub in my haste. But even more liquid floods my greedy pussy.

My palms land on the wet stones and my knees anchor to the porcelain basin, my toes curl to gain purchase. I arch my back to present my ass for punishment to my Dom.

The water ripples like waves in the ocean before me when Baz steps down into the tub. Concentric circles break as they reach my hips. Closer and closer he comes.

I shudder.

"Widen your knees, Naughty Pet," Baz commands.

The waves of desire emanate from his body to hit me more forcefully than the roused water. He bends over my back to press his lips to the shell of my ear. His warm breath tickles the sensitive skin as he breathes.

"Naughty Pet, you were told to wait for me in the tub. You were not told to play with yourself. Your body is my playground alone," Baz says gruffly. "Lean forward. I want your ass on the surface. Those round globes floating, ready for your punishment."

Once again, I hurry to obey.

No sooner than I raise up, the heavy palm of Baz's hand strikes my left ass cheek with a sharp crack intensified by the coating of water.

"Count, Naughty Pet. Miss one and we start anew," he threatens.

I yelp and shift forward as I cry out, "One, Sir!"

Baz grips my left hip to hold me where he wants exactly and proceeds to fall into a steady rhythm.

Left, right, left, crease of my ass and thigh, right, left.

"You do not touch yourself unless I give you permission, Naughty Pet. And be still! Control your body," he rumbles.

As the spanking continues, they get harder and the intensity mounts. I can barely concentrate to count and beg Baz to forgive me. My body strung so tightly from the effort to not cum until he gives me permission, thrums.

"Your ass is a beautiful rose. But I want to see the petals of your pussy, Naughty Pet. On your chest, spread your thighs wider, and hold your butt cheeks apart for me," Baz demands in my ear. "Do you understand?"

"Yes, Sir," I pant.

A dark chuckle slips from Baz's lips. The tip of his thick finger touches my swollen clit.

I whine and undulate my hips, aching to feel his touch inside my pussy. A smack to my pussy lips has me slipping on the wet stone as my hands slide forward and my knees slip on the basin. Before I can fall, Baz slips his arm around my waist and lifts me back into position.

"Oh no you will not, Naughty Pet," he growls. "Keep still, or I will add ten more."

My pussy flutters, and I mewl. A part of me wants to slip for more of a punishment. The other part wants to cum on his massive dick that's pressed against the crack of my ass, wedged between my back hole and my clit.

The dick wins when the tip brushes my rosebud.

More smacks to my pussy lips, and I count every single one like a good girl. Albeit a breathless, quivering mess of one.

Finally, after what seems like a century, I hear those sweet words.

"I'm going to fuck you until you cannot walk, Naughty Pet. Then we will start again," Baz promises with another dark chuckle as he strokes my ass covetously.

Before I can reply, the wide mushroom head of his cock sinks inside of my flooded channel followed by his turgid length in one brutal thrust.

We grunt in unison.

As Baz pummels me relentlessly, I feel every ridge,

every vein, and every one of the ten inches of his massive dick.

"Fuuuck… Pet… I missed your tight, wet heat pulsating around my cock!" Baz growls, his hips buck and jerk with each word.

"Ooooh! I missed you, too, Siiirrr…" I moan as my pussy muscles clamp on his thick invasion.

Baz grunts and leans back. His palm connects with my ass, smacking one cheek, then the other in rapid succession even as his thrusts continue to rock into me.

He pulls his hips back and his still swollen cock slips from my core with a pop. Bereft from the loss, I keen with need.

"Do not fret, Little Pet. Your pussy is not the only hole to service me," Baz says with one more slap to my ass for emphasis.

I whimper and drop my head. My heavy breasts sway below me. Full with milk, awaiting relief from Baz, they ache with need.

The next sound from my mouth is a grunt when his tip breaches the rings of muscles in my puckered hole. His thick dick coated with the natural lubricant juices from my pussy plows into me—two inches in, one inch out—until Baz seats himself fully within my ass. His balls brush my sensitive clit.

"Fuuuuuuck. Me." He roars with feral dominance and desire. "Yessss!!!"

With that cry, Baz grips my hip with one hand and my

throat with the other to hold me in place as he uses my bottom hole for his carnal pleasure.

Each thrust and each groan brings me closer to the edge. I whimper and wiggle my hips to make his heavy balls slap against my clit. I need to cum. Now.

Baz must sense my need. He reaches his hand around my hip to tap, then to tug on my swollen nub. His groin slams into me over and over.

"Cum for me, Little Pet. Cum on my giant cock in your tiny ass!" He shouts ferociously.

When he pinches my engorged clit, I spiral out of control. A long, low keen rips from my mouth as my pussy spasms on air and my ass squeezes his dick. My vision blackens and my hearing fades.

The bliss of subspace overtakes me at last.

* * *

"Have you had enough, or do you want more?"

It's been a weekend of pure carnal bliss. Baz bathes me as we take one last soak in the outdoor tub before we meet Shelley and Morgan for dinner at their residence.

Just as Baz promised, he's fucked me until I can't walk. My wrecked pussy filled again and again with his seed.

I feel wonderful… and deliciously raw.

"Sir, I can never ever get enough of you," I purr. "But our Daddy and Mommy duties call."

I shift position to straddle his thighs and hold his handsome face in my hands. Leaning forward, I rest my forehead against his and breathe his breath.

Baz sighs and cups my ass in his sizable hands. His lips meet mine. A toe-curling kiss ensues. He squeezes my butt cheeks and lifts me from his thighs to stand.

"I love you, Mrs. Steele, and will never ever get enough of your body or of your love," he murmurs huskily. "Now, let's get our son."

Thirty minutes later, we're seated at the outdoor table on the deck, lit with torches. The chef grills steaks, lobsters, shrimp, and corn on the cob in the husk with seasoned melted butter. A fresh green salad with balsamic vinaigrette and raspberry sorbet round out our dinner.

Slade sleeps comfortably in a cot at the head of the table between Baz and Morgan. The men peek at him throughout our meal, even though Slade isn't awake and hasn't made a peep. He's our Sweet Babboo.

"Slade is a pleasure to care for, no problem at all," Morgan says fondly. "Shelley and I are more than happy to babysit him whenever you'd like some time off."

"Indeed! He's a joy!" Shelley adds as she rubs Morgan's forearm. "It's important for the two of you to stay connected. Remember what I told you at your bridesmaids' luncheon, Lola."

I giggle at her sage advice and nod.

"Absolutely, Shelley! So insightful and wise," I respond with a smile.

Baz and Morgan stare between us expectantly.

But what's shared during Girls' Talk stays between the

girls. Shelley winks at me, and we slap our upraised hands before we burst into peals of raucous laughter.

The boys shake their heads and take swigs of their beers.

I have the coolest in-laws imaginable, I think with a grin.

"Hey, guys. I hate to bother you during your baby leaves. If we could have avoided it, we would have done so. But Dad said it's best to run the situation by you."

Malcolm says over the video conference in my beach house office. He's at STEELE International's Asian headquarters in Tokyo to oversee our latest division combined project.

The plan requires Retail, Entertainment, Residential, and Children and Young Adults. Even Lola's input matters since her lingerie boutique will serve as an anchor for the mall—her largest location to date because of the popularity of her lingerie in Japan. Harris and Haley join for their take on technology and cyber security. So the gang's all here, as Harris loves to say.

"Fine, tell us the net net of the situation," I respond as I sit back in my chair at the conference table. The shift from beach bum to multibillion-dollar global company billionaire seamless.

Lola sits across from me with her tablet at the ready. She has a determined expression on her face. Her shift was as seamless as mine.

Despite being on a business call, my cock twitches as I watch her Independent Woman come to the forefront. I've told Lola before how much it turns me on to watch her take charge in the boardroom.

The bedroom however is mine all mine.

The last two weeks we've been fucking like rabbits, wild animals, whatever gets their jollies off to make up for the time we couldn't make love. And it's not one-sided. Lola's more demanding than me! Not that I mind, not one bit.

I thought her body was bodacious before. Now, my Petite Seductress could tempt a saint. Fuller hips, narrow waist, double D-cups full of creamy milk. Yum-my… She attributes it to her yoga and Pilates sessions with Starr and her conditioning and weight training with Borya. He's the only man I trust with my woman, barely. However, I thank them both. Job well done!

Not that her pregnancy body wasn't attractive to me. It abso-fucking-lutely enthralled me, as in mouthwatering. In fact, I can't wait to fill her belly with my baby again. Perhaps she's already pregnant, considering the gallons of jizz I put in her fertile womb.

A man can hope.

Lola must sense my erotic musings. Her hazel eyes survey me from across the table for a moment while Roger makes a comment. She arches an elegant eyebrow in question.

But I shake my head slightly and return my attention to the conversation at hand. Not the ideal impression for the CEO to have carnal thoughts of banging his wife in the middle of an important meeting. Particularly when said CEO's cock hardened to titanium.

"—We can also incorporate the children's clubhouse within the adults' and require a form of recognition to enter the section. The added security would ease my worries for The Twins and Daphne. Don't you agree, *Chérie?*" Leonie suggests as she turns to Lola.

She nods and leans forward, "I most certainly do agree, Leonie. Now, with the mind of a mother, I understand their concerns. The security wouldn't have to be imposing and scare the children. But obvious enough for those who shouldn't be there and warn them off."

Roger and I glance at each other over the screen and grin. Our wives—the mothers of our children—have become not only an integral part of our personal lives, but of STEELE. They prove their worthiness of heading a division, as with Leonie, and holding seats on the board, as with both of them.

Malcolm beams and sits back in his chair. He claps his hands and chuckles.

"Well, ladies, your points provide another perspective and solutions we can use to solve that part of the problem. Do you agree, Haley and Harris?" Malcolm asks.

The Dynamic Duo nod and go into tech lingo that's above my pay grade! Their knowledge of their industry astounds all of us each time we listen to them. They expound upon Lola and Leonie's recommendations.

After another hour, we call it a wrap.

Malcolm will finish his business in Tokyo, then make stops in Singapore, Hong Kong, Beijing, and Kuala Lumpur. He plans to make the most of the Tokyo trip with visits to cities in the area before he returns to the United States. He'll stop by Beverly Hills for business and pleasure. Starr will return with him to Southampton Village for Labor Day.

Harris leaves for site visits in South America. Several of our retail and hotel properties require a review of their infrastructure. He and his team will meet with the leadership and the staff for concerns and feedback before Harris makes changes. Afterwards, he'll fly here.

Haley is over the Pond in the United Kingdom. She's working on a project out of our London headquarters. Some new idea she has for cyber security. Although I believe Lachlan the bigger factor for the choice of her location. Haley can work anywhere in the world with her gadgets. However, London is closer to Aberdeen, Scotland than her base in New York City. How convenient? As though she can fool her big brother…

Roger and Leonie won't leave Monte Carlo until it's time for them, along with Guy, Josy, and Luc to fly here. Roger doesn't want Daphne to fly such a long distance now. She and Slade will celebrate their three-month birthdays when everyone arrives.

Lola uses the video connection for her Girls' Chat. She and Leonie start to catch up on what I do not know since they speak every single day. What might change in less than twenty-four hours, I have no clue.

So, I bid everyone safe travels and kiss Lola on her forehead. Then I head to the nursery for my daily father-son bonding. Nothing compares to being a father. Not my roles at STEELE or my volunteer and philanthropy work. Only my love for Lola ranks as high on my list.

Who'd have thought Alpha Dom playboy solely focused on proving my worthiness as leader of STEELE would fall madly in love with a petite spitfire, marry her, and beg for a baby?

Hell nah!

But here we are, and here I go, striding with a purpose to my son's nursery. I can't help but to chuckle at the irony. I'm ready for family life, but women still flock to me. No ring and no baby keep them away.

Only the other day on Main Street, a woman who's a part of our social circle and knows damn well I'm married, propositioned me. While I was on the line at the Maison Kayser bakery where I was buying Lola a few of her favorite *pain au chocolat*. Unwanted and unbelievable.

As I near the nursery door, I hear Nanny Janice talking to Slade. She's a godsend. The best choice for our needs. Especially since she's not at all interested in me. Thank fuck!

"Hi Nanny Janice," I say as I walk through the door. "How is my son?"

She faces me and smiles as I lift him from her arms.

"Hi, Mr. Steele. Slade just finished a bottle, and I changed his diaper. So he's all ready for you," she responds.

I thank her and give her the rest of the day off. Lola and I prefer to care for Slade ourselves as much as possible. We're hands-on parents. Just as our parents were with us—and mine still! None of that abandoned by the parents for the staff to raise bullshit for our children. The poor little rich kid. No.

A chuckle falls from my mouth as once again I refer to more babies. Hell, Slade just turned eight weeks. Surely Lola isn't ready. But then again, motherhood has changed her.

I've noticed her shift in focus from Lola's Coterie to our son over the last few months, even before she gave birth. Roger says the same happened with Leonie, who unlike Lola wanted a baby. But had to find the balance of being a wife, mother, and her successful careers in modeling and interior design.

Yeah, Roger and I have our Guys' Chats about fatherhood. He's been a great resource—just as my Dad—for me. We don't necessarily speak every day as Lola and Leonie do. But our chats are regular. And we value them.

Slade wiggles in my arms and draws me back to our bonding time. Today I want to take him for a walk on the beach, then sit and watch the waves roll in. He revels in the tranquility just as much as me. The sounds of the waves breaching the sand and the seagulls as they soar above soothe us both.

We walk downstairs and out across the deck to the beach. I strapped Slade in his harness, facing out so he can watch where we go. He's ah-gooing and laughing as we stroll along. His chubby arms wave as his legs kick when a seagull swoops around us, hoping for a bite of food.

Slade's growth and development amaze me. At Nanny Janice's suggestion, we've bought toys and a mobile to stimulate his senses. He's at the stage of learning faster. So Lola and I want to encourage it.

Since the beach is private, we don't encounter other people. I stop at our favorite spot and open the blanket before we settle on the sand. Slade sits on my lap facing the Atlantic Ocean. In the distance sailboats glide by, and a cruise ship makes its way along the East coast.

I take the time to meditate like Starr taught me years ago. Her yoga sessions continue to be a part of my fitness routine for the mind-body benefits. Hell, even Borya MMA champion meets with Starr!

A shift in the breeze brings the scent of Lola's Joy Jean Patou Parfum. It's intense and luscious with an alluring floral composition. Like Pavlov's dogs, my dick jumps to life in my cargo shorts—my go-to bottoms since they have plenty of pockets for Slade's accoutrements.

"Hi, guys," Lola's says. The sound of her voice washes over me like the waves on the shore.

"Hi, babe," I respond as she sits behind me, wrapping her thighs around mine and pressing her front to my back.

Cocooned within her soft, warm body, Slade and I lean back. Her pillowy tits super comfy.

We don't need to speak; just allow ourselves to connect in silence as we watch the waves. Slade falls asleep, and I put a cover over him as he lies on his belly atop the beach blanket. Then I pull Lola around to my lap.

She giggles and kisses me silly.

"How was your father-son bonding today, my love?" Lola asks softly.

She knows the importance of the time for me. Just as her time in the evenings is for her. Lola loves bath time with Slade.

I love how wet her clothes get, then cling to her lush tits. The pebbled nipples ready for me to suckle. Bath time has fast become my favorite evening routine, too. Followed by tucking Mommy in bed beneath Daddy all night long time. Thanks, Slade, for being splashy!

"It was good. He had an encounter with a hungry seagull," I respond and laugh when her jaw drops. "No contact made. It flew around us, hoping for food. Slade thought it amusing."

We stay on the beach for another thirty minutes before we go to my parents' home for a snack on their deck. They too look forward to my walks on the beach with Slade since we include a stop by their place before we return home.

"Malcolm gave me his take on the Tokyo situation update. Tell me your thoughts?" My father asks as we settle at the table with coffee and cookies.

The four of us discuss the strategy, and my father agrees with our decisions. He's retired, but his input is still invaluable. Besides, he'll never fully give up STEELE. He's always willing to step in as necessary.

The maid brings out a few boxes and places them on the table. My mother thanks her, then turns to Lola and me with a grin.

"Nanny Janice and I spoke the other day about the developmental stage Slade is in now. So I ordered a few things. I sent some to Roger and Leonie for Daphne, too," my mother says as she bites her lower lip and raises her eyebrows above twinkling brown eyes.

She's about to burst with excitement.

Lola, my Dad, and I bust out laughing. My mother just can't help herself when it comes to her grandchildren.

"Well, if I'm fully honest, Nanny Janice, Nanny Grace, and I spoke about The Twins' stage, too. So they have a special delivery," my mother continues with a giggle as she claps her hands.

We spend the rest of our time discussing the merits of brightly hued toys that captivate babies because of the high-contrast patterns and bright colors, infant play gyms, mobiles, and anything else two-month-old babies can swipe at. Along with the benefits of pretend play for twenty-three-month-old toddlers' learning and development.

Afterwards, Lola, Slade, and I leave for home. We walk along the beach hand-in-hand. Slade sleeps in his harness peacefully. On the return trip we don't encounter greedy seagulls, just the gentle lapping of the waves on the shore.

All is right in the Sebastian Steele World.

LOLA

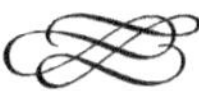

"My, my, my, Mrs. Steele, don't you look lovely this evening."

Baz says with a wolfish glint to his gray eyes as I walk down the stairs of our beach house.

We're headed to the village for Date Night with Leonie, Roger, Starr, Malcolm, Anita, and Norman. They arrived earlier for Labor Day next week.

It's the first time we've been together since Leonie and I gave birth almost three months ago. She and I wanted to take Anita and Starr out to thank them for being our doulas. However, Baz overheard our conversation and invited himself and the boys saying they're just as grateful.

Anita and Norman will stay through the Labor Day festivities and fundraiser. They're offering great silent auction items with custom VIP fitness training sessions with them for a year. The way they whipped Leonie into shape postnatal every person at the event will want to win the bid!

I'm just as happy with my mommy makeover regimen from Borya and Starr. The intense kickboxing, strength training, and conditioning workouts with Borya trimmed the extra pounds and tightened my muscles. The vigorous yoga and Pilates sessions with Starr increased my mind-body connection, flexibility, and core strengthening. Not to mention the much sought-after yoga butt!

So I do a spin for Baz in my white broderie anglaise cotton romper with puffed sleeves and a utility-inspired belt to cinch my waist. The sweetheart neckline outlined in delicate crochet trim enhances my full breasts. Paired with platform ankle-tied espadrilles and my hair in a topknot, I'm ready for our night on the town.

"Thank you, Mr. Steele. You're pretty hot yourself, sexy," I purr, raking my eyes over him.

Baz dressed in all black linen—loose-fitting v-neck sweater and pants—loafers with his five o'clock shadow and tousled hair longer than usual oozes sex appeal. He's leaning against the banister with his hands in his pockets, staring up at me. The predatory gleam in his eyes makes my pussy clench.

Mine, all mine. Hot damn!

He smirks and holds his hand out to help me down the last few steps as I reach him. When my feet touch the floor, Baz sweeps me into his arms and nuzzles my neck.

"Thank you, Mrs. Steele," he murmurs. "I thank you for gifting me with my son truly."

I smile up at him, then my jaw drops when I see a necklace dangling from his fingertips. The extraordinary blue gemstone heart pendant sparkles in the entry chandelier light. My gaze follows the necklace as it moves towards me.

"This is a blue diamond heart. It represents our son Slade, your gift to me"—Baz places the platinum chain around my neck and closes the clasp—"Each child will have a pendant for you to collect on this necklace. I pray we will fill it as many times as you allow, my love."

Tears well in my eyes, and I sob.

Baz hugs me to his chest and strokes my back as he soothes me.

"Let's see how many times we can fill it, my love," I blubber as I cup his handsome face in my palms.

I rise to my toes and slant my mouth over his. We kiss until the front doorbell chimes. Baz grumbles and smacks my ass before he takes my hand.

Shelley and Morgan have all four grandchildren for the night, along with Nanny Janice and Nanny Grace as extra support.

Roger stands at the front door with his Mercedes-Benz G-Wagen behind him. Leonie waves from the passenger window.

"Hey! Ready to go?" Roger asks as he pulls me into a hug, then claps Baz on his back. "Malcolm and Starr are in his SUV on the driveway."

"Yeah, bro! Let's go," Baz replies.

We climb in, and I hug Leonie from behind.

"Of course the boys had to gate-crash our Girls' Night Out!" She laughs. "But I don't mind!"

"Me neither," I respond. "It'll make for a fun time for sure!"

During the drive to the village, we ask about their trip and how Daphne fared with her first overseas travel. The Twins are used to longer flights now.

Roger teases Daphne is a pro since she slept most of the flight. Leonie attributes it to a full belly, empty diaper, and plenty of sleep.

When we arrive at the restaurant, Anita and Norman wait for us at the bar. They're staying at STEELE's version of a bed-and-breakfast just outside of town. It's a luxury property with excellent amenities similar to the offerings found at their large resorts.

We move to banquets at the bar for cocktails while we catch up before we move to our table in the dining room. The Champ tells us about some of his encounters with celebrity clients—without divulging names—that crack us up. Then Leonie adds her handsy times with some of the fashion industries most prominent designers and CEOS of conglomerates. Roger however will hear none of it and growls his dissatisfaction.

Laughter ensues, and we decide it's time to move to our table. As we make our way through the bar and dining room, other patrons follow our progress. Some greet us and others—particularly the women— glower. Their jealousy transparent.

Ha! Again, oh well, ladies. The STEELE Quaternity drops to one, Harris.

Leonie looks fantastic in her fuchsia cotton eyelet off-the-shoulder mini dress. The slim-fitting bodice defined by an adjustable belt around the sheer waist panel and falls to a flouncy tiered hem shows off her toned, postnatal body. Although she's naturally fit, Leonie works hard for her camera-ready body. One would never know she's a mother of three children under the age of two and a newborn to boot!

It's obvious people recognize *The Lion* when their eyes light up as she passes them by. Never one to care about the attention she receives, Leonie struts to the table completely oblivious.

Starr and Anita also look marvelous in a fitted tube mini dress and a maxi dress with boob side cleavage, respectively. Their dedication to health and wellness apparent in their fit bodies any woman would envy, including me, and men drool over, including the men in the restaurant.

However, if I were a man, I wouldn't want to mess with either woman and risk the wrath of The Enforcer or The Champ.

Once we're settled at the table, we order our dinner and wine.

I turn to Leonie and nod. We raise our glasses to Starr and Anita.

"Starr and Anita, thank you for helping me through our pregnancies, from the breathing exercises to the Kegels to the last push. Without your support and friendship, our pregnancies would have been a lot more complicated," I say.

"Oh, so what we're chopped liver?" Baz asks as he nods at Roger.

Leonie laughs and responds, "Of course you and Roger are invaluable, Sebastian! *Merci beaucoup, mon frère!*"

Everyone laughs.

"Well, you're more than welcome," Anita says. "You have a beautiful, loving family, and I'm glad to have had a part in it."

"Absolutely!" Starr replies. "Bringing a baby into this world is a blessing and a joy. Here's to your health!"

We raise our glasses in a toast.

"Hear, hear!"

"Thank you so much!"

"Well said!"

"Here's to family and friends who are as close as our blood relatives!"

The rest of dinner we relish each other's company and delicious dishes. We end the evening with promises to meet in the morning for beach yoga and breakfast. The guys plan for golf and lunch. Then we'll meet for dinner at Shelley and Morgan's residence.

As we leave the restaurant, Leonie loops her arm through mine.

"Your pendant is *magnifique*! For Slade, *non*?" She asks.

"Yes! Baz just gave it to me before we left the house as

my push present," I respond as my fingertips brush the diamond's surface.

Leonie lifts her wrist. A rose gold charm bracelet dangles from it with a lightning bolt, home, heart, and two boy and one girl figures. Some charms sparkle with diamonds and others in solid gold. It's a beautiful piece.

"Roger gave this to me before we left Monte Carlo. I thanked him with a blo—"

I cut her off before she gives me too much information. Leonie giggles and turns to hug Anita good night.

We say our farewells until the morning and hop into our SUVs. Anita and Norman decide to stroll back to the bed-and-breakfast to work off some crème brûlée dessert.

Once we arrive back at the compound, Roger drops Baz and me off while Malcolm and Starr continue to his beach-front home.

"Sweet dreams!" Leonie calls out as she and Roger drive away.

Baz and I wave until their red taillights disappear in the night.

"I know something sweeter than dreams, Mrs. Steele," he murmurs in my ear. "And I'm going to eat it up all night long."

SEBASTIAN

"**D**o you know how important today is for you, Slade? Say again... No, not just our beach time... Really?... I'll give you a hint. Candles, singing... Yup! It's your three-month birthday, son! You and your cousin Daphne will have your party together.... I know exciting isn't it! Your grandparents, aunts, and uncles are here to celebrate with the two of you. Remember how I told you blood in the veins isn't the only requirement for family. Love, loyalty, and respect make family. So *Grand-père* Guy, *Grand-mère* Josy, *Oncle* Luc, Auntie Blair, Uncle Patrick, Auntie Billie, Uncle Norman, Auntie Anita, Uncle Connor, and Aunt Lucie, Auntie Lydie, Uncle Lachlan, Uncle Lucien, Uncle Laurent, and Uncle Borya are here. I suspect Auntie Starr will be more pretty soon..."

Lola and I gave Nanny Janice the day off, so I'm getting Slade ready for his special day.

Their party will kick off our Labor Day festivities with

the family beach bonfire and seafood feast tomorrow night and the STEELE fundraiser the next evening. We'll stay out here through the rest of September, then return to New York City.

I have a feeling Lola may want to stay here until we fly to Verbier for Christmas and New Year's. She'd prefer to work out of her office at our beach house and fly in as necessary to the city or whatever business destination requires her presence. Plus, Blair and Billie handle a lot of the day-to-day responsibilities for her. Lola can create her designs anywhere in the world.

As much as I'd like to do the same, I have business at STEELE's overseas offices to check in on matters since I've been away on paternity leave. Prior to Lola and Slade, I would have booked the trips back-to-back. However, I spaced them out with seven days each over the next three months. In the new year, I'll have Melody schedule the rest.

Hell, I don't mind. I'm living my dream: wife, son, family, STEELE. Perfect!

My parents plan to stay here until the end of the month, then go to the Med for time aboard *Serendipity* for a week. They deserve a break after helping us for months with Slade. But they can't stay away from their grandchildren for long. After their respite, they're going to Paris for time with The Twins and Daphne. Then they'll all fly to Verbier.

Which reminds me... I have to come up with some pretty awesome gifts for all the kids. No way will I let Harris beat me in the coolest presents like he did last year. In fact, I know two puppies are definite. The Bichon Frises

Roger bought The Twins are too damn cute. For Slade, I'm leaning towards a pair of Siberian Huskies. Silver gray with blue eyes for STEELE. I have a breeder on the lookout for them now.

Slade wiggles in my arms, so I hurry to finish dressing him. Almost time for breakfast. And I do not want my son hollering at me. I'm the Alpha male who makes demands in this family, I chuckle to myself.

"Hey there, Daddy. Do you need some help?"

I glance up to find Lola standing in the archway that connects Slade's nursery to our suite of rooms. She's a sexy as fuck MILF. Her hair mussed from my hands gripping her long tresses. Lips swollen from my endless kisses. Toned legs bare beneath my sweater, she ripped off of me last night. Most of all, her heavy tits with nipples poking through like beacons.

I groan with desire at the sight of my gorgeous, curvy wife.

Lola giggles when she hears my need for her. Then she glances down at my burgeoning manhood. Hazel eyes twinkle with mirth as she stalks towards me. Hands behind her back make her bountiful breasts jut out.

I glue my eyes to them, and my mouth salivates.

"The help I need, Little Pet, cannot occur in front of our son," I smirk.

Lola giggles and leans into me, pressing her tits into my back as she reaches up to kiss my lips.

I capture her mouth and nip the full bottom lip between my teeth. Then lave it when she moans.

"Be a good girl and let me finish with our son," I say as I turn back to Slade and put his sandals on.

"I can feed him if you hold this for me," Lola says as I move to the window seat.

As much as I take pleasure in my morning time with Slade, I can't deny him fresh breastmilk. I gesture for Lola to sit, then settle beside her as I hold him out to her.

She smiles lovingly at me with sparkly wide eyes as she bites the corner of her lip. One arm reaches out to cradle Slade to her breast while the other holds her hand out to me. In it is a gift-wrapped box.

I frown and raise my gaze to hers.

She shrugs and holds the box out further.

Assuming it's an early present for Slade, I take it in hand.

"Open it," Lola whispers as she watches me intently.

It's my time to shrug. But I untie the white ribbon and rip off the platinum paper, anyway. When I lift the lid and move the tissue paper, my jaw drops, and my eyes widen in surprise.

Okay, so Lola beat Harris and me in the coolest, most awesome gifts way early…

Nestled on the bottom of the box rest two pairs of dove gray knit booties.

Speechless, I glance up at Lola.

She's sitting still, as though holding her breath. Her eyes scan my face, and she chews on her bottom lip voraciously.

"Booties?" I ask quietly.

Lola nods, unsure of my reaction.

I close my eyes and say a prayer of thanks. When I open them, tears glisten in my love's hazel orbs. With a whoop, I jump from the window seat and pick Lola and Slade up in my arms. I hold my little family close to my chest, lifting Lola from her feet and swinging them in the air.

Tears of joy fill my eyes as Lola hugs me with one arm and our son with the other while our Twins grow in her belly.

The endless hours of making love paid off doubly!

Lola's necklace will have two more diamond heart pendants. I hope at least one is pink.

* * *

Sebastian & Lola's Story Concludes for Now...

Turn the page for the Steele Family, Author's Note, and a Preview of *Capture My Desires Malcolm & Starr Part I*

THE STEELE FAMILY

STEELE INTERNATIONAL, INC

Multigenerational, multibillion-dollar business luxury real estate development and management corporation

Headquarters & Family's Primary Residences:

The STEELE Tower, New York City

A modern, gray-tinted glass fifty-seven story mixed-use skyscraper on southwest corner of Fifty-Seventh Street and Fifth Avenue within Billionaires' Row

Global Offices:

- The United States of America (New York City,
  New Jersey, Chicago, California, Miami, Las
  Vegas)
- The Caribbean (St. Maarten, St. Barth's, St.
  Lucia)
- The French & Italian Rivieras (Nice, Cannes,
  Positano, Capri)
- Monaco (Monte Carlo)
- The United Arab Emirates (Abu Dhabi, Dubai)

STEELE FOUNDATION: A STRONG AND SUPPORTIVE HOUSE

Builds and manages attractive, affordable housing for urban,
lower-income families

Available for download at **bit.ly/STEELEFamily**

Author's Note

Thank you for reading Part III of Sebastian and Lola's sexy, sizzling romance! I hope that you enjoyed the Happy For Now conclusion of their passionate love affair. If so, I'd love to hear your thoughts, please share a review at **bit.ly/ CLBooksSI6Review** and tell your friends.

Yeah baby! *Deepen* gave lots of hints at what's next for the Steele clan in the Desires Series!
Love at last, forbidden love, more babies…

Click below for the answers to one steamy story featuring Power Couple Alpha Dom Malcolm and free spirited Independent Woman Starr as their written-in-the-stars trilogy begins:

Capture My Desires Malcolm & Starr Part I
At **CharmaineLouise.com** take the *Four types of lovers. Which are you?* **Quiz** to match your Sexy Fantasy: sub, Voyeur, Dominatrix, or Dominatrix sub Switch.

Follow me on social media including my CLBooks Coterie Fan Club below or on your favorite channels below and subscribe to my newsletter at **bit.ly/ CLBooksNewsletter** for a **Free Book**.

Fulfill Your Desires.

xoxo

Charmaine Louise

BB bookbub.com/authors/charmaine-louise-shelton
f facebook.com/CharmaineLouiseBooks
instagram.com/charmainelouisebooks
g goodreads.com/charmainelouisebooks

Fulfill My Desires Sebastian & Lola Part I

Heighten My Desires Sebastian & Lola Part II

Ignite My Desires Roger & Leonie Part I

Stoke My Desires Roger & Leonie Part II

Justify My Desires Roger & Leonie Part III

Deepen My Desires Sebastian & Lola Part III

Capture My Desires Malcolm & Starr Part I

Embrace My Desires Malcolm & Starr Part II

Cherish My Desires Malcolm & Starr Part III

A Trilogy of Desires Sebastian & Lola Parts I-III

A Trilogy of Desires Roger & Leonie Parts I-III

A Trilogy of Desires Malcolm & Starr Parts I-III

Series Extras

Series Playlist

COMING NEXT: CAPTURE MY DESIRES MALCOLM & STARR PART I

1 *8 Years Ago*

STARR — 13, Beverly Hills, CA

"—Yeah, right! What makes that loser nerd think anyone wants to go to her corny birthday party?"

"Right! And with her weird hippie parents, too! What'll she have there? Unicorns and rainbows?!"

"Did you get a glimpse of her face when we told her we'd go? She grinned ear to ear with happiness braces on full blast… SIKE!"

"With a name like Starr, she's not very bright, is she?"

"That's the problem she thinks she's so smart, knows more than the rest of us—"

My mind reels as their voices fade out behind the closing bathroom door. I hug my knees to my chest while I rock on the toilet's lid. Tears stream down my heated cheeks, blurring my vision.

I don't need to see clearly to know the voices of Sally, Laura, Gail, Connie, and Jessica—the It Girls of Beverly Hills Junior High School. I could envision Sally, their leader tossing her silky blonde hair over her shoulder as she mimed my glasses. Gail, her main sidekick would have fluffed her curly afro to copy my naturally curly hair.

Obviously, I'm not so smart to have fallen for their easy yeses to attend my thirteenth birthday party this weekend. The It Girls at my simple backyard barbecue? Too good to be true.

For a moment I thought their teasing ways were over since we're in the seventh grade now. Who knew they'd carry over their mean-girl antics from fifth and sixth grades to a new school?

Duh!

A drawn-out sigh slips from my lips when I tilt my head back to stare at the ceiling, hoping to stop the flow of my tears. I'm so tired of them being so nasty to me. And for no reason!

Sure, I like to excel in my classes, and I answer the teachers' questions happily—and correctly. But that doesn't make me a nerd. Just interested in my schoolwork.

The whole braces thing is messed up too. I got them this past summer and grew five inches. So along with a mouth full of metal, thick-lensed glasses, and unruly curls, I tower over the other girls in our class.

Gawky much?!

It was bad enough they teased me ruthlessly about my "hippie" parents, clothes, and crystals in elementary school.

So what if my parents changed their names from Jordan and Belinda to Peace and Sun years before I was even born?! I like my name, Starr Knight. And doggone it, I am bright, and I love my parents—hippies and all!

They're brilliant environmental law attorneys who take on the most challenging cases against big businesses and win billions! The law firm—Knight & Knight LLP—my parents founded years ago after they met at a music festival while at Stanford Law School ranks in the top five of the United States. With offices in LA, Seattle, Denver, Chicago, Houston, New Orleans, Miami, New York City to represent cases in the top environmentally focused cities. They may be hippies, but they're sharks in the courtroom.

And so am I!

After a sniffle, I rise, shake out my vintage, glittery matchstick midi skirt so the layers fall to my Doc Martens' eight-eye, patent leather boots on a whisper. I smooth my off-the-shoulder ruffle top over the white camisole before I grab my well-worn leather crossbody bag.

Loose tendrils of curls fall over my eyes as I bend over. I sweep them back into the big bun at the nape of my neck with a resigned huff as my rose quartz pendant slips along its leather cord. Determined, I straighten my spine and leave the bathroom.

Time to face the music on the school bus ride home.

"Hi, sweetheart, how was school?"

I lift my head from my notebook and smile at my mother. We look exactly alike. Sorrel brown eyes full of love as she peers at me. Smooth chestnut-colored skin glows from healthy eating and regular exercise. Long, curly, dark brown hair pulled up in a topknot. Dimples highlight her sculpted cheekbones when she returns my smile. She's a beautiful woman in her late thirties.

"History class was interesting, and I loved art," I answer as I stand three inches taller than her petite feet-foot-three-inch frame. "But the crew siked me into believing they were coming to my birthday party."

I raise my hand when she speaks. A scowl settles on her pretty face.

"Hey, no worries. 'Be equally thankful for what you perceive to be good and for what you perceive as bad. It all happens for a reason. Either way, you don't let it disturb your inner peace. Strive for tranquility no matter the outer circumstances.' Right?" I ask, reminding my mother of her favorite yogic piece of advice.

She cups my face and beams at me.

"Absolutely, Starr!" My mother exclaims.

"What's the 'absolutely' for?"

We turn to see my father stride into the room. His baritone voice booms around us.

I get my height from him being six feet, five inches. He's opposite of my mom and me, with his obsidian eyes and pecan-colored skin. Equally fit and health conscious, he exudes power at forty-one. He's renowned for his command of the boardroom or the courtroom if negotiations reach that extent.

"A bit of a misunderstanding about my party. But no worries!" I respond as I give him a hug.

It's nearly dinnertime, and they make a point of being home as a family each night if possible. Otherwise the chef makes a meal for me.

"Well, perhaps your gift will make up for it," my father says as his eyes twinkle. "How about you open it early?"

With a shriek, I grasp the envelope and rip it open. An itinerary for a two-week stay at an ashram in Rishikesh, India, the world capital for studying yoga and meditation rests in my hands.

I never thought my parents heard me rambling about the center for spiritual studies a few months ago when I found it online.

Another of their traits I inherited is their focus on well-being. Whenever I have encounters with the crew, I practice breathing exercises to brush off their meanness. It takes the focus away from them and brings it back to me, keeping me centered and at peace.

I whoop and throw my arms around my father, then my mother. Yup, hippies and all, I'd have them no other way!

MALCOLM — 15, Southampton Village, NY

· · ·

"OH SHIT! What the hell is that on your back, Malcolm?! It better not be real, bro!"

My head whips around, my mouth twisted as I glare at my older brother—older than my fifteen by two years barely.

Since we're so close in age, everyone confuses me with him. We share the Steele clan traits of wavy ebony hair and dove gray eyes. Our olive-colored skin tanned further by the bright sun of Southampton Village, where our family's compound spans for a mile along our private beach.

Baz has a few inches on my six-foot-frame, so I have to look up at him.

But I don't look up *to* him. Hell nah!

He's Mister Perfect. The supposed leader of the Steele siblings. A role he's taken upon himself since forever. That's cool for Roger who's fourteen and the fraternal twins Harris and Haley at eleven. They freaking idolize Baz.

Me? Not so much. I refuse to be in Sebastian's shadow. I make my own way and don't need his interference in my life. My identity is my own. Screw looking alike.

"Oh, screw you, Sebastian! You're not my father! Back off, *bro*!!" I snarl viciously as my nostrils flare and my face reddens.

I storm off from the party we're having on the beach, sick and tired of his crap. I push past the others ranging from my age to twenties.

Of course it's a crowd. Everyone wants to be around the

Steeles. Our multibillion-dollar family has deep roots in New York City with our multigenerational luxury real estate development and management company based out of The STEELE Tower.

Even though it's the summer and we're out in the Hamptons for the weekend, each of us interns at the company. Come Monday, we'll be on Fifty-seventh Street and Fifth Avenue in the heart of Billionaires' Row at our respective divisions, learning our family's business from the ground up.

We have our mother to thank for "not being spoiled rich kids who only lounge around the pool all day." Shelley is a native New Yorker who worked as a shopgirl in one of STEELE's retail spaces. She met our father Morgan when he was on a business call to the store. At the time he was President of the Retail Properties Division and our grandfather was the CEO. Now, our Dad is top dog.

Baz assumes he's next in line, so he runs around barking orders at the rest of us.

Well, to hell with that!

I want no parts of STEELE International, Inc. I plan to start my own company for extreme sports lovers like me. Baz can have it all—Favorite Son and future CEO. I'll continue on as the second son; the rebel; the bad boy billionaire playboy of the family. And billions it will be too. Those I make on my own, not handed to me. Thank you very much!

Who the hell does he think he is telling me how to

behave and what to do constantly?! He needs to get off my back already, literally.

That's why I got my tattoo. The wings on my back symbolize freedom from family constraints and the flying as I speed along on my bikes. After I won my latest motocross race, I memorialized it forever in ink. The tattoo artist didn't give me any flack since my height and attitude make me appear older than fifteen. Plus, I flirted with her, then backed it up once she completed my tat. She did a damn good job, and I thanked her royally.

So Baz can shut up with his nagging.

I need to feel the wind in my face to cool down. A quick walk to the garage and I'm astride one of my KTMs, ready to hit the dirt trails outside of the ritzy town. Just as I lift my helmet—I may be a rebel who takes risks, but I value my life—a movement to my left catches my attention.

Damn. Belinda Crane.

Belinda *Baz's Girlfriend* Crane, to be exact.

By her expression, she's not thinking of Big Brother right now. Nor does she mistake me for him. Nope. That heat is all for me.

She twirls a strand of her long silky red hair between her delicate fingers as her eyes travel from my boots to my leather-clad muscular thighs and chest to my smirking mouth. When green meets gray, the lust rolls through us in waves.

I may be fifteen, but this isn't my first rodeo, nor will this be my first ride of this little filly. Poor Baz has no clue. Yeah, height and attitude make all the difference in life.

Belinda sashays over to me, her grip-worthy hips sway, making the strings of her white bikini dance. The round mounds of her tits bounce with each step. Her hooded eyes never leave my face, but my eyes travel the curves of her luscious body. She's a true redhead.

"I love your tattoo, Malcolm… A lot," Belinda says breathlessly as her fingertips skim over my back from shoulder to shoulder, sparks reach through the leather to make my cock jump to attention.

"Do you now, B.?" I smirk.

She nods and licks her full glossy lips.

My eyes dart to them, and I chuckle.

The first time her little pink tongue wrapped around my hardness, I nearly came before she even started blowing me.

I've learned more control since last winter's break. And I plan to use it.

"I'm going for a ride. You wanna cum?" I ask, not missing she picked up on my word choice when her pale cheeks flush bright red.

A quirk of my eyebrow has her nodding and scurrying to hop behind me. The warm, wet folds of her pussy press against my ass.

Yeah, I can't wait to bury my thick ten inches balls deep in her greedy snatch.

The purr of the engine is a precursor to the purrs I'll have Belinda moaning as soon as I get her writhing beneath me.

At times, it's good to be a Steele.

But on my terms.

***

Click the Link Below or visit books2read.com/u/ bPgG2r for Your Copy

Capture My Desires Malcolm & Starr Part I

I dedicate this novel to those whose bond to their loved one proves stronger than steel.

Fulfill Your Desires.

xoxo
Charmaine Louise

WELCOME TO CHARMAINELOUISE — THE SENSUAL LIFESTYLE

GLITZY. GLAMOROUS. STEAMY.

CharmaineLouise New York, Inc. invites you to indulge in *The Sensual Lifestyle* through **CharmaineLouise Books** and **CharmaineLouise Intimates**. CLBrands immerse you in *Sexy Fantasies* with CLBooks contemporary romance novels and give you *Sexy Under Things & Loungewear* with CLIntimates.

Charmaine Louise Shelton the Founder, CEO & Author of CLNY loves all things classic, elegant, feminine, and of course with an erotic edge! Favorite outfit of choice is a cashmere cardigan, leather pencil skirt, and seamed silk stockings with stiletto heels. Sexy Fantasy Type: sub with a dash of Voyeur. When not writing and designing, Charmaine Louise travels and spends time with her Maltese buddies, ZIGGY and Jynger.

CharmaineLouise — *The Sensual Lifestyle*

~ Visit online at **CharmaineLouise.com**

~ Subscribe to **CharmaineLouise Newsletter**

~ Find us on Facebook **@CharmaineLouiseNewYork**

~ Instagram **@CharLouNY**

CharmaineLouise Books *Sexy Fantasies* launched summer 2020. Sizzling, contemporary romance with your soon-to-be favorite Alpha Doms, Powerful Billionaires, and the women they lust after and love for second chances, insta-love, enemies-to-lovers, and more.

Want to chat it up and share your thoughts with other CLBooks Lovers? Read our blog, join our Charmaine-Louise Books Coterie Fan Club and follow us on my author pages and social media to be in the know about the book release dates, exclusive content, giveaways, contests, and more!

~ **Purchase your eBook and paperback novels from my Author Page by clicking here!**

~ Read and subscribe to our blog *The World of Sex*

~ Connect on **Amazon Author Page**

~ Goodreads Author Profile

~ <u>BookBub Author Profile</u>

CharmaineLouise Intimates *Sexy Under Things &* *Loungewear* debuted in 2003. Inspired by the sensuous sirens and sylph swans of the past and present, the hand crochet cashmere and silk collections are for the sexy: hence, the line names Ginger — Bombshell; Diana — Showstopper; Jackie — Timeless; Lena — Classic. Also known as The Movie-Star from Gilligan's Island; Ms. Ross The Boss; Mrs. Kennedy Onassis; Ms. Horne.

Do you thrive on seduction and being sexy lounging at home? Read our blog and follow us on social media to receive the tips, the latest additions to the collections, private sales, and more!

~ Read and subscribe to our blog *The Art of Seduction*

~ Find us on Facebook **@CharmaineLousieIntimates**

~ Instagram **@CharmaineLouiseIntimates**

Fulfill Your Desires.